When you are told, several times a day, that you are filth – vermin; when you drill until your finger-nails bleed, and lie face down in a ditch of yellow fermenting mud, you learn to accept brutality and death.

But the war in the Ukraine was a bitter one, a battle in which Cossacks fought on both sides and exacted a terrible revenge on each other. An enigma of a war where regiments of Russian women were mutilated to death – and German and Russian soldiers swam and ate together.

They had thought, these emaciated survivors from the prison camps, that nothing could ever shock or disgust them again – but the carnage of the Soviet/Nazi war revolted even their blood-sickened stomachs.

LEGION OF THE DAMNED

SVEN HASSEL

Translated from the Danish by Maurice Michael

CASSELL

Cassell Military Paperbacks

Cassell
An imprint of the Orion Publishing Group
Wellington House, 125 Strand, London WC2R 0BB

First published in Great Britain by George Allen &
Unwin Ltd 1957
This paperback edition published 2003

A CIP catalogue record for this book is available
from the British Library

ISBN 0-304-36631-5

Typeset at The Spartan Press Ltd,
Lymington, Hants

Printed and bound in Great Britain by Clays Ltd,
St Ives plc

This book is dedicated to the unknown soldiers who fell for a cause that was not theirs, my best companions in the 27th Armoured (Penal) Regiment, and the brave women who helped me in those grim and dreadful years:

Oberst Manfried Hinka
Oberstleutnant Erich von Barring
Oberfeldwebel Willie Beier
Unteroffizier Hugo Stege
Stabsgefreiter Gustav Eicken
Obergefreiter Anton Steyer
Gefreiter Hans Breuer
Unteroffizier Bernhard Fleischmann
Gefreiter Asmus Braun
    and
Eva Schadows, Student of Law
Ursula Schade, Doctor of Medicine
Barbara von Harburg, Nurse

'Well, the five minutes are up. You must take the consequences!'

He pressed a bell-push. Two big SS men in black uniforms came in. A brief order – and they dragged Eva across to a table covered with leather.

Filthy Deserter

The previous day the big sapper had been before the court-martial and received a sentence of eight years' hard labour. Now it was my turn. I was taken to the court, guarded by two 'watch-dogs'. I was held in a large room, one wall of which was covered with a gigantic painting of Adolf Hitler, while Frederick the Great hung facing him. Behind the president's chair hung four huge flags – those of the Air Force, Navy, Army and SS. Along the wall were lined the standards of the different arms: white with a black cross for the infantry; red for the artillery; yellow for the cavalry; pink for the armoured troops; black with silver trimmings for the engineers; the Jaeger regiments' green with a hunting horn, and all the others. The judge's desk itself was covered with the black-white-red flag of the Wehrmacht.

The court consisted of a legal adviser with the rank of Major; two judges – one a Hauptmann, the other a Feldwebel; and a prosecutor, an SS Sturmbannführer.

A filthy deserter is not entitled to a defending counsel.

The charge was read out. I was examined. The judge ordered the witnesses to be produced. First came the Gestapo man, who had arrested Eva and me when we were bathing out by the mouth of the Weser, and the summery sound of lazily lapping waves suddenly imposed itself upon the proceedings in court. The hot, shimmering white dune-sand . . . Eva standing there, drying her rounded thighs . . . her bathing cap . . . the heat on my back . . . the heat, heat.

'Yes, I jumped up on to the desk and from there out through a window.'

In all, five different police officials had interrogated me, and they came now and gave their evidence. 'Yes, I gave him a false name.' 'No, the explanation I gave him was not the truth.'

It was queer seeing the Kriminalsekretär, who had ordered Eva to be whipped. The others were sadists, but he was just correct. You cannot do anything with people who are correct. There are far too many of them. I began a lovely day-dream: Everybody had deserted, we all had. Only the officers were left. And what could they do? All of us. There were hordes on all the roads. Soldiers going home. The officers were there at the front, and behind the front, with their maps and their plans and their natty officers' caps and polished boots. The others were going home, and they had not forgotten me. In a little while the door would open and in they would come. They would not say anything, and the president, the legal adviser and the two judges would leap to their feet, their faces pale . . .

'Bring in the witness. Eva Schadows!'

Eva! You here?

Was it Eva?

Oh yes, it was Eva, just as I was Sven. We could recognise each other by our eyes. Everything else, all the rest that we knew – the little roundings, the intimate living secrets that only we knew, that we had drunk in with eyes and mouth and seeing hands – all that no longer existed; only our eyes remained, they and their fear and their promise that we were still us.

Can so much vanish in so few days?

'You know this man here, Eva Schadows, don't you?'

'Oily grin' is an expression I hate. It has always seemed coarse, vulgar and exaggerated, but there is no other for the prosecuting counsel's expression – it was an oily grin.

'Yes.' Eva's voice was almost inaudible. A paper rustled, and the sound of it roused us all.

'Where did you make his acquaintance?'

2

'We met each other in Cologne – during an alert.'

You did that in those days.

'Did he tell you that he was a deserter?'

'No.'

The arrogant silence was too much for her and she went on, faltering, 'I don't think so.'

'Think well what you are saying, young lady. You know, I hope, that it is a very grave matter to give false evidence in a court of justice.'

Eva stood looking at the floor. Not for a moment did she look at me. Her face was grey, like that of a patient just after an operation. Fear was making her hands tremble.

'Well, which was it? Did he not tell you that he was a deserter?'

'Yes, I suppose he did.'

'You must say "yes" or "no"; we must have a clear answer.'

'Yes.'

'What else did he tell you? After all, you took him to Bremen and gave him clothes, money and all the rest of it. Didn't you?'

'Yes.'

'You must tell the court about it. We should not have to drag every word out of you. What did he tell you?'

'He told me that he had fled from his regiment; he said that I should help him; he said that I should get him papers. And I did so. From a man called Paul.'

'When you first met him in Cologne was he in uniform?'

'Yes.'

'What sort of uniform?'

'Black tank uniform with a Gefreiter's stripe.'

'In other words, you could not be in any doubt that he was a soldier?'

'No.'

'Was it he who asked you to go with him to Bremen?'

'No, I suggested that. I said that he should. He wanted to give himself up, but I persuaded him not to.'

Eva, Eva, what in all the world are you saying? What are you telling them?

3

'In other words, you kept him from doing his duty and giving himself up?'

'Yes, I kept him from doing his duty.'

I could not listen to this. I leaped up and shouted at the top of my voice, shouted at the president that she was lying to save me, to contrive mitigating circumstances for me, but that she had no idea that I was a soldier, no idea at all. I had taken off my uniform in the train between Paderborn and Cologne. I was in civilian clothes when I met her. You must let her go; she had no idea of it till I was arrested; I swear that.

Perhaps a president of a court-martial can be human; I didn't know, but I thought that perhaps he might. But his eyes were as cold as slivers of glass, and they drew blood from my shouts.

'You must remain silent until you are questioned. If you say another word. I shall have to have you removed,' and he turned his glass slivers back on to Eva.

'Eva Schadows, will you take an oath that your statement is correct?'

'I will. It is exactly as I said. If he had not met me he would have given himself up.'

'You helped him, too, when he escaped from the secret police?'

'Yes.'

'Thank you. That is all . . . except that . . . have you been sentenced?'

'I am serving five years' penal servitude in Ravensbrück Concentration Camp.'

As she was led out she looked across and gave me a long look and pointed her lips in a kiss. Her lips were blue, her eyes both infinitely sorrowful and happy. She had done something to help me. She hoped, she believed that it would save my life. For a fragile hope of being able to make a tiny contribution to my defence she had been willing to sacrifice five years of her life. Five years in Ravensbrück!

I was very far down.

They also brought Trudi in as a witness, but she fainted

4

soon after she had embarked on a crazy statement that was meant to substantiate Eva's evidence.

It is queer when a witness faints in court and is borne off. Trudi was carried out through a little door, and when it closed on her it was as though the whole of my case had been carried out as well.

They did not take long to make up their minds. While the sentence was being read everybody stood up, and the officers and officials present held their arms out in the Nazi salute.

'In the name of the Führer.

'Sven Hassel, Gefreiter in 11th Regiment of Hussars, is hereby sentenced to fifteen years' hard labour for desertion. It is further decreed that he is to be dismissed from his regiment, and that he is to be deprived of all civil and military rights for an indefinite period.

'Heil Hitler!'

Why don't you faint? Isn't everything black in front of your eyes, as it was when they stopped beating you? What is it they call it: shame worse than death? That's it. That's the cliche. You thought you would never use it. But clichés are there to be used: And now you can go and tell people what it means.

No, you are not going anywhere.

I was so bewildered and bemused that I only heard without grasping what the president then said by way of comment on the sentence.

He said that they had tempered justice with mercy; they had let me off with my life. I had not been sentenced to death. They had taken into account that I was an Auslands-deutscher and had been called up in Denmark, and that irresponsible women, women who did not deserve to be called German women, had enticed me into deserting.

2

We were chained together, two by two, with handcuffs and fetters, and, lastly, a chain was run round the whole detachment. We were driven to the goods-station, guarded by heavily armed military police.

We were in the train for three days and nights . . .

They Died by Day,
They Died by Night

'Before I welcome you to our delightful little spa you had best know who and what you are.

'You are a pack of dirty sluts and scroundrels, a swinish rabble; you are the dregs of humanity. That you have always been, and that you will remain until you die. And in order that you may enjoy your revolting selves, we shall see to it that you die slowly, very slowly, so that you have time for everything. I give you my personal assurance that nobody will be cheated out of anything. Your cure will be properly adhered to. I should be most dreadfully sorry if any of you should miss any of it.

'So now I bid you welcome to the SS and Wehrmacht's Penal Concentration Camp, Lengries.

'Welcome, ladies and gentlemen, to Lengries extermination camp.'

He gave his glossy knee-boot a light tap with his switch and let his monocle drop from his eye. Why do people of this type always have monocles? There must be some psychological explanation.

An SS Hauptscharführer read out the rules, which amounted to this: that everything was forbidden and the punishment for all transgressions was starvation, beating, death.

The prison was a five-storeyed erection of cages, there being no walls dividing the cells, just bars. We were searched and bathed, and had one side of our heads shaved. Then all the hairy places on our bodies were smeared with a stinking, searing fluid that burned worse than fire. Then we were all put into a cell, where we remained stark naked for almost four hours while some SS men searched us. They syringed our ears, stuck their fingers into our mouths, and neither nostrils nor armpits were overlooked. Finally, we were given a large enema, that sent us rushing to the WCs, with which one wall was lined. It was worse for the two young women, who had to suffer the guards' indecent witticisms and endure a 'special examination'.

The clothes we were given – striped jacket and trousers – were made of a horrible scratchy material like sackcloth, so that it felt all the time as though you were covered with vermin or ants.

An Oberscharführer ordered us out into the passage, where we lined up in front of an Untersturmführer. He pointed to the right-hand man.

'Come here!'

The man received a shove from an SS man behind him that sent him staggering towards the little, conceited officer, in front of whom he stood stiffly to attention.

'What's your name? How old are you? What have you done? Answer quickly.'

'John Schreiber. Twenty-five. Sentenced to twenty years' hard labour for high treason.'

'Tell me, haven't you been a soldier?'

'Yes, sir, I was Feldwebel, in the 123rd Infantry Regiment.'

'So, in other words, it is sheer insubordination that you don't bother to report correctly. Added to which, you have the impertinence to omit to address me, as you have been taught. Stand to attention, you skunk. Now we'll try to cure you of your bad habits. If this doesn't help, you've only to let us know, and we'll find something else.'

The Untersturmführer looked fixedly at the air and said in a screechy voice:

'Bastinado.'

7

A few seconds later the man lay on his back with his bare feet in a pillory.

'How many, Herr Untersturmführer?'

'Give him twenty.'

The man was unconscious by the time they had finished. But they had ways of dealing with that, indescribable ways, and it was only a moment before he was again standing in his place in the ranks.

The next one, profiting by the other's experience, answered as he should.

'Herr Untersturmführer, former Unteroffizier Victor Giese of 7th Pioneer Regiment begs to report that I am twenty-two and sentenced to ten years' hard labour for theft.'

'You steal! Filthy trick! Don't you know that a soldier mustn't steal?'

'Herr Unterstumführer, I beg to report that I know a soldier must not.'

'But you did it, all the same?'

'Yes, Herr Untersturmführer.'

'So you find it difficult to learn?'

'Yes, Herr Untersturmführer, I beg to report that I find it difficult to learn.'

'Well, we'll be generous and give you a special course. We have one unusually good teacher here.'

The Untersturmführer stared fixedly at the air and said in a screechy voice:

'Cat-o'-nine-tails.'

The man's toes could just touch the floor when they had strung him up by his wrists.

None of us escaped, not even the women. We quickly learned that in Lengries we were not men and women, only swine, dung-beetles, harlots.

Almost everything connected with Lengries is indescribable, revolting, monotonous. The imagination of the sadist is remarkably limited, for all his ghastly inventiveness, while you yourself become blunted; there is even a monotony about seeing people suffer and die in ways that, before, you would have considered inconceivable. Our tormentors had

8

been given a free hand to indulge their lust of power and cruelty, and they made full use of the opportunity. They had the time of their lives. Their souls stank worse than their prisoners' sick, tortured bodies.

I do not wish to reproach our guards in any way. They were victims of a situation others had created, and to a certain extent they came worse out of it than we did. They acquired stinking souls.

There was a time when I thought that I should only need to tell about Lengries and people would be filled with the disgust that I felt and set about improving the world, begin building a life in which there was no room for torture. Yet you cannot get people to understand what you mean unless they have themselves experienced what you have experienced, and to those you do not need to tell anything. The others, those who went free, look at me as if they would like to tell me that I must be exaggerating, although they know that I am not, for they have lapped up the reports of the Nuremberg trials. But they shrink from looking the whole thing square in the face, prefer to nail another layer of flooring over the rottenness in the foundations, to burn more incense, to sprinkle more scent around.

Yet perhaps there is one courageous soul who will dare to hear and see without shuddering. I need such a person, for it is so lonely without. I need, too, to tell my tale, to unburden myself; perhaps it is only to do that that I write; perhaps I am just imagining it when I say that I want to give warning lest history repeat itself over this. Perhaps I am just deceiving myself, when I wish to cry out from the house-tops what I have experienced; that all I want thereby is to attract attention and shuddering admiration, to be the hero who has been through things that not everyone has been allowed to experience.

No, not everybody has had that granted them, but there are enough of them for me to have more sense than to consider myself a phenomenon. Thus, in describing Lengries in the following sketch I cannot say definitely why I do so. Each may attribute to me the motive he or she prefers.

I know, too, that it is those who like to imagine that they cannot believe what I tell who must bear the main burden of guilt that will fall upon every one of us if all Lengries are not done away with, wherever they are still to be found.

There is no need to mention places, countries, names – that would merely distract and lead to squabbling and mutual recrimination between opposing sides, between nations, ideas, blocs, each of which is too busy taking offence at what others do to do anything about their own conduct.

This was Lengries:

A youngish Feldwebel, sentenced to thirty years' hard labour for sabotaging the Reich, was caught one day trying to give a neighbouring female prisoner a piece of soap. The guard called the section leader, Obersturmführer Stein, a man with a ghastly imagination.

'What the devil is this I hear about you two turtle-doves? Have you got engaged? Well, well, this must be celebrated.'

The whole floor was ordered down into one of the yards. The two young people were ordered to strip. It was Christmas Eve and snowflakes were swirling round us.

'Now we would like to see a little copulation!' said Stein.

The pickled herrings we were served on rare occasions were unfit for human consumption, but we ate them – head, bones, scales and all. In the cell we were chained with our hands tied behind our backs. We lay on our bellies and licked up our food like swine. We had three minutes in which to eat it, and often it was scalding hot.

And when prisoners were to be executed:

Such days began with the shrilling of a whistle, while the big bell rang different numbers of times to indicate which floors were to go down. The first time the whistle sounded you stood to attention facing the cell door. At the second whistle you began to mark time: thump, thump, thump. Then a mechanism worked by an SS man flung all the cell doors open at the same time, but you still went on marking time in the cell, till a fresh, piercing whistle rang out.

On one such day there were eighteen to be hanged. Down

in the yard we formed a semicircle round the scaffold, a staging ten feet high with eighteen gallows on it. Eighteen ropes with nooses hung dangling from them. The sight of a dangling rope with a noose has become part of my life. In front of the scaffold stood eighteen coffins of unplaned deal.

The male condemned wore their striped trousers, the women their striped skirts, but nothing else. The adjutant read out the sentences of death, then the eighteen were ordered up the narrow steps on to the scaffold and lined up, each standing by his rope. Two SS men acted as hangmen, their shirt-sleeves rolled up well above their elbows.

They were hanged one after the other. When all eighteen were hanging there, with urine and excrement running down their legs, an SS doctor came, threw them an indifferent look and gave the hangmen the sign that all was in order. The bodies were then taken down from the gallows and flung into the coffins.

I suppose I ought to say a word or two about life and death at this point, but I do not know what I should say. Of hanging, I only know that it is quite unromantic.

But if anyone is interested in hearing more about death, there was Sturmbannführer Schendrich. He was quite young, handsome, elegant, always friendly and polite and subdued, but feared even by the SS men under him.

'Now let's see,' said he at roll-call one Saturday, 'If you have understood what I have told you. I will now try giving some of you an easy little order, and the rest of us will see if it is carried out properly.'

He called five out of the ranks. They were ordered to stand facing the wall that ran around the whole prison. Prisoners were strictly forbidden to approach within five yards of this wall.

'Forward – march!'

Staring straight in front of them, the five marched towards the wall, till the guards in the watch-towers shot them down. Schendrich turned to the rest of us.

'That was nice. That's the way to obey an order. Now go

down on your knees when I tell you, and repeat after me what I am going to say. On your – knees!'

We dropped to our knees.

'And now say after me, but loudly and distinctly: We are swine and traitors.'

'*We are swine and traitors!*'

'Who are to be destroyed.'

'*Who are to be destroyed!*'

'And that's what we deserve.'

'*And that's what we deserve!*'

'Tomorrow, Sunday, we will go without our food.'

'*Tomorrow, Sunday, we will go without our food!*'

'For when we do not work.'

'*For when we do not work!*'

'We do not deserve food.'

'*We do not deserve food!*'

Those crazy shouts rang out across the yard every Saturday afternoon, and on Sundays we got no food.

In the cell next to mine was Käthe Ragner. She looked dreadful. Her hair was chalky white. Almost all her teeth had fallen out as a result of vitamin deficiency. Her arms and legs were like long, thin bones. On her body were large suppurating sores from which matter trickled.

'You're looking at me so,' she said to me one evening. 'How old do you think I am?' And she gave a dry, mirthless laugh.

I did not reply.

'A good fifty, I expect you would reply. Next month I shall be twenty-four. Twenty months ago a man guessed that I was eighteen.'

Käthe had been secretary to a high Staff officer in Berlin. She got to know a young captain in the same office, and they became engaged. The date for their wedding was fixed, but there was no wedding. Her fiancé was arrested, and four days later they came and fetched her as well. The Gestapo had her under treatment for three months, accused of having made copies of certain documents. She did not understand much of any of it. She and another young girl were each sentenced to ten years. Her fiancé and two other officers were condemned to death. A fourth was sentenced to hard labour for life. She was made to witness her fiancé's execution and was then sent to Lengries.

One morning Käthe and three other women were ordered to crawl down the steep, long flight of stairs that connected all the storeys. It was a form of exercise with which the guards liked to treat us. You were put in handcuffs and fetters and thus had to crawl down the stairs head first, and you had to keep going.

I do not know whether Käthe fell, or let herself fall, from the fifth storey. She was utterly broken, so it might have been either. I just heard the shriek and then the smack, followed by a few seconds of deathly silence, after which a shrill voice cried from down below:

'The harlot's broken her neck!'

3

A few days after Käthe's death I and a number of others were transferred to Fagen Concentration Camp near Bremen. They told us that we were detailed for 'special work of extraordinary importance'.

What this work was did not interest us. None of us believed it would be more pleasant than that to which we were accustomed. We were used to working as draught animals in front of a plough, harrow, roller or wagon, pulling till you dropped dead of it. We were used to working in the quarry, till you dropped dead of that. We also worked in the jute mill, where you dropped dead with haemorrhage of the lungs.

All work was the same: you dropped dead of it.

Fagen

Fagen worked on two fronts, as it were; it was really a camp for experimental medicine, but there were also the bombs.

The first few days I was put to hard navvying. We worked like galley-slaves, digging sand from five in the morning till six in the evening on a thin gruel that was served us three times a day. Then came the great opportunity, which I seized at once: the chance of a pardon!

The camp commandant informed us that those who volunteered had a chance of earning a pardon. You had to do fifteen of them for every year of your sentence left to run. That meant that I had to do two hundred and twenty-five.

But I have not explained. You had to dismantle fifteen unexploded bombs for every year of your sentence that you still had to serve. When, as I, you had fifteen years it meant that you had to dismantle two hundred and twenty-five bombs. Then, perhaps, you would be pardoned.

These were not ordinary duds, but the ones neither the Civil Defence nor the Army's units dared touch. Some people had managed to do fifty before they were killed, but I argued

14

that sooner or later someone must get up to two hundred and twenty-five, so I volunteered.

Perhaps that was what decided me, or else the fact that each morning before we went out we were given a quarter of rye bread, a small piece of sausage and three cigarettes as extra rations.

After a short training in dismantling bombs we were driven round by the SS to the various places where there were unexploded bombs. Our guards kept a respectful distance, while we dug down to where they lay buried, which could be ten or twenty feet in the ground. Then they had to be freed of earth; a wire had to be placed round them and derricks lowered into the holes, and they had to be hoisted a fraction of an inch at a time, until they were upright. As soon as one of these brutes was hanging in its derrick, everyone vanished – carefully so as not to wake it, swiftly so as to get well away and take cover. Only one man kept the bomb company, and that was the prisoner who was to unscrew the fuse. If he bungled it . . .

We kept a couple of wooden boxes in the workshop lorry for those who did bungle, but it was not every day that there was need of them – not that people did not bungle, but because we could not always find anything of them to put in the boxes.

You sat on the bomb while unscrewing the fuse, for that makes it easier to hold the fuse in one position; but I discovered that it was better to lie at the bottom of the hole under the bomb when the dangerous thing had to be eased out, as it was easier to let the tube fall down into your asbestos-gloved hand.

My sixty-eighth bomb was an aerial torpedo, and it took us fifteen hours to dig it free. You do not talk much when you are on such a job. You are on the alert all the time. You dig cautiously, thinking before you exert much force on your spade or with your hands or feet. Your breathing must be calm and even, your movements deliberate and made one at a time. Hands are good to dig with, especially as you must be careful that the earth does not slide. If a torpedo moves a

15

mere fraction of an inch it can mean the end. In its present position it is silent; but no one knows what it would take it into its head to do if it changed position; and it *has* to change position, has to be hoisted up into the derrick; the fuse has to be removed. Before that it is not safe, until then we dare not breathe; so let's get it over – no, not too hastily, slowly does it, every movement deliberate and calm.

Such an aerial torpedo is a cold-blooded opponent; it gives nothing away, absolutely nothing. You cannot play poker with an aerial torpedo.

When we had dug it free we were told that the fuse was not to be removed until the torpedo had been taken out of the town. This, perhaps, meant that it was a new type which no one knew, or that it lay in such a position that it would explode if anyone breathed on the damned fuse, and if a brute like that exploded it would blow up that whole part of the town.

A Krupp-Diesel lorry fitted with a derrick arrived and stood waiting for its monstrous load. It took four hours to hoist the bomb up into the derrick, lower it into place and lash it so that it could not move.

That done, we looked at it and felt relieved. But we had forgotten something.

'Who can drive?'

Silence. When there is a snake climbing up your leg you must turn yourself into a pillar of stone, a dead thing that does not interest a snake. We made pillars of ourselves, mentally withdrawing into the depths of the shadows, so as not to be seen, while the SS man's gaze travelled from one to the other. None of us looked at him, but we were so keenly aware of him that our hearts pounded, and the life in us darted, crab-like, sideways, avoiding craters, in and out among the debris.

'You there! Can't you drive?'

I did not dare say no.

'Up with you!'

The route was marked out with flags. One bright spot was that it had been cleared and repaired, so that the surface was

16

fairly level. All for the sake of their blessed houses! I did not see a soul. The other vehicles came crawling along a way behind me. They felt no urge to approach the danger. At one point there was a house in flames, burning in the silence. The smoke from it stung my eyes, and I was scarcely able to see; but I did not dare increase speed. It was five agonising minutes before I was breathing fresh air again.

I do not know what I thought of during that drive. I only know that there was plenty of time to think, and that I was calm, a little elated perhaps, even a little happy for the first time for a very long while. When the next second may be your last you have plenty of time to think. I know, too, that for the first time for ages I was aware of being myself. I had lost sight of myself, had ceased to have even an opinion of myself, my personality had been expunged – and yet it had survived the degradation, the daily degradation. Here you are, I said to myself, here you are. Good day to you. Here you are. Doing what the others dare not do. So, after all, you are a person who can do something, someone they have use for. Look out for those tram-lines there!

I got out of the town, past the last allotments and tin shanties, where only tramps lived, bums and down-and-outs. Perhaps decent people lived there, too, now that there was war and the city was becoming more and more pitted with holes every night. A solitary man was digging. He leaned on his spade and looked at me.

'Aren't you going to take cover?' I called to him.

He said something, though what it was I could not hear for the noise of the engine, and remained as he was. Perhaps he said 'Pleasant journey.' Strange to be driving so slowly along a completely empty highway.

In the town they would now be creeping back to their flats and shops. The most courageous first. Then the others would come, relieved and delighted. Look, it's all there still.

I could perhaps have escaped; there had been many opportunities in the empty streets. I could have jumped off the lorry and leaped into cover, while the bomb continued without a driver for another minute or so, till it went bang.

Why I did not take the chance I do not know. But I did not. I was really quite enjoying myself. We were alone, my dear aerial torpedo and I, and nobody could do anything to me.

Flags still marked the route, but out there on the heath the intervals between them were longer. Now my instinct of self-preservation awoke from its queer intoxication: weren't we there yet? Hell, but it would be too bad if, after all these miles, after close on twenty-four hours . . .

Eight miles out on the heath I was able to stop. As they considered it impossible to unload the torpedo, it was exploded as it hung in its sprung derrick.

For driving it, I was given three cigarettes with the usual remark that I had not deserved them, but was given them because the Führer was not devoid of human feelings.

I considered three cigarettes good payment. I had only expected one.

The worst thing happened to me that could happen to any prisoner – I became ill; and that perhaps saved my life. I kept going for five days. If you reported sick you were at once sent to the camp hospital, where they experimented on you, till you could be used no more; and you could only be used no more when you were dead from having been used. Therefore you did not report sick. But during a roll-call I collapsed, and when I recovered consciousness I was in the hospital.

I was never told what was wrong with me – no patient ever was. The day I was well enough to get up, it began. I was given various injections. I was put in a scalding-hot room, and from there taken to an ice-box, while they kept taking samples of my blood. One day I would be given all that I could eat, the next I was starved and kept without liquids until I was on the point of collapse; or they shoved rubber tubes into my stomach and pumped me empty of all that I had eaten. One painful state succeeded the other, and, finally, they took a large and painful sample of my spinal marrow, after which I was hand-cuffed to a barrow filled with sand, and this I had to push round and round a large enclosure without stopping. Every quarter of an hour they took a sample of blood. All that day I trundled my load, while my head swam. For a long time after that treatment I had intolerable headaches.

I was luckier than so many others. One day they thought I had had enough, or perhaps I was not interesting any more. I was returned to the camp. There, a grinning SS man told me that I had been taken off the bomb-disposal work. The bombs I had dismantled no longer counted.

I went back to slaving in the quarry.

Then, suddenly, I was sent back to the bombs after all; but just when I had worked up quite a good figure I was sent back to Lengries, and the whole thing went for nothing.

Seven months in the gravel-pits at Lengries. Monotonous, lethargic insanity.

One day an SS man came for me. A doctor examined me. I had a mattery rash all over my body; the spots were washed and smeared with ointment. The doctor asked if I were well. 'Yes, doctor, I am well and in a good state of health.' You did not complain of things there. You were well and the state of your health good as long as there was still breath in your body.

I was taken in to SS Sturmbannführer Schendrich. He had curtains at his windows. They were even clean. Just think, curtains! Light-green curtains with a yellow pattern. Light green with a yellow pattern. Li—

'What the hell are you gaping at?'

I started. 'Nothing, Herr Sturmbannführer. Excuse me, I beg to report that I am gaping at nothing.' And inspiration made me add in a low voice, 'I beg to report that I am just gaping.'

He looked at me confused. Then, brushing his thoughts away, he held out a piece of paper.

'Now will you sign here that you have been in receipt of ordinary army food, that you have not been subjected to hunger or thirst of any kind, and that you have no ground whatsoever for complaining of conditions here during the time that you have been here.'

I signed. What did it matter? Was I being transferred to another camp? Or was it my turn to be hanged?

Another document, a very formidable-looking one, was shoved across to me.

'And you sign here that you have received strict, but good, treatment, and that nothing has been done to you contrary to international law.'

I signed. What did it matter?

'If you should ever say as much as a syllable about what you have seen or heard here you will come back and I will prepare a special welcome for you, understand?'

'I understand, Herr Sturmbannführer.'

So I was being transferred.

I was put in a cell where there lay a green army uniform without badges of any kind. I was told to put it on. 'And clean your nails, you swine!' An SS man then took me to the commandant's office, where I was paid 1 Mark 21 pfennig for seven months' work, from six in the morning till eight at night. A Stabscharführer roared at me:

'Prisoner 552318 A – for release. Dis-*miss!*'

So they tortured you that way, too. I was quite proud that I did not let my hopes be raised. I turned smartly and walked away, expecting to hear their peals of laughter. They were more subtle than that. They kept straight faces.

'Sit outside in the corridor and wait!'

They were not laughing in there. In the end it began to get on my nerves, for I had to wait over an hour. I began to think silly thoughts, wondering how people could be so petty, so wicked. But you can see for yourself that they can be, I told myself. I thought you had got over that sort of childish thought.

Even today I can still be overcome by that utter, speechless bewilderment in which I followed the Feldwebel into the little grey Opel car, after being told that I had been pardoned and was going to serve in a penal battalion.

The great, heavy gate fell into place behind us. The grey cement buildings with their many small, barred windows disappeared, and I was driven away from the nameless horror and fear.

I did not understand it. I was stupefied – no, consternated – and I did not even recover properly when we were driving across the barrack square in Hanover.

Now, many years later, I no longer remember the nameless horror and the many fears except as something that is past and over.

But why my consternation when I drove away from it? I have not yet answered that question.

4

Twenty times a day we were told with much swearing and cursing that we were in a penal battalion, and that that meant that we were to be the best soldiers in the world.

For the first six weeks we had drill from six in the morning till half-past seven at night. Only drill.

One Hundred and Thirty-five Corpses

We drilled till the blood spurted from our fingernails – not as a figure of speech, but in grim reality.

Or we goose-stepped in full equipment: steel helmet, pack, ammunition pouches filled with sand, and wearing great-coats, while other people went about in their summer clothes, groaning at the heat.

Or we slogged through mud that reached halfway up our legs; stood up to our necks in water and did rifle drill without a twitch being visible on our set faces.

Our NCOs were a pack of howling devils, who shouted and bawled at us till we were on the verge of madness. They never overlooked an opportunity.

There was no such punishment as deprivation of freedom, for the simple reason that we had no freedom. It was just duty, duty and duty. It is true that we had an hour's interval for dinner, and that in theory we were free from half-past seven until nine o'clock, but if we did not devote every minute of that time to cleaning our muddied uniforms, leather, equipment and boots, we were taught to do so by the most fearful reprisals.

We had to be in our bunks by nine. But that was not the same as being able to sleep. Every single night there were practice alerts and practice in the quick changing of uniform.

When the alarm sounded we tumbled out, put on full field equipment and fell in. Then back we were sent to change into parade dress. Then into drills. Finally, back into field dress. It

22

was *never* good enough. Every night for a couple of hours we were hounded up and down the stairs like a herd of frightened animals. Gradually we got into such a state that the mere shadow of an NCO was almost enough to make us swoon with panic fear.

Once the first six weeks were past we began rifle practice and field exercises. That taught us what fatigue was.

We learned to crawl on our stomachs across miles of training ground, across sharp cinders and flints that tore our palms to gory ribbons, or through inches of stinking mud that almost suffocated us. But it was the route-marches we feared most.

One night we were turned out. Our NCOs came bellowing into the rooms, where we lay sleeping the sleep of the deadbeat:

'Alarm! Alarm!'

Heavy with fatigue, we tumbled out of our bunks, flung open our lockers and in feverish, cursing haste got into our uniforms. A strap proving difficult, a stubborn clasp, half a second lost, those were catastrophes. Before two minutes had gone the whistles were shrilling out in the corridors. Our doors were kicked open.

'No. 3 Company – fall – IN! What the hell, you stinking pimps, aren't you down on the square yet? And your bunks not made? Do you think this is a home for the aged? Lazy camels!'

We tumbled down the steps, tightening a last strap as we went, and in a few seconds we were standing in two wavy lines on the barrack square. Then there was a bellow:

'No. 3 Company – to your rooms – DOUBLE!'

Fancy their not bursting something in their heads when they bellowed like that! Or perhaps they had done something to the place where normal people keep their common sense. Have you ever noticed how they talk? They cannot talk normally. The words in their sentences are joined together till they are baying, and the last word is made into the crack of a whip, if that is any way possible. You never hear them end a sentence on an unaccented syllable. They chop every-

23

thing into military pieces, making it incomprehensible. That bawling, that ever-lasting bawling. They are mad, those people.

Like a flood sweeping everything before it, we one hundred and thirty-five recruits hurled ourselves at the stairs to get back to our rooms and change into drills, before 'Fall – IN' was shouted again.

After being hounded up and down a dozen times to the accompaniment of crazy oaths and curses, we were again on the square, sweating and wild-eyed, in full marching order, ready to go out on a night exercise.

Our company commander, one-armed Captain Lopei, stood surveying us with a slight smile round his mouth. He required iron-discipline of his company, inhuman discipline; yet we thought that he, alone of our tormentors, had something human about him. He at least had the decency himself to do everything that he made us do, and he never expected us to do what he could not do himself. When we came back from an exercise he was as filthy as we. Thus, he was fair, a thing to which we were not used; we were used to the person in authority selecting a scapegoat, a poor wretch whom he was always after, never leaving him alone till he was done for, collapsed, disabled, killed with fatigue or driven to suicide. Captain Lopei had neither scapegoats nor favourites – he was that rare type of officer who can get his men to go through hell for him, because he himself will lead them there, and because he is fair. If that man's courage and fairness had not been harnessed to Hitler's car, if he had been an officer in almost any other army, I would have liked him. As it was, I respected him.

The commander briefly inspected his company's dressing. Then he walked out from it, and his incisive, commanding voice cracked out across the square:

'No. 3 Company – atten – tion! Eyes front! Shoulder – arms!'

Three rhythmical smacks rang through the night as one hundred and thirty-five rifles were shouldered. A few seconds of absolute silence – every officer, NCO and private standing as stiff as ramrods, staring rigidly ahead from under their steel

24

helmets. Woe to the poor wretch who moved as much as the tip of his tongue!

Again the captain's voice rang through the tall poplars and the grey barrack buildings.

'By the right – forward! Right – turn – quick – MARCH!'

There was a thunderous crash as our iron-shod boots thudded down on to the cement, sending sparks flying. Out of the barrack square we swung and on down the rain-sodden road, flanked by tall poplars. In a penal battalion all singing and conversation are naturally prohibited; fourth-rate people cannot enjoy the privileges of the German soldier. Nor did we have the right to wear the eagle badge or such symbols of distinction; all we had was a narrow, white band (that always had to be white!) low down on our right sleeves, and on it the word SONDERABTEILUNG in black letters.

Since we had to be the best soldiers in the world, all our marches were forced marches, and thus it was not a quarter of an-hour before we were steaming. Our feet began to get hot; we opened our mouths and began breathing through them as well; the nose alone being unable to supply sufficient oxygen. Our rifle-slings and shoulder-straps were heavy brakes on the blood circulating in our arms, and our fingers were becoming white and swollen and slightly numb. But those were trifles we no longer heeded. We could do a forced march of sixteen miles without feeling any particular discomfort.

Then came exercises: advance in open formation, in short bursts, one man at a time. With lungs working like bellows we dashed across country, running, crawling across sodden, icy fields, digging ourselves in like frightened animals with our short trenching tools.

But, of course, we never did it quickly enough. Each time the whistles called us back, and we stood gasping for all too few seconds while they cursed us. Then off again. Advance – advance – advance. We were caked with wet, ploughed earth; our legs shook, and then the sweat came, running in rivulets down our bodies and burning and stinging our skins, where the fretting straps and heavy equipment had rubbed and made sores. The sweat soaked through our clothes, and many had dark patches on the backs of their tunics. We could scarcely see, because the sweat blinded us; our foreheads itched and tingled from being wiped with dirty hands and coarse tunic sleeves. If we stood still our soaking clothes became ice-cold. The insides of my thighs and my crotch were skinned and bleeding. We sweated with fear.

Exhausted, we became dully aware that day was breaking. Then it was time to practise being attacked from the air.

We set off at a heavy run down the rough road. Every stone, every little puddle, to say nothing of the damned deep ruts slipping away from our fearfully staring eyes, meant that we had to concentrate on seeing that our feet reacted correctly, so as not to stumble or trip or put a foot wrong. The mere business of getting our feet to work properly, of just running and walking, things you normally do without thinking about them, became an agonising physical and mental effort. Our legs felt so heavy, so crushingly heavy. But stubbornly we jog-trotted and reeled and staggered along in step, at the double. Our otherwise ashen, hollow-eyed faces were as red as lobsters; our eyes rigid and staring, the veins in our foreheads swollen. We gasped for breath; our mouths were dry and slimed; and every now and again a gasp would spatter flecks of white foam.

The whistle shrilled. We dashed to either side of the road, flung ourselves blindly into the ditches, no matter whether there were nettles or water at the bottom, or someone quicker already there. Then the frantic race to get mortars and machine-guns into position. It all had to be done in a matter of seconds, so better tear your fingers to shreds or get kicked in the back than that it should be too slow.

On we marched, mile after mile. I believe that I know everything worth knowing about roads: soft roads, hard roads, wide roads, narrow roads, stony, muddy, cemented, boggy, snowy, hilly, gravelled, slippery, dusty. My feet have taught me everything worth knowing about roads, callous enemies and tormentors of my feet.

The rain stopped. Then the sun came out. That meant thirst, heavy heads, headaches, spots before the eyes. Your feet and ankles swell in your burning boots. We dragged ourselves along in a strange kind of trance.

At noon a halt was ordered. Our muscles were so tortured that it hurt even to get them to stop walking; and a few simply did not have the strength to stop, but staggered on after the command was given, until they barged into the man in front and stood there swaying with drooping heads, till the others shoved them back into their places.

We were on the outskirts of a little village. A couple of young boys came running up to stare at us. We were to have half an hour's rest. Without stopping to consider that we were fifty miles from the barracks, we flung ourselves down where we stood, without even loosening our straps, just flung ourselves down and were asleep before we even reached the ground.

That same second, or so it seemed, the whistle shrilled again. But thirty minutes had passed, all our precious rest. The next quarter of an hour was a hell of a torment: stiff muscles and feet protested; they did not want to get going again. Every step was a series of stabbing pains shooting right up to our brains. The soles of our feet registered each nail in our boots, so that it was like walking on glass splinters.

But there was no help – no lorry to pick up those who fell in the ditch. No, they, poor devils, were given special treatment by a lieutenant and the company's three harshest NCOs. They were hounded and hectored, till either they went off their heads and ran amok, or they lost consciousness, or were transformed into will-less robots that obeyed all orders automatically and would have jumped from a fourth-floor window if told to do so. We could hear the NCOs bawling and shouting, threatening to have some wretches up for refusing to obey orders if they did not obey more quickly.

Later in the evening we marched into the barrack square, ready to drop.

'Parade – MARCH!'

We pulled ourselves together with a last effort. Our legs flew out horizontally and our feet thudded against the paving-stones. Sparks swirled in front of our eyes; we actually felt our blisters bursting. But we must do it. We must. We brought our lame feet smashing down, smashing the pain. We summoned up our last reserve of strength.

The camp commandant, Oberstleutnant von der Lenz, was standing at the point, where we had to swing round up to our barrack. Captain Lopei ordered:

'No. 3 Company – Eyes – LEFT!'

Our heads turned to the left all right, and we all stared at the slight figure of the colonel; but the stiff movements that are part of the salute were not stiff at all. We even got out of step! Captain Lopei gave a start, halted, went out to the side and watched his company. Then came a sharp:

'No. 3 Company – HALT!'

It was the colonel. There was a moment's deathly silence, then came the colonel's snarling voice:

'Captain Lopei, do you call this a company? If you want to go to the front with the next infantry battalion, just say so. There are plenty of officers who would be more than glad to have your job in the garrison.'

The colonel's voice rose in a fury:

'What in hell is this collection of filthied curs you have here? What undisciplined rabble is this? One wouldn't think they were Prussian soldiers. You'd think they were mangy curs. But that can be cured!'

Arrogantly, he surveyed our exhausted company. We stood there in a stupor. If only he would finish soon, so that we could get to our quarters, get our things off and sleep.

'That can be cured,' he repeated threateningly. 'Curs require occupation, a little training. Don't they, Captain Lopei?'

'Yes, indeed, Herr Oberstleutnant, a little training.'

Dull hatred mounted within us mingled with self-pity. This was going to cost us at least an hour of the most exhausting drill in the German Army, the most devilish, exhausting drill in the German Army. It could only mean parade-marching.

Have you ever had the glands in your groin swollen and hard from overwork, so that they hurt at every step, the muscles in your thigh hard balls on which you must thump with all your might every now and again to get them to work, your leg muscles contracted in cramp, either boot feeling as though it weighed a hundred weight and each of your legs a ton, and then try to swing your legs up to thigh level with toes pointed, and do so as lithely, briskly and rhythmically as a chorus girl?

Have you tried, after that, when your ankles are weaklings that have long since given up the game and your toes are curled together in a bloody lump and the soles of your feet are on fire, large blisters filled with water, or burst blisters that bleed and are both fire and splintered glass, have you tried lithely moving forward on one foot while you bring the other poised boot down on the stone-flags with a smack? And this has to be done in time, with a precision as though one hundred and thirty-five men were one; it must produce such a report that people stop and listen and say: 'There's marching for you! That's magnificent! What an Army we have!' The parade-march always impresses the immature.

It did not impress us. It is the most accursed, most tiring drill in the Army. It has torn more muscles and damaged more lymphatic glands than any other form of training. Ask the doctors!

But we had underestimated our Oberstleutnant. We were not to have an hour's parade-marching. He had gone now, smartly saluted by Captain Lopei, but before he went he said, 'Yes, by Jove, that can be cured. Captain Lopei!'

'Sir!'

'You'll march that lot to the training area and teach them to be soldiers and not a pack of mangy curs. You will not come back before nine o'clock tomorrow. And if by then your company cannot manage a parade-march that smashes the paving-stones you'll go back again. Understand?'

'I understand, Herr Oberstleutnant.'

All night we practised attacking across open country and parade-march.

The next morning at nine o'clock we rhythmically thundered past the Oberstleutnant. He was taking no chances. He made the company march past him seven times, and I am sure that if but one of us had for one second been a tenth of a second out of time we would have been sent back a second time.

It was ten o'clock when we were dismissed and tottered blindly to our rooms and slept.

It was an inhuman performance – but then, we were not proper humans. We were mangy curs – a pack of famished curs.

This picture of our training requires one finishing touch. To put everything in its proper light and perspective you must add – hunger.

We were never able to eat our fill. We were all, in fact, slightly crazy on that point, as on so many others. At the end of the war in 1945 the entire German people was living on starvation rations, but in 1940–41 we had less than the worst situated group of the population – that is, the ordinary civilians – had in 1945. We could buy nothing, because we got no coupons. Dinner was the same every day: a litre of thin beet soup and a handful of sauerkraut to put in it, but we had the sauerkraut only every other day. We were not to be spoiled or allowed to become finicky. Meat was a luxury we did not know. In the evening we were issued our dry rations for the coming day: a hunk of rye bread, that, with a little practice, could be cut into five slices, three for that evening, two for breakfast. As well, we had twenty grammes of rancid margarine and a morsel of cheese, cheese with the world's highest water content – there must have been 5 per cent of water in that cheese. On Saturdays we had an extra ration of fifty grammes of turnip marmalade. For breakfast we had a thin brew of ersatz coffee, the colour of tea, which both tasted and smelt revolting, yet we gulped it down with relish.

Sometimes, when out on an exercise, you might find a potato or a turnip. If you did, you gave it a wipe to get the worst of the earth off, stuffed it into your mouth and ate it. The whole thing was over so quickly that a spectator would have thought you were doing a conjuring trick. It did not take us long to discover that birch bark and a particular kind of grass that grew beside the ditches were quite palatable, perhaps even nourishing, but at any rate things that stayed down and dulled the pangs of hunger. Here is the recipe: Take some birch bark or grass, grind it between two steel helmets, add a suitable quantity of ersatz coffee and eat as gruel.

If, by a miracle, one of us was sent a bread coupon there was feasting in the fortunate one's room. A whole loaf!

5

We always dreaded the Monday inspection. At the morning roll-call we had to fall in wearing steel helmet, parade tunic, chalk-white trousers with creases as sharp as knives, pack, belt, ammunition pouches, trenching tool, bayonet, haversack and rifle. Your greatcoat had to be rolled up in the regulation way and hung across your chest.

Every man had to have a clean, green handkerchief in his pocket. And that handkerchief had to be folded in the regulation way.

Spit and Polish

Cleanliness harms no one. Nor does order. And in an army there must naturally be both cleanliness and order, all worked out to an appropriate and detailed scheme. The conscientious soldier spends an incredible amount of time on cleanliness and order, but the soldier in a penal battalion devotes all his time to it – that is, all the time not otherwise occupied. We did nothing all Sunday but wash and clean and fold together in the regulation manner, hang things up in the regulation way, and put others in the place laid down by the regulations. Our leather had to have a gloss on it, as though it were varnished; there must not be a speck on our uniform or equipment, either inside or out. I can assert with utter truthfulness that when the men of a German penal battalion go on parade on Monday they are immaculate from top to toe.

But I also think that there must be something wrong with military order and cleanliness if, after toiling a whole Sunday to achieve it, you do not feel any of that satisfaction, that ease of mind that one should normally feel after such a clean-up.

That parade was no festival of purification. It was a night-mare of fear. The immaculately clean, tidy soldier did not feel clean; he merely felt like a hunted animal.

I find that I keep using these expressions 'hunted animals', 'panic fear', and 'wild with terror'. I know that repetition is bad, that good literary style calls for variety in expression, but I am afraid that I shall have to go on sinning, for how can you find a variety of expression for what is uniform? Some perhaps could, but I am not sure that I can. I am too tired, too bemused, too desperate, sometimes also too angry, to be able to devote time and energy to the search for shades of meaning and fine distinctions. What I have to tell is so tragic; and even now, all these years afterwards, I am sometimes so oppressed by it that I feel that I have the right to ask for your help in making good where I have failed from your own vocabulary. As long as you understand what I mean, I do not mind if now and again you shake your head and say: 'He could have told that better.'

We, the immaculate, felt like hunted animals. We knew that whatever happened we were going to get it in the neck. The most paradoxical thing about the whole performance was that if the Hauptfeldwebel could not find anything over which to catch us out, he was furious, and one or other of us immaculate soldiers would catch it worse than ever. Woe betide him who catches it in the neck over nothing – he catches it ten-fold. It is not easy to do right in such a situation.

'Front rank one step forward – rear rank one step backward – MARCH!'

One – TWO.

For two long minutes after the ranks have opened, the Hauptfeldwebel stands watching. He who sways even slightly catches it for refusing obedience. But we have learned to turn ourselves into pieces of wood, as such, can stand without moving for half an hour at a time. It is a sort of trance or catalepsy, to be able to achieve which is worth untold gold to the soldier who knows the value of being able to stand and just be a piece of wood.

The Hauptfeldwebel roars: 'Is all ready for inspection?'

The company replies in chorus: 'Yes, Herr Hauptfeldwebel.'

'No one forgotten to clean something?'

Chorus: 'No, Herr Hauptfeldwebel.'

He glares at us ferociously. Now he has us.

'You don't say so,' he says ironically. 'It's the first time in the history of this battalion, if it's true. But that we shall have to see.'

Slowly he approaches the first piece of wood, walks round it once or twice; circling your opponent without saying a word is a very effective form of the warfare of nerves. The back of your neck grows hot and your hands become clammy, and the thoughts in your head start whirling round hysterically in all directions but their natural one. You stand stock still and work yourself into a state of nervous breathlessness, and you suddenly feel that you stink both figuratively and in actual fact.

'Yes, yes – that we shall have to see,' he repeats behind the third man in the front rank.

There is dead silence, while he inspects number four and number five. Then comes a bellow: 'No. 3 Company – shun!' which is followed by the usual flow of verbal filth. We said of the Hauptfeldwebel that he could not talk filth without saying filth first; perhaps a poor witticism, but we were easily satisfied on that score – and it is at least a good description of this brutal, thoroughly unhealthy petit bourgeois who had been given a small share of the sweets of power.

'What the hell is this, you – company. You can't have done anything yesterday but dipped each other in –. Wallowing in a dung heap, that's something for a herd of swine like you. I have looked at five men now, and they all resemble pimps born of syphilitic harlots and delivered with forceps . . .'

It was not human speech but a stinking effusion. One of the brute's favourite expressions was 'the French disease'. He himself had the Prussian disease in an advanced degree, that pitiful urge to humiliate. It is a disease, and one not confined to penal battalions; it has permeated the whole German Army, where it is like a plague of boils. And in each boil you can be pretty sure of finding an NCO, a man who is something without being much.

We are now given the regulation punishment drill, which

lasts about three hours. The finale is a long ditch several feet deep and half full of fermenting mud with a rather yellowish, greasy scum on the surface. We have to scrape it from our eyes each time the order 'prone' sends us to the bottom. Then it is dinner-time. We march back to the barracks and gulp down our food as we are. Then we have to get busy, for we must be spick and span once more when we fall in for afternoon drill in half an hour's time.

We wash our uniforms and ourselves by the simple expedient of standing fully dressed under the shower. Our rifles and other equipment must first be washed, then carefully dried with a rag and finally oiled. The barrel has to be pulled through carefully. The normal soldier does his equipment thus thoroughly once, perhaps twice a week, if there has been an especially dirty exercise. We have to do it a couple of times a day.

When we fall in after this, our uniforms, of course, are dripping wet, but that does not matter as long as they are clean.

There was only one thing we feared as much as this ghastly Monday inspection, and that was the room inspection every evening at 22.00 hours. It was incredible what the Duty NCO could think of to make dead-tired men do after an exhausting day.

Before the Duty NCO came in each man must be lying in his bunk and naturally in the regulation position – on his back, arms along his sides on top of the blankets, and feet bared for inspection. The room orderly was responsible for there being not so much as a speck of dust anywhere in the room, that all feet were as clean as those of a new-born babe, and that everything in our lockers was placed and folded in accordance with the regulations. At the start of the inspection the room orderly had to report:

'Herr Unteroffizier, room orderly recruit Brand reports all in order in Room 26, complement twelve men, eleven in their bunks. The room has been properly cleaned and aired and there is nothing to report.'

The Duty NCO naturally did not pay any attention to that, but looked round. Woe betide the wretched room orderly if the Duty NCO found the least smear, or a locker that was not fastened properly, or a pair of feet with a mere hint of a shadow.

NCO Geerner – I believe he was a real mental case – used to howl like a dog. It sounded as though he were always just on the point of bursting into tears – and, in fact, it was not unusual for him to weep real tears of rage. When he was on duty we scrubbed and washed and tidied everything feverishly. I remember one unfortunate evening when Schnitzius was room orderly. Schnitzius was the room's scapegoat, good-natured as the day is long, but so hopelessly undertalented that he was the self-appointed victim of every one of his superiors from the Stabsfeldwebels down.

Schnitzius was as nervous as the other eleven of us, who lay there waiting for Geerner, wondering what we had forgotten. We could hear Geerner in one of the other rooms. It sounded as though all the bunks and lockers were being kicked to matchwood, and in between we heard his screeching, howling and sobbing voice: mangy swine, curs, etc. We blenched, pale as we already were. Geerner was in real form. He would be properly warmed up by the time he got to Room 26. We jumped out of our bunks and went over the whole room again, but we could find nothing.

The door flew open with a bang.

Oh, if only someone else than Schnitzius had been room orderly, someone with a little more gumption!

Schnitzius stood there rigid and deathly pale, quite short-circuited. He could only stare at Geerner with terrified eyes. Geerner reached him in one bound, and from a distance of two inches roared at him:

'What the hell, man! Am I to wait all night for you to report?'

Schnitzius got his report made in a quavering voice.

'All in order?' snorted Geerner. 'You're making a false report!'

'No, Herr Unteroffizier,' replied Schnitzius, his voice trembling, while he slowly turned round on his heel, so that he kept facing Geerner, as the latter prowled round the room, peering and looking.

For some minutes all was silent as the grave. We lay in our bunks, our eyes following Geerner as he walked slowly round looking for dust. He raised up the table and wiped under each of the legs. No dirt. He examined the soles of our boots. Clean. The windows and the lamp flex. Nothing. He glared at our feet as though he would drop dead if he did not find something to object to.

In the end he stood and surveyed the room with mournful, intent gaze. It really looked as though he was not going to be able to get us this time. He was exactly like someone whose girl has not turned up at the rendezvous, and who thus must go home and to bed with himself and his fearful, unsatisfied longings.

He was just shutting the door behind him, when he spun round on his heel.

'All in order, you said? I wonder.'

In one great bound he was beside our coffee-pot, a large aluminium pot holding three gallons. Each evening it had to be polished bright and filled with clean water, and that it was so Geerner had regretfully discovered a moment before. But now we realised – and our hearts missed a beat – that Geerner had thought of something new.

He stood and peered at the surface of the water from the side. It was impossible to avoid a few grains of dust settling on the water once it had been standing for some minutes.

Geerner's howl was fantastic.

'Call this clean water! Who the hell is the filthy pig who filled this pot with – ? Come here, you dung-covered splash-board!'

Geerner mounted a chair and Schnitzius had to hand the can to him.

''Shun! Head back! Open your gob!'

Slowly the can was emptied into Schnitzius' mouth. He was almost suffocated. When the can was empty the insane NCO flung it at the wall, then he rushed out of the room and we heard him making a clatter in the washroom and a tap being turned on. Shortly afterwards he flung a bucket of water into the room. When he had sent us six pailfuls, we were told to dry it up. Having only a couple of ragged floor-cloths, it took some time before the floor was dry.

He repeated that joke four times before it palled. Then Unteroffizier Geerner went comforted to bed, and we were left in peace.

Furor germanicus is what the old Romans called the special kind of battle-madness they encountered when waging war with the tribes north of the Alps. May it be some slight comfort to the Romans and to the other hard-tried enemies of the Germans to know that the Germans are as demented in dealing with themselves as with their neighbours.

Furor germanicus – the German or Prussian disease.

Geerner was a poor NCO, a diseased wretch who had to content himself with rendezvous with dust.

Peace be with him.

6

The commandant thereupon handed the company over to the chaplain.

'No. 3 Company – for prayers – KNEEL!' roared the chaplain.

One Kind of Soldier

Our training ended with an exercise that lasted seven days and sleepless nights. It took place on a huge training area called Sennelager. There they had built whole villages, bridges, railway lines, all complete except for the inhabitants, and there we had to fight our way through tangled under-growth, bogs and rivers, over swaying bridges that were just laid loosely across deep chasms.

That, perhaps, sounds romantic, like playing Red Indians on a large scale; but we lost a man while we played. He fell off one of the unsteady bridges and broke his neck.

One of the games consisted of digging holes in the ground just deep enough for us to be below the surface when we curled up in them; whereupon heavy tanks came up and drove over the holes, while we cowered in them, shaking with fear.

This 'thrill' was immediately followed by another. We had to fling ourselves flat on the ground and let the tanks drive over us. We felt the steel bottom of the tank brush our backs, while the heavy caterpillars clattered past to right and left.

We were to be hardened to tank-shock.

At any rate we were scared, and that is the normal thing. The German soldier is brought up on fear, trained to react like a machine through sheer terror, not to fight bravely because he is fired by a great ideal that makes it seem obvious to sacrifice himself if the need arise. Perhaps you could call this moral inferiority the characteristic feature of the Prussian mentality and the chronic ill of the German people.

The day after the end of this exercise we took the oath of

allegiance. For this, the company formed up along three sides of a square into the middle of which a tank drove, and on either side of this a machine-gun was placed. As soon as this neat little tableau was arranged, the commandant appeared, accompanied by his adjutant and the chaplain, who, to make the occasion more solemn, was got up in all his trappings.

The commandant then made a speech:

'Men of the Prussian Army! Your training is now complete. In a short while you will be attached to various field regiments like grenadiers, anti-tank, fusiliers, scouts or even a home-defence unit. But no matter where you are sent, you must do your duty. You are outcasts, but if you show that you are brave and courageous, the day may perhaps come when the great Führer will take you back into favour again. You are now to take the old oath of allegiance, the oath you have once forsworn, but I am sure that from now on, and for the rest of your lives, it will bind you in loyalty to your country. I expect of each one of you that you will never again forget your oath and your duty to our ancient land and our great people, your duty to the Führer and our God.'

Shortly after that we all kneeled, removed our steel helmets and folded our hands over the muzzle of our rifles. It must have looked very moving, just the stuff for a news-film. The chaplain then spoke a short prayer to the great, almighty and, of course, German God, who would bring the Nazis victory. The idiot did not actually use the word Nazis, but what else could he have meant when he said:

'Almighty God, our Lord, show us Thy greatness and goodness and grant to German arms victory over our barbarian enemies.'

Their barbarian enemies, mark you, being peoples who had bred men like Ibsen and Nansen, Hans Andersen, Rembrandt and Spinoza, Voltaire and Rene Clair, Tchaikovski and Gorki, Shakespeare and Dickens, Abraham Lincoln and Theodore Dreiser, Chopin and Copernicus, Socrates and Homer, and women like Florence Nightingale and Emmeline Pankhurst, Marion Anderson and Mrs. Roosevelt, Marie and Irene Curie,

Catherine II, Joan of Arc, Isak Dinesen, the Brontë sisters, Anna Pavlova.

After that he blessed the weapons with which we were to exterminate barbary, but I do not think that helped. For a miserable little priest to stand up and make the sign of the cross at a great tank can scarcely be very effective magic, even if you believe in magic, which I cannot. At the most you might imagine such a creature bewitching small arms. And, anyway, they lost the war.

Then we took the oath. The chaplain recited it a few words at a time, and the company repeated them in chorus, while one of us stood out in front of the company with three fingers touching the point of the commandant's drawn sword. That was part of the tableau.

A buzz of voices rang out across the silent square:

'I swear by God – our Holy Father – the sacred oath – that I in everything – will fight dutifully and faithfully – and will give up my life – if that be required – for the Führer, people and fatherland – he who swears this oath – must know – that it is branded on his heart – and if he breaks his sacred oath – may God the Almighty have mercy on his soul – for he will then have forfeited – his right to live – and he will be tormented – for all eternity – in Hell fire – Amen.'

Then we sang *Deutschland, Deutschland, über alles!*

Thus were we confirmed, but we were given no confirmation present.

The next day we were split up into small groups of from five to fifteen men and issued with new field equipment. I and a few others were given the black uniform and beret of the tank troops, and the following morning we went under command of a Feldwebel to the barracks in Bielefeldt, where we were at once thrust into a company on the point of leaving for the front and loaded into a troop train.

7

'Is this company to be burdened with more of you bloody criminals? Disgusting! Don't let me catch you committing the least irregularity, or I'll have you sent back to the gaol where you ought to have had the decency to die long ago, devil take me if I don't. Gaol's the place for your sort.'

Such was the greeting with which I was welcomed by the commander of No. 5 Company, obese Hauptmann Meier, tormentor of recruits. But one was so used to that sort of thing.

I was assigned to No. 2 Squadron under Leutnant von Barring, and then things began to happen to which I was not accustomed.

Our First Meeting

Barring held out his hand and took mine in a strong, friendly clasp. That is the sort of thing an officer in the Prussian Army simply cannot do, yet he did it; and when he had done it he said, 'Welcome, lad, welcome to No. 5 Company. You've come to a hellish awful regiment, but we have to stick together and make a do of it. Go across there to truck No. 24 and report to Unteroffizier Beier, he is leader of No. 1 Section.' And then he smiled – a big, open, bright smile, the smile of a nice, friendly young man.

I was completely bewildered.

I soon found truck No. 24, and Unteroffizier Beier was pointed out to me. He was sitting beside a large barrel playing cards with three others – a short, powerfully built man of about thirty-five. I halted the regulation three paces from him, brought my heels together with a bang and in a loud, clear voice began my report:

'Herr Unteroffizier, I beg—'

But I got no further. Two of the four leaped off the buckets on which they were sitting and stood as stiff as ramrods, with their fingers down the seams of their trousers. The Unteroffizier and the fourth fell over backwards, sending the cards flying like dead leaves in an autumn storm. For a moment all four stared at me. Then a tall, red-haired Obergefreiter said:

'What the hell, man! You scared the life out of us. Hitler's got into you, I do believe. What can have possessed a flat-footed dung-beetle like you to come and interrupt peace-loving burghers at their innocent occupations? Tell us, who and what are you?'

'Report, Herr Obergefreiter, that I come from Leutnant von Barring and am to report to No. 1 Section to Unteroffizier Beier,' I replied.

Beier and the fourth man, who was still on his back, stood up, and all four stared at me in horror, looking as though they would run shrieking in all directions if I took one step towards them. Then all at once they burst into a roar of laughter.

'Did you hear him! Herr Obergefreiter. Ha, ha, ha! Herr Unteroffizier Beier, ha, ha, ha!' exclaimed the red-headed Obergefreiter, who then turned to the Unteroffizier, bowed low and said, 'Honourable Excellency! Your Worshipful Grace, your captivating Magnificence, Herr Unteroffizier Beier, I beg to report . . .'

I looked in bewilderment from one to the other, quite unable to see what was so superbly funny. When they had recovered from the paroxysm the Unteroffizier asked me where I had come from. I told them, and they looked at me sympathetically.

'Off with your wooden legs,' said the red-head. 'Penal battalion in Hanover. Now we understand why you behave as you do. We thought you were trying to make fools of us when you clashed your heels together like that; but I suppose it's a God's miracle you still have them to clash. Well, here you are!'

With those words I was received into No. 1 Section, and an hour later we were rolling along towards Freiburg, where we were to be formed into a fighting unit and sent to one place or another in crazy Europe for special training. As we rattled along, my four companions introduced themselves, and it was with these four that I went through the war.

Willie Beier was ten years older than the rest of us, and because of that he was called The Old Un. He was married and had two children. By trade he was a joiner, and his home was in Berlin. His politics had earned him eighteen months in a concentration camp, after which he had been 'pardoned' and sent to a penal battalion. The Old Un smiled quietly to himself:

'And here I will certainly remain, till, one fine day, I run too fast into a bullet.'

The Old Un was a stout companion. He was always calm and quiet. Never once during those four, frightful years that we spent together did I see him nervous or afraid. He was one of those strange beings who radiate calm, the calm that the rest of us so badly needed in a tight corner. He was almost like a father to us, although there was only ten years difference in our ages, and many was the time I rejoiced at my good fortune in being put in The Old Un's tank.

Obergefreiter Joseph Porta was one of those incorrigible wags who can never be bested. He did not care a fig about the war, and I believe that both God and the devil were slightly afraid of having anything to do with him in case they made fools of themselves. At any rate, he was feared by all the officers in the company, whom he could put off their stride, sometimes for good and all, just by looking innocently at them.

He never omitted to tell all whom he came across that he was a Red. He had been a year in Oranienburg and Moabit charged with Communist activities. What had happened was that in 1932 he had helped some friends to hang a couple of Social-Democrat flags on the tower of Michaelis Church. He was caught by the police and given fourteen days, after which the matter was forgotten until, in 1938, he was suddenly arrested by the Gestapo, who made great efforts to persuade him that he knew the mysterious hiding-place of the fat but ever invisible Wollweber, leader of the Communists. Having starved and bullied him for a couple of months, he was hauled before a court and accused of Communist activities. A huge enlargement of a photograph was placed before the judges, on which you could see Porta complete with enormous flag on his way to Michaelis Church. Twelve years' hard labour for Communist activities and profanation of God's house. Shortly before the war broke out, like so many other prisoners he was pardoned in the usual way, by being flung into a penal battalion. It's the same with soldiers as with money – it does not matter where they come from.

Porta was a Berliner and had all the Berliner's raffish humour, ready tongue and fantastic cheek. He only had to open his mouth to make all round him collapse with laughter, especially when he gave his voice an affected drawl and assumed so arrogant and insolent a manner as you would otherwise only encounter in the valet of a German count.

Porta was also highly musical and the possessor of a real, natural talent. He played equally bewitchingly on Jew's-harp and church-organ, and wherever he went he took his clarinet, on which he made magic, his shrewd piggy eyes staring rigidly in front of him and his red hair bristling like a haystack in a storm. The notes seemed to come dancing out of the instrument, whether he was crooning a popular tune or improvising on classical themes. A score was double-Dutch to Porta, but if we happened to come across some music it only needed The Old Un to whistle the melody for him and Porta would play it, as though it were he who had composed it.

Porta also had the true gift of the story-teller. He could make a story last for several days, lies and invention though it was from beginning to end.

Like all self-respecting Berliners, Porta could always tell where there was something to eat, how you could get hold of it, and if there was a choice, which was the best. Perhaps they had a Porta during the wandering through the wilderness.

Porta maintained that he had great success with women, but his appearance made you doubt his word. He was endlessly tall and correspondingly thin. His neck was like a stork's neck protruding from his uniform collar, and in it was a huge Adam's apple which made you giddy every time he talked, because you could not help watching it jump up and down. His head was a triangular affair at which a fistful of freckles had been flung haphazard. His eyes were small, green and piggy, had long white lashes and twinkled craftily at the person to whom he was speaking. His hair was fiery red and stood out in all directions like thatch. His nose was his pride, the Lord knows why. When he opened his mouth, you saw one tooth, alone in the middle of his upper jaw. He insisted that he had two others, only they were molars and well-hidden. Where the quartermaster found boots for him was a mystery; he must have taken size fourteen.

The third of the quartet, Pluto, was a mountain of muscle. He was a Stabsgefreiter and his real name was Gustav Eicken. He had thrice been in a concentration camp, and with him it was not politics but good honest crime that had sent him there. He had been a docker in Hamburg, but he and some of his companions had done quite well for themselves by purloining a little of this and a bit of that from warehouses and ships. Then they were caught, and that cost them six months. Two days after his release the police came for him again. This time it was his brother, who had faked a passport, for which they chopped off his head. Pluto himself was kept in prison for nine months without being interrogated, and was then thrown out without explanation, after being thoroughly beaten up. Three months later he had something worth calling a theft foisted upon him, that of a whole lorry-load of flour. Pluto knew nothing whatever about it, but they beat him up just the same, and then confronted him with a man who swore that Pluto was the accomplice with whom he had stolen a flour lorry. The trial lasted exactly twelve minutes and earned Pluto six years. He was in a Fühlsbüttel for two of them, then he was sent to the usual penal battalion, and in 1939 he rattled into Poland along with the rest of the 27th (Penal) Regiment. If you wanted to get Pluto really wild you only had to pronounce a sentence in which the words lorry and flour occurred.

The fourth, Obergefreiter Anton Steyer, was never called anything but Titch. He was four feet eleven and a half inches. He came from Cologne, where he had worked in the perfume industry. A rather noisy altercation in a Bierstube had earned

46

him and two companions three years in a concentration camp. The other two had gone long since, one falling in Poland, while the other had deserted, been caught and executed.

For six days our troop-train rattled round Germany before we reached our destination, the picturesque South German town of Freiburg. We did not expect we would be allowed to stay there long. The rear is not the normal place for penal regiments, whose duty it is to be ever to the fore and to write the gory pages of history. There were wild rumours that we were to be sent to Italy, and from there to Libya, but no one knew anything for certain. The first day was taken up being classified, with driving instruction and other pleasant duties. Our free time we spent pleasantly enough in the restaurant Zum Goldenen Hirsch, whose genial host was naturally called Schultz, and, equally naturally, proved to be an old friend of Porta.

The wine was good, the girls willing and our voices were at any rate strong.

It was so long since I had taken part in that kind of activity, and such ghastly things lay close behind me, that I had considerable beginner's difficulties in burying the past, or rather in suspending it for a night, when the occasion offered. If I succeeded now and again, it was thanks to Porta, The Old Un, Pluto and Titch. They had been through the whole gamut of it, just as I had, and it had made toughs of them, and when there were wine, girls and song in the offing they gave not a damn for anything else.

8

At first, the railwayman refused. A good National-Socialist did not run errands for convict-soldiers. But when Porta breathed something about a whole bottle rum the railwayman forgot for a while that he was a superior being. He went across to the platform of our fat restaurateur Schultz, and shortly afterwards returned with a bulky parcel, which he duly handed over. Porta gave him a look of infinite geniality.

'You are a Party member, aren't you?' said Porta, with his most innocent expression.

'Of course,' the railwayman replied, and pointed to the large Party badge that graced the pocket of his uniform. 'Why do you ask?'

Porta narrowed his green, piggy eyes. 'I shall tell you, dear fellow. If you are a Party member you will obey the Führer's commandment that the good of the whole comes before that of the individual. And therefore you will say something like this: 'Brave warriors of the 27th Fire-and-Sword Regiment! To help you to fight still better for Führer and People, I, in my gratitude, will make you a gift of the bottle of rum that Herr Joseph Porta, by God's Grace Obergefreiter, in his infinite goodness wished to give to my unworthy person.' Wasn't it just that you were wanting to say? Weren't those very words trembling on the tip of your tongue? Dear fellow, we thank you from the bottom of our hearts, and now you may go.'

Porta flung out his hand with a magnificent flourish, raised his cap and shouted, 'Grüss Gott!'

As soon as the wretched Nazi railwayman had gone, furiously gnashing his teeth, we opened the parcel.

There were five bottles of wine; there was a whole roast of pork; there were two roast chickens, and there was . . .

Curiosities of the Balkans

'But we must remember that we are going to war,' he said in a quavering voice, 'and war can be a pretty dangerous thing. You hear of all sorts of things, and people dying of them. Just suppose a bullet suddenly came and killed all five of us at once. Or suppose' – his voice sank to a horrified whisper – 'suppose it did not hit any of us, but went through these three bottles while there was still something in them. That would be – that would be the real horror of war!'

Even so, we put the bottles aside for later.

Shortly afterwards the train started.

'We're off! We're off!'

God knows why we shouted that, for it was perfectly obvious both to us in the truck and to those standing outside. The sliding doors were open on either side and we stood in them, hanging over each other, shouting ourselves hoarse. It did not matter what we saw: a cat, a cow, to say nothing of a woman, we gave it a ringing cheer.

'Tell me, what the devil are we really cheering for?' said The Old Un suddenly. 'Are we so happy at going off to be butchered?'

Porta broke off in the midst of a hurrah and thought this over.

'Why we cheer? Well, my dear little piggy-wig, you see, we cheer – but why?'

He looked round at the rest of us.

'I think I know,' said Titch.

'Well, why?'

'Because' – he looked at us solemnly – 'because, have you ever heard of a war when people don't cheer?' And he added, like an afterthought, 'And then we're off on a great mission. We are on our way to help the Führer, to help our great Adolf to a real, big defeat, so that this filthy war can stop and the wonderful collapse at long last become a glorious reality.'

Porta lifted Titch up, kissed him on both cheeks and set him down again. Then he stretched his long swan's neck over the rest of us and emitted a jubilant bellow that the Führer must have heard but perhaps would not have understood.

It is not for me to express an opinion, but seen from the angle of the private soldier the famous German talent for organisation did not appear up to much, at any rate where troop transports were concerned. The impression of the General Staff's brilliant planning and lauded organisation that the private gets is that when he has to be transported anywhere he is taken there in a zigzag. To transport a private from A to B along a straight line and without day-long halts at fortuitous places among cornfields or in the sidings of a marshalling yard – in a word, to transport him without waste of time or fuel, would be equivalent to revolutionising the conduct of war, and would have the fateful result that their fine plans would not get in a muddle. And it is a well-known fact, which private soldiers in all countries will be able to confirm, that you cannot wage a war without muddles. The amount of muddle and the tremendous waste of human life, food, material and brainwork that lie behind such expressions as 'advance according to plan', to say nothing of 'straightening the front' and 'elastic retreat', is so immeasurably tragic that you could not conceive it, even if you tried.

It seems to me that there is a sort of explanation for the muddle of war. It is perhaps this, or this among other things, that if there were no muddle it would be possible to pin down responsibility. If you take Muddle $= \div$ Responsibility, then my explanation becomes quite plausible:

If War = Muddle
and Muddle = no Responsibility
then War = no Responsibility

and this is an equation to which we shall frequently revert.

Without responsibility we rolled across the Serbian border, where we were told that until further notice we were the 18th Battalion of the 12th Panzer Division and that we were being sent to a training area somewhere in the Balkans, where we were to be trained in the use of a new tank, after which we would be sent to the front. When we were told this Porta grinned, delighted.

'At the present rate, that will scarcely be for the next thirty-four years,' he said. 'Our good fortune is assured. We shall be wonderfully happy and become fantastically rich, and I'll tell you for why. In the Balkans business flourishes as nowhere else in Europe, because all trade is done by the direct method: you steal from each other and no fuss is made. And what is a soldier if not a good businessman? Be good soldiers now, remember what you have learned and apply it. I shall leave the lovely Balkans a well-satisfied, rich and well-equipped young man.'

From Zagreb to Banja-Luka; from Banja-Luka to Serajevo; from there a sudden dive north to Brod, then eastwards again across the Hungarian frontier to Pécs; thus did the 18th Battalion roll to and also from, performing great and long-remembered feats, though not quite of the same kind as those the telegrams from the front proclaimed to Neuropa, and which held breathless audiences spellbound in the cinemas, when the 'Documentary' news-films were shown to the accompaniment of very martial music. No, 18th Battalion was never filmed or mentioned in orders. It was just one of the unknown, grey battalions that were wiped out, reformed, wiped out, reformed and wiped out – again and again and again, for a cause that we abominated, though we could not express our feelings with such enviable conciseness as Porta, who was never at a loss for a fart with which to put a 'full stop' at the end of the improbable 'surveys' of the wireless commentator.

We almost left Porta behind in the little town of Melykut, north-east of Pécs. He came running up at the last moment and had to be pulled into the truck. A couple of minutes later, as we rattled past a hovel on the outskirts of the town, we saw three gypsy women standing waving eagerly. Porta waved back and bellowed:

'Goodbye, little girls. If you have a baby and it's a boy call him Joseph after his father. And for the Holy Virgin's sake don't let him be a soldier; far rather a pimp, that's more respectable.'

51

Then Porta settled himself comfortably in a corner of the truck, produced an incredibly greasy pack of cards from his pocket and soon we were deep in a game of the inevitable vingt-et-un. When we had been playing for four hours, the train stopped at the frontier station of Makó, a little south-east of Szeged.

We were told that there was to be a halt of ten hours before we went on into Roumania. We jumped down from the truck and strolled off to have a look round. As usual, Porta went off on his own, and, as usual, he came sauntering up to The Old Un and me a little while later, looking most innocent, and whispered:

'Come!'

The town – it was something between a country town and a village – lay dead in the quivering heat of the afternoon. Our clothes stuck to us as we strolled, hot and sweating, down the main street, where ragged peasants lay asleep in the shade of the trees. Suddenly Porta clambered over some fences and through a hedge, and we found ourselves in a little street of small houses with little gardens.

'I can scent things,' said Porta, and broke into a trot.

The upshot was that The Old Un and I suddenly found ourselves hiding behind a hedge, each clutching a strangled goose, while Porta ran for his life pursued by a dozen bellowing men and women.

We hurried back to the train, stuffed the geese away out of sight, and then set off to rescue Porta.

We met him, striding along with a grand escort consisting of a Hungarian lieutenant, two Honved Scouts with fixed bayonets, two of our own military police and a good fifty shouting, gesticulating civilians, Hungarians, Roumanians, Slovaks and gypsies.

Porta took it all with the utmost calm. 'As you see,' he said to us, 'the Hungarian Regent Horthy, our Führer's best friend in this country, has given me a guard of honour.'

Luckily it was Major Hinka who received this procession, when it reached the Staff truck. Hinka was young and decent, and Porta's particular protector. Calmly he listened to all the accusations of the Hungarian lieutenant; then, when the lieutenant had finished, he began:

'What the hell is this you have been up to now, man? Robbery and attempted murder. Not only have you been stealing geese and so brought the entire population down upon us, but, devil take me, if you haven't also been attacking Hungarian soldiers, our brothers-in-arms. And kicked a valuable dog. Smashed the bailiff's false teeth. Been the cause of two miscarriages. What have you to say to that, you bandy-legged ape!'

All this was roared out, so that the excited crowd could see that Porta was catching it.

Porta bawled back: 'Herr Major, this lot of maundering idiots are such appalling liars that my pious soul is shaken to the quick. By the sacred, knobbly mace of St. Elizabeth I swear that I was walking along quietly and peacefully, in innocent enjoyment of the lovely view and the wonderful weather. I was just in the middle of a silent prayer of thanks to God for allowing me to be among the fortunates who have become our great and beloved Führer's soldiers and thereby had an opportunity of getting out to see the wide world beyond our good city of Berlin, when, with an abruptness that was exceedingly bad for my delicate nerves, I was torn from my pious and beautiful thoughts by a band of savage devils suddenly rushing out from some bushes, where they had been lying in wait for me. I have no idea what I have done to them; but is it any wonder that I gave a shout of terror and took to my heels? I could only conclude that they wanted to murder me, for I could not possibly have imagined that they just wanted to borrow a match, and, as I had noticed that one of them wore a watch, I knew it could not be the time they wanted to know. Then, as I turned a corner at the highest permissible speed, there stood one of these operetta warriors with feathers in his imbecile hat and a paintbox on his chest. When he tried to stop me there was nothing I could do but give him a slight push, but I assure you there was no discourtesy intended. I believe he did fall fairly hard, but if he is still not on his feet I will gladly help to get him to hospital.

53

After that, a whole flock of these feathered fowl came up howling, exactly like the Indians used to do when on the warpath, according to that lovely book – Herr Major will surely know it – *The Deer Slayer*, it's called, and if you haven't read it I'll write home to my Granny for it, for I know she has it.'

'That's enough, Porta,' bawled Major Hinka. 'Can I have an explanation of the geese?'

'Herr Major,' said Porta, and to our great delight tears now began to roll down his dirty face, 'I have no idea what geese these people are talking about; but you know yourself how often I am mistaken for someone else. I am the most unfortunate of men, and I am convinced that I have at least two doubles. My Granny says so too.'

Major Hinka's cheek muscles quivered, but he managed to keep a straight face, as, turning to the Hungarian lieutenant, he assured him that Porta would be duly punished for plundering.

That evening Major Hinka also had roast goose.

9

We crawled over and under an infinity of goods-trucks and came to a large covered one, the door of which had been sealed with the Wehrmacht's seal. Both seal and heavy padlock were broken, however, and swiftly The Old Un pushed the door aside.

'Take a look at that, and tell me what you think,' he said.

We almost fell over backwards at the sight that met our goggling eyes. Ye gods! – did such things still exist? Tins of pineapple, pears, fillets of beef, ham, asparagus, lobster, shrimps, olives, Portuguese sardines, jars of ginger, peaches. Real coffee and tea, chocolate, cigarettes and wine, white wine – red wine, brandy, champagne. A grocer's shop on wheels, a poem, an Eastern play.

'Almighty God!' gasped Titch. 'Who is this truck meant for?'

'You mean, who was it meant for,' said Pluto. 'Even a monster like you must be able to see that God has guided your steps. And God did not do that for you to stand up on your hind legs and ask silly questions.'

The next day when we reached the big goods-station at Bucharest, where we were meant to detrain, Porta disappeared with a case of wine, and shortly afterwards a shunting-engine moved our truck across to a remote siding, where it was hidden from inquisitive glances. Porta even got a Stabsfeldwebel to fill out a freight-note for the truck, so that it really belonged to 18th Battalion.

The Glories of the Balkans

We were quartered in the Roumanian barracks by the River Dombrovitz, a little way outside the city. One Saturday evening Porta went into Bucharest to play poker with some Roumanians of his acquaintance, and he had not returned by the time we had to go on parade on Sunday morning. There was nothing for it but for me to call 'Here' in answer to his name.

Pluto's idea was that Porta, having staked and lost everything, including his clothes, was now with some girl waiting for help. The rest of us found that difficult to believe, for Porta was a genius at cheating at cards. The more likely and more disquieting explanation, we felt, was that he had cleaned the others out – and then been set upon.

As soon as we had eaten we hurried out into the town to try and find him. That was by no means an easy task, since Bucharest is a large city with a million inhabitants. Not only that, but it is spread over a considerable area and is full of large parks, broad boulevards and endless streets of houses standing in their own gardens.

But we had no need to worry. As we were walking down a street in one of the best residential districts we saw a strange procession coming towards us, so strange that everyone stopped and stared. Four men – two Roumanian privates, an Italian Bersagliere sergeant and a man in full evening dress – came staggering along with a sedan-chair the size of a compartment in a railway carriage between them. As they went, they bawled out 'In a Persian Garden' to the accompaniment of a flute. The flautist could not be seen; he sat inside the monster of red lacquer and gilt. Suddenly he shouted:

'Halt, slaves! Prepare to land! Attention – *land*!'

The two front bearers let down their end with a thud that could be heard for miles, and out tumbled Porta. He, too, was in stiff shirt and tails, wearing a top hat and a monocle. He greeted us with a gesture of the kind that the bad French novelists of the turn of the century called 'indescribable', and hailed The Old Un and the rest of us in an affected voice:

'*Chéris! Mes Frères!* My name is Count de la Porta, by God's Grace von und zu. If I am not mistaken, I know you gentlemen?

'Goes all well with Germany's arms? Let me see a list of today's victories.'

'What the devil's that you're going round in?' said Titch. 'Is our honest cattle-truck no longer good enough for you?'

'I am thinking of having myself transported to the Eastern

56

Front in this special conveyance, which is now reserved exclusively for the best soldier in the German Army. James' – this was addressed to me – 'you shall walk just behind me and hand me my rifle when I have to shoot. See that Germany's best man has aimed properly before I pull the trigger. We don't want any misses in this war.'

'And where's your uniform?'

'Gentlemen, this war is a gentleman's war. I have put on a gentleman's uniform . . . As well as this sedan-chair and these irreproachable tails I have won 2,300 lei and a very fine musical-box, which I shall now play for you.'

Porta dived into the depths of the sedan-chair and emerged with a magnificent rococo musical-box, which played a little minuet while two porcelain shepherdesses danced. It was undoubtedly a valuable piece. A couple of days later he presented it to a tram conductor.

'And lastly I have won a mistress – with thighs and the rest of it.'

'A what?'

'A what?' Porta echoed. 'Don't you know, child, what a mistress is? It's a toy for counts and barons. It has thighs and breasts and buttocks. That's what you play with. You can buy them in very expensive shops, where you drink champagne while you inspect the models. It has to be wound up with a cheque before it will move. It moves up and down till it becomes tired, then it has to be wound up with another cheque. If you have enough cheques it will never stop.'

Porta thrust a bottle of wine at his four bearers and bellowed:

'Here, slaves, petrol! Drink and be merry!'

Then he handed us a couple of bottles of schnapps and said with a flourish:

'Let us sing the praises of the good old gods!'

He put the flute to his lips and began to play, while his four delighted bearers chorused:

'*Now it is the time to drain the flowing bowl,*
'*Now with unfettered foot to beat the ground with dancing,*

'Now with Salian feast to deck the couches of the gods, my
   Comrades!'

'Where the devil did you get your Horace from?' said I.

Porta replied impudently that he had penned the lines
himself.

'Did you really?' said The Old Un interestedly. 'I never
thought you were so old. The Romans used to sing that two
thousand years ago.'

Porta's slaves now gave us a vivid description of the events
of the night. Porta had played poker with a young baron.
Both had cheated so grossly that a child must have seen it. In
the end Porta had won everything, including the clothes off
the baron's back. After that, he had gone feasting with the
four merry lads, and they were now carrying him to Bazar
Street and the young lady he had won from the unlucky
baron.

Then they picked up the sedan-chair and bore it swaying on
its way, while we stood there, shaking our heads and clutching our bottles of schnapps.

Late that afternoon the four slaves deposited Porta, flute
and all, by the wall outside the barracks. We managed to haul
him inside and bribed one of the junior doctors to have him
admitted to the sick bay, where he slept for two solid days.
We packed his evening dress at the bottom of his kit-bag, and
he carted it round with him all the war. On festive occasions –
or rather when he thought there was occasion for festivities –
he would dress up in it, even doing so in the trenches on
more than one occasion.

Perhaps that sedan-chair is still standing by the wall of the
barracks outside Bucharest as a sort of peaceful war memorial.
If so, the Roumanians will certainly look more kindly upon it
than on the ruins, which were the true memento the German
Army left behind it.

If there had been more Portas and considerably fewer
Hauptmann Meiers there is no doubt that we would have
conquered the peoples, vanquished the enemy and made him
our friend and brother toper. We would have vanquished the

enemy, not in bloody battle but in a drinking contest, which is never such a grim business, and has the advantage that the means satisfy everyone, while it is also easier to recover from a hang-over than from having a leg shot off.

We did not come to Roumania as welcome tourists, far less as fêted brothers-in-arms, though the newspapers proclaimed that Germany and Roumania were close allies fighting like brothers, shoulder to shoulder, for a great cause. People like Porta and The Old Un, and many others of the galley-slaves in the German Army, were more to the Roumanians' liking than one might have imagined, but our uniform was not, and it was that which they saw. They only saw that we were allies of the Iron Guard, of the barons, of the anti-semites, of the dictator General Ion Antonescu, of all the gentry who harried the land with the scourge of under-development. It was, in fact, almost more difficult in the land of our brothers, the Roumanians, to fraternise with the people, or certain sections of them, than it was in many of the countries which the German Army had occupied as an enemy. We were brothers-in-arms for whom none could have anything but profound mistrust. It was typical that Porta made his way into the Roumanians' hearts via a dissolute baron. The upper classes were the only ones who would have anything to do with us. Of course, we were there to defend their money and civic rights, to defend them not only from the Soviet or Socialism but from the maltreated, dissatisfied Roumanian workers and small farmers who needed repressing with a bloody hand. A barefooted, under-nourished, coerced and defiant people will not take foreigners to its bosom straight away, however much those at the top may say that they are brothers and fellow-countrymen of a kind because both are neo-Europeans. Life in Roumania at that time was more or less what I imagine it must be in Spain now, well nigh impossible because of having to mistrust everyone and everything, with murderous inner strife beneath the surface, yet so close to it that you had to be blind not to discover it.

Unfortunately many German soldiers were both blind and deaf. They did not discover the proper connection between

59

things. They were blinded by Hitler and deafened by Goebbels. They believed all they were told, and therefore could not understand why the Roumanians did not receive them as conquering heroes. They did not like it; they were hurt. Others were able to smell the rottenness of everything, but they were too bemused and terrorised from home to dare face up to the problem. They let things take their crooked course and dared not look each other – far less their 'brethren-in-arms' – in the face.

Porta's was a happy expedient; he plundered a baron, had an evening out on the proceeds, and then presented the remains of the booty to a tram conductor. He managed better than we did. We had more or less to content ourselves with visual pleasures, with scenic beauties, the unending melancholy of the puszta; the flatness and extensive fertility of the Roumanian wheatlands; the picturesque realm of the mountains; the station communities asleep at noon but lively in the evening; the flocks of sheep with solitary shepherds walking along in white, coarse coats and sheepskin caps, with a leathern bottle on a string strung across their shoulders, and all the time in the world; groups of thin adults and large-eyed, rickety children. And Bucharest, the white, splendid city with its magnificent residential quarters, expensive motor-cars, arrogant rich and murmuring, miserably ragged poor; inquisitive peasants in colourful national costume.

The life of the people was just for us to look at, not to take part in, unless you were a God-forsaken gallows-bird like Porta. Only occasionally did one or other of us succeed by the use of slight shades of tone in voice and behaviour in achieving a certain amount of tacit sympathy – it never found expression in words – with those in whose country we found ourselves under the most difficult of all circumstances – that of being unwelcome friends. Nor could we have been anything else, for it was the old story: we had entered the country on the pretext of coming to fight a common foe. In reality we were a necessary addition to the country's police force. On the pretext of protecting the Roumanian people from being conquered by the Soviets, we had come first and foremost to help prevent the oilwells, the mines, the railway concessions, the big estates, the wine-, match-, textile-, sugar-, paper-, cosmetics-, and an infinity of other monopolies, in fact the whole rich country with its impoverished population, from taking the sad, sad road that leads to nationalisation.

What right has a people to its own oil?

None – as long as *we* were in Roumania with Hungarians, Italians and other foreign 'friends' to help us. The rich were indecently rich, the poor indecently poor – and the concentration camps . . . Ugh, the whole thing was indecent.

It was there in the Balkans, I believe, that I learned the need not only for revolt but for *organised* revolt against war. I came to the conclusion that the war was not so pointless, as in moments of sentiment and emotion we sometimes felt it.

The point of it was that we were to pull certain chestnuts out of the fire. When we had done that, we could then see whether we might not be able to live on the ashes.

Those ideas were not clear in my head then, but they were there. I had not learned to reflect then. I lived for the moment and never thought very much. I had to get properly over what I had been through before I could embark on anything so exacting as the business of thinking.

10

We had written each other many affectionate letters since we parted in Freiburg, but in all Ursula's letters I found a discouraging note, that at times almost sent me out of my mind with the misery of unrequited love, with longing to be able to persuade her that she was mistaken, that she did love me, only would not admit it to herself.

Her reply to my telegram came in the evening:

MEET ME VIENNA STOP WAIT IN FIRST CLASS RESTAURANT STOP URSULA.

Ursula

Ursula was not there. Her train must be late. She would be coming soon. I sat down at a table, from which I could keep watch on the door. There was a continual stream of people coming in and out. Now and again so many came in at once that I could not take them all in at one glance and I stood up in a sort of semi-fury.

More than an hour passed.

I took her letters from an inner pocket and began reading them for the thousandth time, reading a line at a time with a look at the door in between. Suddenly I became panic-stricken: suppose she had been there while I had my eyes on a letter; suppose she had stood there and looked round without catching sight of me and so had gone again, got into a train and gone back to Munich.

After sitting there for two hours I went out and asked if the train from Munich was delayed. I was told that it had arrived an hour before mine. The man was polite and friendly, but quite uninterested in my important problem, of which I told him nothing, but which was certainly there for all to read on my face.

Feeling empty with irresolution, I walked about haphazard.

What the hell had I come to Vienna for? I returned to my seat in the restaurant and sat there staring, trying to think, loving, weeping inwardly, hating, building up theories, making ingenious plans for finding her, inventing plausible improbabilities that might have happened, while round about me voices buzzed, crockery clattered, two cash registers whirred and their tills opened and shut. Everybody else was busy either serving or eating or smoking, talking, laughing – but living. I was the only one no one knew, and therefore I could not live, but must just sit, growing more and more haggard, while my inner life assumed more and more fantastic forms. I do not believe there is a more abnormal being than the person who is sitting waiting for his beloved. It was now three hours past the time; she was not coming. Mine was a very painful madness, one that perhaps would never have been cured if she had not come.

But she came, as soft and graceful and rounded as a little flame. My fingers crushed the cigarette they held, and the glowing end fell into my palm, but my brain did not hear the palm's call that it had burned itself, my eyes drowned the sound of it as they looked and looked – looked at the grey suit, the confident shoes, the fleeting smile, the little brown suitcase with the silver letters US and the hand that held it, just made to fit at the back of a man's neck.

'I came with the wrong train. I am so sorry.'

She protested, but I kissed her hand nonetheless and shoved the table forward, so that she could sit beside me.

'Darling.'

'Now, my lad, first you must order your darling some food – no, no, be good now, order something nice and a bottle of wine. Then I'll tell you what we are going to do.'

I ordered paprika chicken with rice and pointed to some number on the wine list. I was still shaken and non compos, but I retained sufficient presence of mind to confine my utterances for the next quarter of an hour to the one word 'darling'. It was an honest admission of not being quite right in the head, and thus an admission that could only please her and be accepted.

We were going to Hochfilzen. In an hour.

'I like the place so much, and when you telegraphed that you had got leave and wanted to come, that you had five days, I thought that that was where we would go. You're mad about mountains yourself, aren't you?'

'Darling.'

'You're quite impossible. You must drink lots of wine. We must get you normal again. I don't want to travel with an imbecile. Not that I'm quite right in the head myself. What have I let myself in for?'

I emptied my glass and then refilled hers and mine. The food on my plate remained untouched, but she shovelled in chicken and paprika sauce and rice and bread, and chattered away and displayed great, comforting activity. I was slightly disappointed that she did not tell me I ought to eat. She always used to say that. She always used to say that I was too thin, that I ought to eat well. She did not say it now. Something about her had changed, and I was not sure that she was not just as nervous as I, that we were not sitting there groping round the outside of each other, away from each other.

'You've let yourself in for a honeymoon,' I replied thoughtfully. 'Our honeymoon.'

She laughed; then having sat for a while looking ahead of her with wrinkled brow, she suddenly grasped my hand and pressed it to her cheek. We sat thus looking out across the restaurant.

'I don't know about that,' she said. 'I don't know about that. But because you have only five days, and because you will perhaps never . . . you shall have your wish, you shall. Are you happy?'

That took me completely by surprise, and it fooled me into looking at her with a great hope. But she had not granted me that great hope; she was just indulging me, because she wanted to be kind to me.

'It is not my wish I want,' I said, 'but yours . . . and you shall have *your* wish all right. Shall we go to that train?'

As we were walking along the platform she took my hand again, stopped and looked at me.

'Go back and buy a bottle of cognac.'

When the staff captain saw us in the compartment, a smart woman, a bottle of cognac and a shabby private from a penal regiment, he turned on his heel. Shortly afterwards the military police appeared. An abrupt silence fell between us, while I produced my papers and showed that I had a supplementary ticket for second class. Ursula answered their looks with dark-red, silent indignation. It was a good thing that she said nothing. The captain got out at Linz. He had not had a pleasant journey, for Ursula's gaze had not left him for a second. The civilian couple got out at Setztal, and so we had the compartment to ourselves. To my surprise she gave me a long, lingering kiss, that left her breathing in little trembling gasps.

'You shall have everything you want,' she said breathlessly, while she looked out through the window. 'There are limits to what they can be allowed to do to you.' She turned towards me, her eyes still angry. 'You shall have it now, if you want.'

It was lovely to be able to laugh, laugh properly. 'Don't mind what they say. We don't ourselves. They are petty and despicable. You sometimes slip on one, then you wipe your shoes clean and walk on. Scrape yours clean, my girl, and we'll go on.'

I opened the bottle.

'Shall we drink to clean shoes?'

Outside, the mountains were filing past the window, along with the rain and the telegraph poles and the twilight. In the end came the darkness, and it stayed out there, keeping us company. When we woke it was three o'clock and we should have got out at Hochfilzen at a quarter-past twelve.

The loudspeaker on the platform woke us with its:

'Innsbruck. Innsbruck. Innsbruck.'

We staggered out, drunk with sleep, and while Ursula went to tidy I rang round to the hotels.

'Have you got a room?' she asked when we met beneath the clock.

'Hotel Jägerhof,' I replied.

'Was it difficult? Now I'm cold.'

I had rung twenty-three different hotels, but I said it had

been easy, that they had not been able to refuse my melodious baritone. The huge station hall was deserted and lay half in darkness. Someone was rattling a bucket somewhere, and nearby a man with a broad soft broom was methodically sweeping oiled sawdust across the terracotta-coloured flags.

'So we're to have our honeymoon in Innsbruck,' she said. 'Are you sorry?'

'No. There are mountains here too. Let me take your case.'

The square in front of the station was also deserted. It had been raining and the air was chilly. What now? Where was Hotel Jägerhof?

'Wait a bit,' said I, and went back into the station to find someone to give me directions or to ring for a taxi. There was not a soul to be seen, but beside the newspaper kiosk was a telephone-box. I was just about to open the door.

'One moment!'

I let go of the handle and turned round. Slowly the door closed with a sigh.

'Follow me.'

It was very light in the military police office. I began to sweat. The light was far too white. A white light can still make me sweat, even now.

The Duty NCO looked interrogatively at the two who had brought me in, and then searchingly at me.

'What's up?' he said.

The two stood stiffly at attention. 'We came across this man in the hall.'

The other looked at me again. 'What were you doing there at this time of night?'

I stood to attention. 'I wanted to telephone for a taxi. My wife and I came by the night express from Vienna to spend my leave here. Here are my papers.'

He looked at them. 'Leave for a convicted soldier. That sounds peculiar.'

We looked at each other. A fly was buzzing somewhere – buzzing and buzzing, as it zigzagged about the room.

'Where is your wife?'

'She is standing outside by the main entrance.'

He nodded to one of the other two. 'Fetch her.'

I listened to the man's steps outside, squinted up at the fly. The NCO shifted in his chair. A side-door opened and a sleepy head appeared in it. 'What's the time?'

'Half-past three.'

The head withdrew again.

'Meanwhile, let me see your ticket.'

That gave me a start. Should I say I had thrown it away? Then he would ask if I had not had a return to Vienna. He would also ask to see Ursula's ticket. There was no getting out of it.

'This is only for Hochfilzen. How do you explain that?'

'We fell asleep, and only woke here in Innsbruck.'

'You mean to say that you have travelled without paying from Hochfilzen here?'

'Yes. There was no time to pay. We had to hurry to get out of the train. But, naturally, I will gladly pay the extra.'

He did not reply. His telephone rang. He picked up the receiver.

'Station police – who? One moment.' He ran his finger down a list pinned up on the wall beside him. 'No, we haven't got him . . . It must be a mistake . . . Yes, it's the usual mess. They always have their things in a muddle there . . . I'll gladly have another look, but you won't get anything out of it . . .'

Ursula came in. She looked at me, frightened. We waited. The fly buzzed. Penal battalion. Penal battalion. Convicted. Conviction. Convict. The man at the desk laughed into the telephone and replaced the receiver.

When he saw us he asked for Ursula's papers, and then we had to confess that we were not married. 'Not yet,' said Ursula, 'not till tomorrow.' Suddenly she pulled herself together. 'Now listen,' she said, 'let us go. The whole thing is an unfortunate mistake, and if we had not overslept we would have got off where we meant to, and none of all this would have happened. You know yourself how difficult it is for a man in – a – well, in a penal battalion to get leave. My husband has got leave. He has not done anything wrong; it was my fault that we overslept. You understand, we had not seen each other for so long, and I badly wanted to make it a really happy reunion; I wanted to make everything really nice for him. And then we had something to drink' – she held out the bottle of cognac a little way – 'and it was I who got him to get it, and also to – to—'

'Yes?'

She was magnificent. Blushing furiously, her eyes sparkling and flashing, she bored right to the man's heart in woman's unscrupulous way.

'You see, we had the compartment to ourselves. And it was so long since I had seen him. He has not done anything wrong; he has behaved like a good soldier.'

The last remark was a stroke of genius. The man at the desk handed us our papers. 'You may go.' Then he turned to me. 'And keep on behaving like a good soldier.'

As the door closed behind us the men inside guffawed noisily.

'Let's get away,' she whispered and pulled me along almost at a run. 'I am afraid.'

When we were back outside in the rain-sodden, deserted square, I saw that her face was white and her forehead beneath her black hair covered with tiny beads of sweat. 'Hold on to me,' she groaned. 'I think I'm going to faint.'

There I stood with a bottle in one hand, a suitcase in the other and Ursula in my arms. I had to put the suitcase down hastily and support her, till I got her seated on one of the steps. 'Head down between your knees,' I said. 'Now stay quite still. It will go off in a bit.'

'I'm fine now,' she said, when she had recovered. 'Are you very angry?'

'Over what?'

'Over my fainting like that? I'm not much help.'

'I like that! If you hadn't saved the situation, you never know what it might not have developed into. At any rate, by the time they had investigated my statement and rung round from Herod to Pilate I would never have got away until sometime in the morning. That sort of thing can take an awful time, and you don't get a telephone call through to

Bucharest in a quarter of an hour, I can assure you. I think you have been magnificent and very brave . . . You must be horribly tired now. Shouldn't I try to get a taxi?'

'No, no. We won't leave each other any more. I'll come with you. If I can just sit another couple of minutes we'll go together and look for a cab . . .'

So we sat for a while, with her snuggled close to me. Then she gave herself a shake. 'I'm cold.'

'Come. Let's go.'

We found a horse-cab and rattled to the hotel. It was large and white and asleep, with open balcony doors and a drive with a deep layer of gravel that made the horse suddenly go slower. The old night porter scratched out Ursula's name when I wrote it in the register, telling me in a friendly tone that I did not need to put my wife's maiden name. 'Now we'll just put "and wife",' said he with a slight smile. 'That's sufficient.' I was as red as a peony. We even thought the liftboy smiled, and I looked rigidly ahead of me. While the chambermaid was turning down the bed Ursula went out on to the balcony, and I said 'Hm' and went into the bathroom, and shortly afterwards we were standing alone in the middle of the floor, looking at each other.

'Well – here we are! Cigarette?'

The match broke, and her hand trembled slightly.

We were appallingly embarrassed. The dry air in the strange hotel room, where everything was clean and unhomely. The emotional excitement. Was the whole thing just emotional excitement? The tiredness. I felt as drained and heavy-limbed as after manoeuvres; and she stood there with drooping shoulders and had hazel eyes, and no eyes can look so infinitely sad and weary as hazel eyes; and neither knew whether the one expected it in a little of the other, or thought the other expected it; and could we, did we want to, or would we both fumblingly exert ourselves to please each other without knowing what was the right thing to do? Or do it wrong? Tense the wrong muscles and in the end draw apart out of reluctant necessity, tormented by tiredness and im-aginings?

'Now I'll go and finish my cigarette on the balcony, while you get – undressed.'

This was awful. Didn't I dare even say 'bed'?

Is there anything so still as the night? The mountains were a massive, enormous something in the darkness, waiting for the day to be able to show what they looked like. Big mountain, great mountain, tomorrow I shall see you, and Ursula shall see you. Tomorrow we will have slept, and we shall have breakfast with you, and talk about visiting you. Tonight it is dark, and you have nothing to show us.

'Now you may come.'

In the bathroom one tooth-glass was almost half full of cognac. The other was empty, but I could smell that there had been cognac in it too. The bottle was empty. I picked up the glass.

If I say that we are too tired, she may think that I am just being considerate, and so she'll say that, yes, we are, and so we'll come to a standstill and we will both be afraid to be the first to fall asleep. Perhaps, too, she will be slightly disappointed, even if she is dead tired. And if I say . . .

It is really not easy to know about that sort of thing. Those human bulls and stallions in the hard-boiled American novels, the Hemingwayish, sensitive, sexual heroes with bursting hearts . . . At that decisive moment I envied them. But no, no moment is decisive before you are dead.

'Here's to clean shoes,' I said aloud and drained the glass.

'You are sweet,' she said in a subdued voice from the room. I put her head on my shoulder and pulled the quilt up over her breast.

'Tomorrow,' said I, 'I will be one of Hemingway's most emotional, sexual heroes. The mountain asked me to tell you that tomorrow it will show us all that it has. And now, by heaven, I want to sleep.'

She laughed. 'You are sweet.'

I got out of that one very well.

Shortly afterwards she added: 'Thanks, darling.'

She put her head on her own pillow, bent my left arm and tucked her right one through it, and so we fell asleep. We

70

slept a heavy, good, cognac sleep, and woke several hours later simultaneously and in the same position, and the mountain did show us everything, and we climbed it together and afterwards rested on it.

You just have to sleep on it.

11

'I love you. I love you with all my heart.'

Big, shining tears glistened on her long lashes and ran down her cheeks. She kept her eyes shut.

The Last Days

The morning sun was shining in upon us through the open door of the balcony. We sat, each in a chair, having the breakfast that the waiter had just brought us. She held out a well-buttered slice.

'You're to eat something more!'

'I can't eat so much,' I said. 'I've so long been accustomed not to eat much. That's why.'

'You must get rid of your bad habits. You eat too little. Good heavens, boy, you're just skin and bone.'

I looked down at myself. She might well say that. My arms were so thin that I could span them with one hand. Heavens, what did she want with a person like me? She, a woman who was well-covered, lissom, buxomly graceful. Heavy behind, strong and nicely rounded. Made to be the centre of a sun-burned brood; podgy toddlers, big long-haired boys and cackling girls continually coming in demanding something to eat and so out again. And a tall, big man to come home in the evening, a bear of a man. A mighty man. Not me.

'Now eat, and don't sit being sorry for yourself. You are good enough as you are. I expect a lot of you when we've finished. A lot. But you must eat first. You must have two eggs. And then be fearfully oriental.'

'You can't do that,' said I peevishly. The bread was so dry in my mouth. It just went round and round.

'What can't you?'

'Sit there coldly and calmly eating and waiting for after-wards.'

'You just stop waiting for afterwards. Eat up now, darling.

Here, drink a glass of milk; perhaps you're thirsty. If I have to stuff you myself, you're not getting away till you've got a tummy. You mustn't forget that I'm a doctor, and I can see you've got the English ill, you're suffering from lack of vitamins and a lot of other lacks, even if you are a skilful orientalist.'

'I am very, very skilful.'

'Where did you learn it all? Most men are just violent and think that is being skilful.'

'When I got your telegram I practised on nine thousand women and a Turkish drummer-boy specially ordered from Constanza.'

She had her way. I ate everything and drank what she gave me, and then she and I were very, very skilful. It is nonsense that men only want *that*. Men want the same as women. They want what is the root and food of all culture: *to know*.

Afterwards we walked in the mountains right up to a little monastery, where a white-haired priest showed us round. We saw everything there is in the mountains. At one place we met a flock of goats and parti-coloured cows being watched by a picturesque herdsman with full beard and alpine boots. Further on, we sat for a while and looked down on a little village with twisting alleys and bright, childish colours. A couple of chalet girls sang to the gay clangour of the cow-bells, and from higher up came an answer: 'Holidorio! Holidorio!' And there was an eagle up in the blue sky. A real eagle, a living creature, not a heraldic eagle that held Europe in its gory talons.

A scene that is so obtrusively idyllic as that can become intolerable. It is too beautiful, too clear, the snow peaks too calm. It does not fit in with man's restless soul. You must either get up and go on, or sleep in the fragrant, myriad-buzzing heat.

The idyll continued. I, the soldier, was pelted with idyll. And while we sat and ate mountainous helpings of good food and quaffed Rhine wine in amber-coloured stone mugs, and I ran my hand down her thighs so that she drew away from the tickle of it, I was suddenly seized by apprehension and forebodings: we had only two days left.

73

'Just think,' she said suddenly, 'we have two whole days yet.' That's how she said it. Yet she wept and was just as unhappy as I. The innkeeper said 'Grüss Gott' and looked gravely after us as we left. When we had gone a short distance she turned. He was still standing in the doorway, and waved, still gravely.

'How sweet he was,' she said.

'Wasn't he.'

She put my arm round her shoulder. 'Don't you understand, boy, that it would be hell for me if I fell in love with you?'

'Fall in love with me?' I said, surprised. 'I thought you were.'

'But I've told you the whole time that I'm not. Only you won't believe it. But that's another matter. I just couldn't not come. You – you are someone women aren't used to. Not I, at least. Perhaps because I am not particularly . . .'

'You are very, very,' said I, and lowered my hand to clasp her breast; but she removed it and put it back on her shoulder again.

'No, don't let's talk of that,' said she. 'It will just make us confused. But . . . I don't know what to say.'

'I do,' said I. 'You want to say that you are not in love with me. Don't let's use big words, Ursula. I know that I've been guilty of that myself, but for a long time you kept me so at arm's length, and yet you didn't. So it is really difficult to express oneself strictly objectively.'

'And you are so thin and maltreated. Do you know that you cry out in your sleep?'

'Perhaps. But things are hellish for me.'

Suddenly she became quite wild. She flung herself at me and sobbed and sobbed. 'You mustn't leave me, will you?' she sobbed. 'They won't take you from me, will they?'

'No, no,' said I; 'no, no.' That was all I could say. I patted her back and whispered, 'No, no.' I could not make head or tail of it all.

That evening, she put on a simple, close-fitting black dress and a necklace of green and black beads. It looked very expensive. I knew that my black tank uniform lent me a sort of grim elegance that was emphasised by my having no Iron Cross or other ribbons, just the mere, ordinary unit badges. It gave me a certain feeling of pride when I saw that people looked at us as we walked to our table.

While we were eating, a lieutenant walked past, almost brushing the table, dropping a folded piece of paper in front of me as though by accident. Puzzled, I picked it up and read:

'If you are here without permission, hurry and get out. The Military Police are next door. If you need help I shall be in the hall.'

I looked at Ursula and she at me. We agreed that I should go out and thank him for the warning and tell him that my papers were in order.

I discovered him standing smoking in a corner of the hall. After a brief introduction, I thanked him and then said: 'Would it be impolite to ask the reason for your kindness?'

'You are in the tanks, and so is my brother. Do you know Hugo Stege?'

I told him that Stege was one of my best friends in the company.

'You don't say so?' said the lieutenant gaily. 'That calls for a celebration. Won't you and your lady be my guests this evening? I know an amusing place where we can go when we have eaten.'

Together we went back to Ursula. He introduced himself as Paul Stege of the Engineers. When, after a colourful night, we took leave of each other outside our hotel, he told us to ring him up if there was anything he could do to help us.

Up in our room we flung ourselves wearily into chairs and smoked a last cigarette without speaking. Outside it was beginning to grow light, so I got up and pulled up the Venetian blind from the balcony door. Then I switched on the wireless. There was usually good music at that hour, a so-called 'programme for the Front'. A symphony orchestra, surely the Berlin Philharmonic, was working its way up towards the final burst of Liszt's *Preludes*. Hitler and Goebbels had ruined even this stirring, romantic piece, turning it into programme music for their damned war. It was what UFA used as a background for the newsreels of the Luftwaffe's raids. It was the Luftwaffe preparing the way for us tank troops. It was the Luftwaffe literally razing the Warsaw ghetto to the ground in three days and nights. When quiet returned and the smoke had drifted away there was nothing in that huge expanse more than five feet high. Only a handful of the many hundreds of thousands of Jews escaped alive through the laughing cordon of SS troops. A handful of Jews and some few million rats.

To the sound of Liszt's festival music.

'Shan't we switch off?' said Ursula. 'That piece gets on my nerves.'

I switched off and undressed.

'What a lovely day it has been. Look, it will soon be light. It's almost a shame to sleep.'

'I think it will be lovely to sleep – at any rate for a few hours. We are pretty tired.'

'Life should always be as lovely as this. What a lot one really has to be glad of! Eating when you are hungry. Drinking and becoming slightly elevated and witty. Opening your eyes and being wide-awake, because a wide-awake day full of light air awaits you. Being tired in the proper way. I am tired in the proper way; at this moment I ask for nothing.'

And taking off her necklace. And her shoe. And then the zip-fastener, yes, the zip-fastener; ah, the zip-fastener – there!

'How calm your hands are. They know a lot. When shall I have the other shoe off? No, not those now! Those last.'

'No, those now.'

I removed the shoe as well.

'Be careful the meshes don't catch on your nail. It is the last decent pair I have. Oh, didn't you say we were going to sleep?'

I did not reply. I had my doll to play with. I gave her a doll to play with, and so we fell silent, acquired a heavy, tranquil pliancy, that immeasurable slowness in which clouds pile up, huge, in a sky large enough for all kinds of lightning, rolling, rumbling and the sudden rain before the storm comes overhead.

One waits for so many superfluous things, and because they are superfluous you become impatient, restless, vehement and urgent, and meanwhile the clouds drift across your head and are gone, and you have only been appallingly confused.

But when the thing is a thing that is not superfluous, you wait confidently, and make the little wave quite ready, so that it can course on contentedly and give the great desire to follow it.

'Now I have eaten you.'

To look up into a pair of eyes, in which a wave comes and goes. To be such good friends with oneself that the gods lend you their senses and you can feel a pressure of a milligramme, a shift of a fraction of a millimetre. That is to unite body and soul.

'Move a tiny bit up,' said I softly. 'That's it. *There.*'

'Well . . . and what now?'

I did not need to answer. Bigger waves came of themselves and washed across our faces.

Ursula flung herself abruptly on her side and lay with her back to me. Quivers coursed through her at regular intervals. I was the same. We were both shaken to our depths, felled, the two of us. Neither of us spoke. There was nothing to say. I picked the eiderdown off the floor before we grew cold.

I have written that as a memento, as a reminder that I did achieve what is called complete happiness, before I switched the wireless on again:

'. . . the Soviet Russian armies to be used in the attack. The offensive has flared up from the Northern Arctic Ocean to the Black Sea, and already reports are coming in of advances and victory for the combined German – Italian – Roumanian—'

I looked across at Ursula, went right up to the bed, called softly. She was asleep. God be praised.

Some people are sure to be offended and others will smile wry, superior smiles at my memento. But these, you will find, are people who still cherish ideas about spirit and matter, body and soul, and that one is on a so-called higher plane than the other. Let them be offended or smile their superior

smiles. The day they are felled themselves they will understand it all much better.

The next day we got married at the little monastery. Paul
Stege gave Ursula away. He brought her a large bouquet of
white roses, which touched her. The white-haired priest was
reluctant to marry us, because I was who I was; but we pressed
him, and when he heard that I was an Auslands-deutscher of
Danish-Austrian descent and as good as naturalised Scandi-
navian, he consented. 'I spent a number of years of my youth
in that little country in the north. An oasis in the middle of
Europe. Let's hope it will be spared, and if it is, then go and
settle there as soon as you can.'

For her morning gift she got Roumanian treasure: a silk
nightdress with real lace, two sets of gossamer-thin undies,
five pairs of real silk stockings and a ring Porta had got me. It
was a gold ring with a big sapphire in the middle of tiny
diamonds. All together, the things were worth a fortune on
the black market.

I have only fragmentary recollections of most of the last
day:

'What does the silly war concern us? We know we have
each other.'

'No, no, no, you must promise me. If anything happens.
You must promise me to get rid of it. We must wait till the
war is over and see what the country's like.'

'Darling! Do you remember, you said nothing but "darling"
in Vienna. Now it's I who says "darling" and nothing but
'darling".'

'Promise me that you will take good care of yourself. Stop
volunteering for everything. Promise me that you will write
really often. Oh, Sven, Sven!'

'There, there. You mustn't cry now. There, there.'

'Goodbye, Sven. Have you remembered . . .'

Ursula, Ursula. A white face receding, faster and faster now.
Ursula, Ursula, Ur-su-la, dum – dadum, dum – dadum,
wheels, whe – els . . .

The telegraph poles were going the other way. The compartments were over-full. People talked and talked. They

believed the reports of successes, and that, perhaps, made me feel more depressed and foreign than did the parting. To which of these gabbling, thoughtless, well-broken creatures could I explain that a perfect military machine like that of the German generals was going to come to a miserable end before long? Which of them could I tell, that in the first place the perfection was not really so very perfect; that it consisted only of conditioned reflexes cultivated to perfection: the ability to stand at attention; that could not lay claim to any respect whatever, nor had they the cleverness *not* to demand anything more than perfection in standing to attention. What was utterly lacking was the ability to know and value the path down which one was marching in step. You were told to go this way, and you went that way.

The machine was marching at an enemy who possessed that which gives victory: moral superiority.

It was only to people like The Old Un and Porta that I could have said that we were just rotten old boots; but they knew that already. You had to keep that sort of thing to yourself in those years.

12

'For my part,' answered The Old Un, 'it was a very nice leave with my wife and the kids. Lovely – but what use are a few days? The wife's become a tram-driver on the 61 route. That's always better than being a conductor. Now they can make the money go round at home all right. Hellish that one has to come back to this filth. If only one could have the luck to have a leg sent flying, then one would be done with this rotten Nazi war.'

'An arm would be better,' said Porta.

'We have not even been in it yet,' said I. 'But, good Lord, perhaps we'll come through.'

The Old Un hid his face in his hands. 'I think we've been in enough,' he whispered. 'I'm not asking for any more. I am in no need of magnificent victories. I'm in need of peace. Come through! Who will have anything to do with us when we have come through? No one. Not even we ourselves. Hell take it.'

Porta put the flute back in its case. He had not played it.

Porta's Leave

'They can take their report and – it. Before it comes in I shall be in the desert, and I should like to see them doing anything to me there, just because a snotty railwayman received a well-deserved kick in his strawberry.'

Porta blew his nose in his fingers and spat at the wall, hitting a notice announcing that spitting was forbidden.

'I've been darned unlucky with my leave. I had scarcely got inside the door before some hag from over in Spandau came running with a baby and had the impertinence to tell me straight to my innocent, handsome face that I was its father. I told her in a civil and well-bred manner that there must be some regrettable mistake, and that she could go and – in the garden.

'Darn me, if the mare did not take me to court – and I had

to go and stand before some bellowing creature, who sat raving behind a tall desk and spouted away that I was father to that bawdy strumpet's residual product.

'I told him quietly and calmly what was a fact, that anyone must be able to see that it was an utter physical impossibility for such a handsome young man as I to sire a baby that looked like that, and I pointed to the product which the hag had brought with her.

'There was a lot of noise about a blood-test, and a squint-eyed individual who asserted that he was a doctor arranged that side of it, and happy I was, for now I believed that it would all be cleared up, but it just shows that you should never trust doctors, for, devil take me, if they did not say afterwards that I must be held to be the child's father.'

'But, Porta, they can't do that! If your Soldier's Book shows that you have not been in Berlin they can't . . .'

'They can do anything. Just as I am in full swing taking tender farewell of my dear old folk and it's all ruddy idyll and gnashing of teeth, then a rickety old sow comes walking in and informs me that she is going to farrow.

' "Very interesting," says I, "and good luck with it – the Führer will be most happy. My regards to your husband and tell him from me that he must take the dustbin down every day till this is all over."

'It was not a thing that concerned me, of course, but then one has one's manners after all. So, I chatted a bit with the mare about the great happiness that was coming to her, and so that she too should know it was Christmas we went into the other room and ate a sweet together.

'I, idiot that I was, never thought of anything, till the mare whispered into my shell-like ear: "You're the father, me dear; aren't you glad?"

' "Glad?" I bellowed. "You must be stark raving!"

'And so she was dismissed without my blessing. One's just dogged by misfortune. I don't know how it is with others, but it only needs a woman to sit on my lap and there it is.'

'You ought to try buttoning up your flies,' said The Old Un.

'Tell me honestly, Porta, *weren't* you in Berlin at all ten months ago?'

'You can see for yourself, in my Soldier's Book,' said Porta.

'Yes, yes, but what's in a Soldier's Book is one thing, and what isn't is another.'

'*Et tu, Brute*,' said Porta, hurt. 'I was in Berlin ten months ago – but, hell, it was only for half a day.'

'That doesn't matter if you were on the thigh-path,' said The Old Un.

13

Just let me get my hands on the throat of the poet who wrote that the Mediterranean was blue and lovely and smiling.

Destination: North Africa

With legs dangling over the edge of their cattle-trucks, the 18th Battalion rolled through Roumania, Hungary and Austria, and from there we cheered our way down through Italy. Five times we got Porta to the door to look at a macaroni field. He was never properly convinced that macaroni is not a plant.

We were quartered in Naples, equipped with brand-new tanks and put into tropical uniform. Porta refused to exchange his old black felt beret for a helmet, and there was such an altercation between him and the depot Feldwebel that the noise of it could be heard on Vesuvius. The result was a compromise: Porta accepted the helmet, but the Feldwebel did not get his beret.

Just before we were to be loaded, an epidemic broke out in the battalion, and in a few days we lost so many that we had to remain where we were a bit longer, till replacements arrived from Germany.

When we eventually embarked there were five battalions of us, five thousand men divided between two ships, former passenger steamers. We roared hurrah as our boat slid out of the harbour. We hung over the rail and up in the masts and rigging, and cheered and cheered.

Each man was issued with a life-belt and we had strict orders never to take them off, but they made too good pillows for anyone to respect such an order. The lifeboats were kept swung out hanging on their davits. There were AA guns mounted on the deck, and we were escorted by three Italian torpedo-boats with oily, black smoke pouring from their stocky funnels. The boat pitched violently, and you could not stay down in the hold for the stench of the vomit. Porta, The Old Un and I wrapped ourselves in our greatcoats and lay in the lee of the deckhouse. I cannot remember what we talked about, but I do remember that we were quite satisfied with our lot. I believe we just smoked and talked quietly of things in general, thoughtful little observations uttered at sober intervals. We talked rather like navvies sitting on the edge of a trench during the lunch interval. For a while we ceased to be the gallowbirds we normally were, and Porta did not even lard his talk with the words descriptive of the human sexual organs, as he usually did. Even he behaved normally. I found myself longing for Ursula to lend reality to the peace, of which we were being allowed a momentary taste in a troop-ship heavily laden with men and tanks.

Porta felt that he wanted music, but discovered that his suitcase was gone. 'Help!' he yelled. 'Help! I'm dead! Murdered! Thieves, murderers, damned lot of Nazis! I've been robbed! Plundered! My flute and my tails!'

He refused to be comforted, even when we assured him that he could buy a new flute in Tripoli. No flute from Tripoli could ever be as good as his old one.

Gradually we fell asleep.

We were awakened by a tremendous noise of motors in the darkness just above our heads. Spiteful red tongues of flame stabbed down at us from the air. Screechings and whistlings tore at our ear-drums; there was a banging and smacking against the steel plates of the ship's sides. Our own gun stuck its tongue out through the darkness back at the attacking bombers. Boom-boom-boom it went, and the machine-guns barked furiously.

We stood pressed against the deckhouse, both afraid and pleasantly thrilled – this, after all, was the first time we had been in action – while we tried to make head and tail of what was happening. Now the planes were back again, roaring as they dived.

Then a whine rose above the roar. The Old Un gave me a push and shouted:

'Down! This is it!'

Then came the roar, and the big boat shook. Again we heard the dreadful howling, but this time it was the other ship they were after. Along with the crash, several pillars of fire shot up over there, and in the glare of them we saw each other's faces. Within a few seconds the other ship was a roaring sea of flames. Red and yellow tongues shot upwards through thick smoke with reports as loud as gunfire. An aeroplane dropped on to the foredeck and lay there. Then that, too, was ringed by flames. Suddenly, I thought that my ear-drums had burst. I could not hear a sound. It was like a film, when the soundtrack has failed. I got up and looked out across the dark-red sea, but suddenly I was flung over and found that I could hear again. Fountains of fire and water rose towards the heavens. From inside the ship came the sound of resounding explosions. One of our three big funnels rose and sailed off slowly in an arc into the darkness. It was a remarkable, unreal sight.

'The ship's capsizing!'

Rumbling crashes were still coming from inside the ship, whence rose a thousand-voiced cry of terror from those in the holds. We looked confusedly at each other. Then we jumped.

The water was so fantastically far beneath me that I thought I should never reach it; but all at once it had closed over me, and I sank and sank, feeling as though my body were broken in half. There was a roaring and seething in my ears, and inside my head something was throbbing faster and faster, louder and louder. In the end I could stand no more. I gave up. Now you're going to die, I thought, and at that instant my mouth came above the surface and my aching lungs snatched at the air. But I was under again at once. Frantically I laboured with arms and legs to get as far as possible from the sinking steamer so as not to be sucked down with her when she went. All the colours of the rainbow danced and flickered before my eyes. I have no idea whether I swam in the right direction, but I assume that I did, although I do not remember taking a bearing. I just kicked out for dear life, while my muscles yelled with pain and begged to be allowed to stop what they were doing, preferring to die. My instinct of self-preservation, however, was stronger of all and made me cling, sobbing, laughing, only semi-conscious, to a life-buoy that suddenly appeared.

I floated, my arms resting on the life-buoy. The black, foam-covered waves sent me shooting up like a rocket till I was dizzily perched on the top of a huge mountain of water, staring in horror down into a gurgling trough. Several times, as I plunged into such a valley, I cried out hysterically.

Far away, a blaze was colouring the heavens reddish-purple; otherwise there was nothing but water, water, savage, mighty water and terrifying, pitch-black night.

Sharks! What about sharks? Were there sharks in the Mediterranean? Yes, there were! I kicked out hysterically, again and again, but I soon tired and had to stop. Then I thought of The Old Un and Porta and started yelling out their names into the darkness:

'OLD-UN! PO-R-TA! PO-R-TA!'

Only the roar of the waves answered, and again I sobbed wildly and desperately. In my fear I called to my mother and to Ursula.

'Pull yourself together, man!' I shouted, and then I began to laugh. I howled like a hyena, was beside myself, uttering lunatic sounds that were no longer mine, then I recovered and went on sobbing. All night I was tossed about among the waves, sea-sick, vomiting and weeping.

Was that someone shouting? I listened. Yes, someone was yelling away in the darkness. There it was! Definitely. Nonsense. They were all dead. There's no one. Some time you'll die in the dark too. Everybody's dead. They have other things to think of. There isn't one who thinks of you. They are evil and cold; you are ridiculous if you expect anything of people.

Yes, but there must be *someone*. You don't just lie in the water and are forgotten. When they have gone through the lists and found out who is missing, they will send out every-one available . . .

To look for you? *You?* A convicted soldier! Ha-ha-ha-ha!

It began to grow light. Isn't that something there to the right? Isn't that a man lying on a life-buoy, as you are?

You're seeing things, things you want to see. You're a fool, and you're seeing things that aren't there.

But it was Porta. With a broad grin, he pulled his black beret from inside his tunic, put it on his head and raised it as though it were a hat.

'Good day to you, my boy! So you've come down to the beach too? I've got a bit damp about the feet, but an occasional bathe does you no harm.'

'Porta!' I shouted delightedly. 'Oh, thank God, you old muck-spreader!' I was slightly crazy, and I could see from his eyes that he was too. 'Where's The Old Un?'

'He's somewhere in the pond here,' said Porta with a flourish of his arm. 'But don't ask me whether he's lying with his snout in or out of the water.'

We tied our life-buoys together so that we should not risk drifting apart.

'Perhaps you're waiting for the same tram, sir?' said Porta.

'And why the devil are you so thin?' said he, glaring hungrily at me. 'There isn't even a square meal on you. But it will be fun a hundred years from now, when I can tell my grandchildren how once I saved my life with a bag of bones called Sven. Doesn't it make you proud that you should end your heroic career as a meal for Hitler's best soldier? When I get home I shall see that you get a memorial. Would you prefer granite or bronze?'

All at once he uttered a great roar and pointed to a ship in the distance.

'Our tram!'

We called and shouted ourselves hoarse, but the ship disappeared.

'Glad you had to go!' yelled Porta, as it vanished below the horizon. 'Just leave us in peace. We haven't done anything to you!'

The grey, overcast morning passed in talk. The sun was scorching when it did occasionally break through the clouds.

87

In the end I became half-stupefied from exhaustion, but Porta kept up a long monologue.

'Now a couple of gulls like that, they can laugh at everything. There would be nothing to it if we had wings; but instead, here we are sitting with our bottoms in the foot-bath. You spend a long life taking the greatest care not to get too near the darned sea, and of course the filthy Army has to send you right into it. It's what I've always said: no good ever came of being a soldier. Promise me you'll never be a general, my son! If only it wasn't so wet here.'

'Porta . . . do you think we'll come through?'

'Come through? No, you can take your oath we won't, so bow your head, my boy. But if you snivel, I'll catch you such a one on your snout that you'll have to be issued with a harp. You are to keep your ugly mug out of this ——pot here. I'll tell you all right when you can stop. Meanwhile, be glad you're not lying in a stinking shell-hole with the big guns giving a concert. Of course, those little holes out in no-man's-land are excellent for those with a tendency to constipation, but this is better. You see – and this is a unique, undeserved piece of luck where you are concerned – here you can not only mess your pants but be washed clean simultaneously. You can't do that in a shell-hole.'

'Porta . . . do you believe in God?'

'Who, him? If you mean the chap the clergymen preach about, you can go home to your vicar and tell him he had better resign from the union and find someone better to tout for.'

'It's my opinion, too, that the Church and everything about it is a despicable swindle. Strange, my saying "It's my opinion". I don't normally talk like that.'

'Good! So you've not gone altogether mad. I was getting quite afraid that I was lying here savouring the joys of bathing with a mental defective who wanted to convert me to the Church and religion. But swindle – that depends how you look at it. In any case, don't waste your energy despising religion. It's not worth it. Let people believe in it if they like. As long as they don't embarrass me with their belief it doesn't

88

concern me; and if they can find comfort in it, well, good luck to them. Personally, I prefer to confine my attention to communion wine and nuns. I can assure you that if you've once broached a well-assorted nunnery you won't be disappointed with religion.'

Porta, of course, had also been gardener's boy at a nunnery. I listened dully to a juicy account of his exploits, while my thoughts occupied themselves further with the question of an almighty, omniscient and supremely good Creator.

'You're not listening, boy,' said Porta, and came to a sudden stop. Our situation was not really conducive to improvising on the theme of the deeper joys of life in a nunnery. He saw that. But then his face brightened again.

'There's one thing, though, that the Church has given me that isn't humbug.'

'What's that?'

'The organ. If only we had one here. I don't believe I'd mind lying here getting my feet wet and catching my death of cold. I knew an organist once, and he taught me to play the organ. Yes, give the devil his due, even though all that about prayers and how the poor ought to be glad because they'll get into heaven is just eye-wash and nothing at all for Daddy here, it's a darned fine sight when they put on a proper Jesus feast with Christmas-tree and what have you. And when they sing and make church music, I can tell you – you want to blub quietly from sheer ruddy emotion. When you hear their music the water fairly pours down your mug.'

Thirst was racking us, and we fell silent.

Just after daybreak of the second day an Italian plane flew low over us and dropped a rubber boat that landed only twenty yards away. We laughed and wept, and Porta shouted up at the plane:

'Thanks, old spaghetti-eaters! So there's some good in you after all.'

It proved more difficult than we thought, both to paddle the twenty yards to the boat and to get ourselves into it. We went one to either side. I was to try first, and I struggled and jumped up and down in the water and slid under and nearly

drowned myself, because I started laughing from sheer tiredness and could not stop. But in the end we both got in and
shook hands.

'Now we only want a pack of cards.'

We could not find one, but the water-tight locker contained
some tins of milk, dried meat, biscuits and four bottles of
schnapps. We ate and drank, then we stretched out under a
studding-sail in the stern and slept. Cold woke us in the middle
of the night. We started pummelling each other, and that and
a couple of good swings of schnapps soon made us warm again,
so we settled down once more and slept on. About noon the
next day we made a further investigation of the boat's lockers
and this time we found a box of rockets and a tin of some
yellow fluid. This latter was to pour on the water, which we
did, and the next moment the oily stuff had spread and made a
huge, bright-yellow patch that must have been easy to see
from the air. We let off a couple of rockets and cheered, as if it
were a garden party. Then we sang one German, one English
and one French song, sampled the remaining provisions,
taking great delight in cheating each other, but towards the
end we shared like true brothers, and in our hunger we ate up
everything that was left except for a few biscuits.

We began talking about the others, most of whom were
presumably dead.

'We'll be kept busy writing letters when we get ashore,' said
Porta, 'to all those mothers and sweethearts and wives.'

Ursula.

The next morning we drank the last of the schnapps and
ate the last biscuit.

'The next treat will be our boots. How would you like yours
done, with truffles or vanilla sauce?'

Shortly afterwards we came across a body floating in a life-
belt. With great difficulty we managed to heave it in. He was
an Unteroffizier, badly burned about the legs and abdomen.
In his pocket was a note-book full of jottings and addresses,
and we also found his Soldier's Book and a pocket book. From
this we learned that his name was Alfred König and that
he was an Unteroffizier in the 161st Artillery Regiment; that

he had been a soldier for three years, was twenty-two and married to twenty-year-old Irma Bartels from Berlin. His pocket-book contained a number of snapshots of himself with a young, fair-haired girl.

We kept his things and sent him overboard again.

'Greetings to all the others in the aquarium there,' said Porta. 'I'll write a nice letter to Irma and tell her that you died like a hero; erect and alone, you kept a superior attacking force at bay for four days, till you dropped with a bullet in your heart, killed outright. Yes, I know what's needed, so that your little Irma can proudly tell her girl-friends that her Alfred popped off in regulation fashion, fighting for his filthy, great fatherland. Nothing about his first having been roasted like a goose and then soaked in the sea. Your Irma is perhaps lying at home in Berlin now, thinking of nothing, but just longing for her Alfred. She'll re-read your last letter in which you wrote that you were well and faithful to her and thinking of her a lot, and that consequently you would not dream of sticking your nose or anything else into the temptations of Naples. Then she'll wipe away a tear and let the gas-man go without having done anything but read the meter. And that's life for Irma. Each day she doesn't get what she ought to have, because the Führer has taken it from her and sent it down to the bottom of the sea. And one day she'll get a postcard from the Army, simple, brief and military:

Unteroffizier Alfred König, of 161st Artillery Regiment, fell on 30th September 1941 fighting heroically for Führer and Fatherland

and underneath the elaborate flourish of some filthy officer's illegible signature. And beneath that in fine, Gothic lettering, as though a quotation from the Bible:

The Führer thanks you – Heil Hitler!'

Porta broke wind loudly and surveyed the grey uniformity around us.

'For a couple of days or so little Irma will go about with red eyes and that card in her handbag, and some people will be sorry for her, but not many, for she isn't the only one, and if one were to be sorry for them all it would be more than one could manage; no, where can I scrounge half a pound of butter? And the next time the gas-man calls he will be allowed to do more than read the meter, and in that way the loss of Alfred will turn out a good thing, for Alfred came only once a year, while the gas-man comes every quarter, and he can't fall for the Führer and Fatherland, for he has a wooden leg . . . God knows, perhaps we'll end up in Spain. Now, a nice little black-haired thing with a carnation behind her ear, you . . .'

I was tormented by thirst and found that Porta's everlasting bawdiness was becoming irritating. 'Shut up, you great swine,' said I peevishly. 'How can you think of wenching when we're lying here on the point of turning up our toes from hunger and thirst?'

'Turn up our toes? Are you mad? You don't think that the Royal Italian Air Force has presented us with this fine rubber dinghy, in which we shall paddle ourselves to Spain, for us to turn up our toes in it? Pop off in the middle of the Royal Italian Mediterranean – you're crackers, man! It would almost be an insult to the King of Italy to lie down and die here. Wonder if kings have gold aunts with plush seats?'

He pulled his trousers down and sat with his behind over the dinghy's stern. Now and again a wave rose up and gave his bare bottom a smack.

'Ugh! How that tickles! But it's hygienic. You should try it. It's a healthier way than the King of Italy's.'

'Porta, you're no longer amusing.'

His vitality stupefied me and exhausted me; it was like a white wall in the midday sun. Yet each time that I felt like seizing him by the throat his eyes stopped me. I could see from them that, for all his *galgenhumor*, we were in the same state.

But then even that began to get on my nerves, and if we had not spotted a ship in the distance just before darkness fell

I believe that I should have gone for him during the night in blind, crazy hatred. We called and waved and fired off rockets, and so we were picked up by an Italian destroyer. We washed the oil from the sinking ship out of our hair under a hot shower; we were put into dry, warm bunks and fed with a mountain of spaghetti, which we washed down with two litres of red wine; and then we slept like logs. The next morning, the sailors told us that quite a number from the two troopships had been rescued and that they had all been taken to Naples, to which we too were to put in. The ship's doctor came and looked at us, asked how we felt, and left without doing anything. We began talking about the others. Porta sighed gloomily.

'It won't be pleasant writing to The Old Un's wife. I went out to see them when I was on leave, and she and The Old Un and his old father and I agreed that we would be home again in six months, for the war would be over then and we would have got through the revolution. Hell! I hope the spaghetti-eaters' Royal Pirate Club fished him up and that he's lying in some Neapolitan inn or other, sullying his fair name and reputation in the company of sots, gamblers and loose women . . . But what the hell are we lying here blubbing for? Of course they've fished The Old Un up. What would Rommel do in North Africa otherwise? He could never manage without The Old Un, even with us helping.'

When we got to Naples we dug our heels in and made a scene.

'I don't care a damn if you are a major. There'll be no army for us till we've found out where The Old Un is. It wasn't for our pleasure that we let ourselves be torpedoed and then lay there kissing Mediterranean sharks for days on end, nor was it so that we should stand here getting flat feet for the sake of your rotten ration lists and clothing receipts. The Old Un's our pal, and until we know about him you aren't a major or anything else as far as we are concerned. We sit here and we're not budging; so just shoot us or shove us in clink, or what you bloody well like.'

To put it mildly, we were not quite right in the head. It was reaction. We could take no more. Fortunately they could see the state we were in, and luckily the major was a sensible man. He gave us as good as he got, and when we discovered that he had been in the other troopship and had been through it all, too, we became more amenable.

When the Feldwebel in the clothing depot saw us he gave Porta his hand with a great grin, and when we had told him about our rescue and asked him if he had heard anything about The Old Un, he told us to look out our own things while he went and saw what he could do. He disappeared into his little office, and after a short while he came out again and told us to go in there and wait. He would have news in ten minutes. He gave us schnapps and cigarettes and asked us various details about the loss of the ships, but we just told him anything, for we were anxious and thought the ten minutes were taking a very long time to pass. It was as though The Old Un were there but not allowed to join us. Each time the telephone rang he leaped out of it, as it were.

'Hallo . . . Yes . . . Where? . . . Thanks.'

The Feldwebel turned to us. I can still remember his smile.

'He's in one of the naval barracks down by the port.'

I hope that Feldwebel understood that it was not ingratitude or rudeness that sent Porta and me rushing out of his office without thanking him. But in the field a friend is a very special being. At first you live in noisy solitude, in violent loneliness; then you find a friend, and you know the whole time that he may be gone the next second, leaving you alone again in the din and solitude, with nothing.

We spent the next four or five days drifting about doing nothing. Of course, we had paid a visit to Pompeii and went up Vesuvius, whose crater naturally was an obvious victim for Porta's rhetoric.

Then, one morning, we were loaded into transport planes, so-called Auntie Jusz's, and off we flew, twelve planes in V-formation, protected by fighters. The Mediterranean disappeared behind, and there were black mountains far beneath us. Now and again we saw a lake or a town. Twice we landed before we reached our destination, the Westphalian town of Wuppertal. We marched through the town to barracks in the suburb of Elberfeldt. There we were to be reformed into three companies, that being all there was enough for, and after that we were to be sent to the Eastern Front and incorporated in the 27th Tank Regiment.

14

The Old Un shook his head and said contemptuously:

'Now don't be naïve, Hans. As long as there is one single officer who sticks to discipline we will keep silence, step and direction. Just look how it went in 1918. It wasn't till the whole ruddy thing collapsed that the lads in field-grey revolted. But God preserve us from a revolution. Pointless, aimless stupidity. No, my lad, the little German sausage-eater is so frightened of everything that he doesn't dare think, and you don't make revolutions with frightened men, whose stomachs turn at anything strong. It ended as it had to; the clever ones ran off with the swag. The bloodhounds were allowed to go scot-free, and today there they are, cracking their whips over us again. I have no doubt that the whole ruddy thing is going to collapse again, but you may call me Adolf if that leads to revolution. It will be the same ruddy story again. The clever ones will find their like and take care of No. 1, and when a suitable time has passed they will help the bloodhounds up again and shove nice new whips into their paws, and then we will have to put our backs into it all over again. Until my highly-esteemed fellow-countrymen begin to discover what it's all about, I have no confidence in them. Hitler and his dregs will be slaughtered, of course, and the sooner the better, but what are they but filthy puppets? And it's not making a revolution if you just smash the puppets and let the director run off with the takings.'

Thus The Old Un in 1941.

Three Girls

Among the many new men who came to fill up our company, I found a new friend, Hans Breuer. He had been a police lieutenant in Düsseldorf and had come to our dear little outfit because he refused to volunteer for the SS, as Hitler had ordered that all policemen should. He was convinced that Germany would soon lose the war, for he knew from his brother, who worked in Goebbels' propaganda ministry, that Nazism was on the verge of bankruptcy.

The Nazis could rely on no more than a fraction of the armed forces, and it was only a question of time before the generals settled accounts with Hitler and his crazy gang. Hans and I several times talked of deserting again, but The Old Un advised us not to try.

'Not one in a thousand gets away with it, and if they catch you you've had it. You're for the wall. It's much better to get wounded – only, for heaven's sake, don't do it yourself, for they examine you pretty thoroughly to see if it could have been self-inflicted. Remember there is always a little fouling left in the wound if you put a pistol to an arm or leg, and if you're caught with that, my lad, then you're for it. Typhus or cholera are the best; they can't prove anything with those. Syphilis is no good. They chuck you into hospital and shove you out again a fortnight later, after giving you such treatment as you'll never forget. Keep off VD, for they'll impale you alive if you come in with it bad. Some people drink the petrol we use for the tanks and that's quite good; it gives you bubonic plague that you can keep going for four or five months, if you know the dodge. Or you could pull a cigarette through an exhaust-pipe and eat that; that's pretty good too, gives quite a nice fever, but it doesn't last so long, and you have to smuggle a bottle of petrol and a bag of lump sugar into hospital with you, and eat a lump soaked in petrol every day; that keeps your temperature up at 39C., but don't let them catch you or they'll have you for "lowering the will to fight". If you can give a hospital orderly a couple of hundred cigarettes he can arrange a gangrened leg for you; then you lose a leg and the war is over, as far as you are concerned. You can also get typhus-infected water. But there is always a snag about these tricks and most other wangles; either they don't act with you – Porta has tried them all; he has even eaten some dead dog full of maggots, but on Porta that sort of thing acts more like a health cure – or you become paralysed, or you end in the cemetery. Many have done that.'

On Sunday, October 12th, our train crossed the Polish

frontier at Breslau. While we were standing in the goods-station station at Częstochowa we were issued with emergency rations. Each ration consisted of a tin of goulash, some biscuits and half a bottle of rum. There were strict orders that we were not to touch these rations until we were told that we might; and, above all, the rum was not to be drunk before the time.

With its usual taste for bombastic nonsense, the Army called this an 'iron ration'.

The first thing Porta did, of course, was to drink his rum. The bottle never left his lips until it was empty. Then he sent it flying over his shoulder with an elegant swing, smacked his lips, and let himself subside on to the straw that covered the floor of the truck. Before he fell asleep he broke wind and said: 'Take a sniff, dear children. There're vitamins in the air.'

A couple of hours later Porta woke, belched, stretched and then, to our amazement, produced yet another bottle of rum from his haversack and polished that off with a blissful expression. Then he called for cards and made us play vingt-et-un with him. Things went nicely, until someone outside called:

'Obergefreiter Porta, come out here!'

Porta remained where he was, unconcerned.

'Porta! Will you come out here at once!'

Porta never even looked at the door as he roared back:

'Shut your mouth, you flat-footed swineherd. If you want me, you maundering numskull, come in here, but remember to wipe your muddy feet first, and next time you call me you call "Herr Obergefreiter Porta", remember that. You're not at home in the barracks, you lousy lout!'

A deathly silence followed that salute. Then the whole truck burst into a great guffaw. When the laughter had died away there was a roar from outside:

'Porta, if you don't come out here this moment I'll have you court-martialled!'

Porta stared at us. 'Dear me, I believe that's Haptmann Meier,' he whispered. 'Now Porta'll get a spanking.'

He jumped down from the truck and smacked his heels

together before our bully Meier, who stood with legs straddled and arms akimbo, his face purple with fury.

'So you've deigned to come, *Herr* Obergefreiter! I'll teach a dirty skunk like you to obey orders. And how the hell dare you call me a swineherd and a lousy lout? What? Stand to attention, man, or I'll smash your face. Have you gone crazy? What possessed you to insult an officer? What the hell's this? You stink of rum, man! You're drunk. Now I understand. You've taken from your iron ration, have you? Do you know what that is? That's insubordination! And, by God, I'll have you punished for it!'

Porta did not reply, but just stood to attention looking incredibly dim-witted. In the end Meier lost the last vestiges of his self-control.

'Answer, you muck-rake! Have you been drinking rum?'

'Yes, Herr Hauptmann, but it was only a little dash that I poured into our otherwise so savoury National-Socialist ersatz tea. But it was rum that Herr Kücheunteroffizier owed me from the time we were fighting over in France. I can thoroughly recommend Herr Hauptmann to try it. It makes the splendid ersatz tea our beloved Führer gives us even more splendid.'

'What the hell, man! Are you trying to make a fool of me? Let me see the rum you were issued with your iron rations.'

At that, Porta produced yet another bottle of rum from one of his many homemade and roomy pockets, and with a smile held it up to the light so that the astonished Hauptmann could see that it was full.

Some squealer must have told Meier that Porta had drunk his rum. We did, in fact, discover later that Meier had promised a Gefreiter an extra fortnight's leave if he could provide proof that would enable him to run Porta in.

'I understand,' said Porta, all meek and mild, 'that Herr Hauptmann thought it was Herr Hauptmann I meant with all the things I called out just now, but it could never enter my head to say anything like that to my Herr Hauptmann and admired company commander. I thought it was Unteroffizier

Fleischmann I was shouting at. His father has had lice, you see, and he got them from him.'

Meier, as usual, made a fool of himself by sending for Fleischmann, who told him, grave-faced, that he and Porta had a bet on which could curse best. And it was also true, he said, that he had had lice. The whole family had got them from his father. The lice originated in the 1914–18 war, when his father had fought at Verdun.

'Children,' said Porta, one afternoon when we were in a siding between Kilsu and Częstochowa, 'we have lived in this royal suite for several weeks now, and we still have no idea what is behind this door here.'

This was the sliding door on the left-hand side of our truck. So far we had only opened that on the other side.

'We know that outside that door,' Porta went on, pointing to the right-hand door, which was open, 'we have Poland. We know that. But what great mysteries are hidden here,' pointing to the other, closed door, 'we do not know. Perhaps we shall find behind it' – here he laid hold of the door – '*Victory* itself, which must be somewhere or other, for has not the Führer said that it is ours? Or perhaps something even better – perhaps behind this mysterious, never-opened door' – here his voice sank to a whisper – 'there stands a whole crowd of lovely . . .'

With the extravagant gesture of a tout he pulled the door open.

He was as taken aback as the rest of us, for there in actual fact were three young women. They stood looking at the train and smiled uncertainly at us. To the soldier a woman is a remarkable, complicated being. She is a romantic, remote and lofty goal for aching unsatisfied longings, conjured up in lonely dreams of a lost, normal, civilian existence, so distant as to have become unreal, scared off by the swagger and bluster of army life; and at the same time she is an objective for woman-less man's accumulated salacity. A soldier is a being in uniform, one of a herd, among his own, and therefore he dares give expression to sexual fantasies, things that, when living an ordinary life among people, he never utters. His uniform is a protection against identification; he allows himself to play freebooter in his poor little way. He is a whole company, and that gives him backing.

We jumped out, the whole lot of us, and began delivering ourselves of the most hair-raising indecencies. We meant no harm by that, had no desire to wound the girls, and I have noticed that women do not take the remarks of a lot of soldiers very much to heart. When even Porta's stock was exhausted, most climbed back into the truck, for it was bitterly cold; but Porta, Pluto, Hans and I could not tear ourselves away. We looked at the girls and they at us, and only then did we realise the unusual aspect of the situation. We had, of course, been aware of it the whole time, but the overwhelming surprise of seeing women there, where we least expected them, had driven any other thoughts from our minds.

The three women were in striped prisoner's clothes, and there was a nine-foot fence of barbed wire between us and them.

They were prisoners in a concentration camp. All three, they told us, came from France and they had been a good fourteen months in the camp. One of them was Jewish. When they heard that we were going to Russia they asked us to take them with us. Naturally, that was meant as a joke.

'Can't be done, little girls,' Hans answered. 'The Gestapo would shoot us.'

One of them, a tall, fair-haired girl with intelligent eyes, said teasingly:

'Are you afraid? Show us that you're men!'

And suddenly, without any of us really wishing it, we all felt that we were taking the thing seriously.

'We'd better go,' said Hans nervously. 'If the SS see the girls standing talking with us they'll beat them till they're crippled. I know that from being in the police.'

'We'll stay till it suits us to go,' said Porta.

'Yes, but we shan't get it in the neck nearly as much as they,' said Hans, and looked anxiously to right and left in case he could see a guard.

There was something in what he said. By standing there, we were exposing the girls to the possibility of being maltreated in the most appalling fashion. We looked at them irresolutely. They looked at us resignedly.

'Hell and damnation! We ought to take them with us,' said Pluto. 'The poor kids. Look how thin they are.'

'And sweet, nevertheless,' said I.

There was no resisting their friendly smiles. We threw cigarettes over to them. Then we just stood there, helpless and filled with hatred of those who had imprisoned the three women.

'There's no point in dithering,' said The Old Un, who, for some reason or other, came crawling out from under the truck with Asmus.

'Are they coming with us, or aren't they? If they are, then it must be now.'

The Old Un was self-possessed and as quick as lightning. Before we knew what we were doing we had formed a pyramid by one of the posts, and The Old Un was standing on the shoulders of Pluto and Asmus. Our belts were joined together and lowered down to the girls, who were hauled up one by one, helped over with a heave from The Old Un, and caught by Hans, Porta and me, as they fell. Then Asmus, Hans and Pluto climbed back into the truck and turned out all who did not belong there and shut the door on the far side; in this way no one saw the girls get up into the truck.

We looked at the three wretched girls with pounding hearts. What had we let ourselves in for? Almost the most dangerous thing we could have thought up. Something had taken us by surprise. Could we use a big word and call it life? At all events, mortally afraid of this adventure into which we had dived headlong, we were also proud and glad; we felt that swelling joy that comes when you find that you are capable of excelling yourself, doing far, far more than you had thought yourself capable of. I wish I could express this really well, without making it sound boastful as it so easily can, but the fact is that when there is talk of heroic deeds I always use this situation as a touchstone of what is a truly heroic action and what not, and by that criterion there are many vaunted feats for which I cannot, with the best will in the world, feel any great admiration.

This was an occasion when fellowship had gained a great victory over loneliness.

'But to get down to things practical,' said The Old Un, once we had recovered from our first breathless, conspiratorial delight. 'They can't go around in prison stripes. We'll have to get them rigged out in something else. Produce what you have, boys, and no holding back!'

In a moment forty packs had been tipped up, and socks, pants, sweaters, shirts, drills, caps, boots were offered for the girls to choose from.

When the girls calmly drew their dresses off their otherwise naked bodies forty filthy soldiers turned their heads and silently looked the other way. God knows, we were a collection of pretty putrid rotters. I suppose that it was civilisation which had made us what we were, so here you have an example of why we should not be too pessimistic over the veneer of civilisation being so thin, since the fact that it is so still gives natural breeding a chance to make itself felt. It was not merely embarrassment that made us let the girls change their clothes in peace; it was at the same time a demonstration against the guards, who, for fourteen months, had mocked at and trampled on all that is called human decency. We wanted to show those sweet girls that consideration, modesty and humanity still existed, even though we were just a lot of filthy soldiers.

We hid them behind a pile of kitbags; then The Old Un, Porta and I went out to see if the alarm had been given in the camp, while the others sat in the open doorway to deny access to those with no business in our truck.

Our train left before the escape was discovered.

We stuffed those three little girls with the best we had. The eldest, Rosita, was a music-teacher. Porta was her particular protector. She would not say anything about why she had been sent to the camp.

Jeanne, just twenty-one and the youngest, had been at the

Sorbonne. Her two brothers had been lieutenants in the Army and were now POWs. Her father was wanted by the Germans, and the Gestapo had taken Jeanne as a hostage.

Maria, the Jewess, had been arrested in the street one evening and sent to the camp in Poland without comment or examination. She was married to a businessman in Lyons and had a son of two and a half. Three months after arriving in the concentration camp she had given birth to another boy, but he died a fortnight later.

When we had had them five days all forty of us were naturally hopelessly in love with all three of them; and, rather like boys who have found a nest of baby birds, we had no idea what we were going to do with them. We were continually discussing this and producing the most fantastic and impractical suggestions. We agreed, however, that in no circumstances could they come with us right to the front and then try to find an opportunity of escaping across to the Russians. This was partly because it would have been too awkward for us having them in the field, and partly because, as many insisted, if they were unlucky enough to cross on a sector held by men of some remote, primitive Asiatic people, they would be raped by the whole lot of them on the spot.

It was Fleischmann's brother who solved our problem for us. One day Fleischmann came rushing up and told us that his brother was Oberfeldwebel on an armoured train that was halted a little farther along in a siding. The train was going to France and the girls could go with it. We hurried to get them ready for the journey. They did not immediately grasp what was being done with them, but thought that the Gestapo had caught up with our train, with the result that Maria began to cry. But Porta said with a grin:

'Quietly now, little Maria, you're off to the heavy artillery. You're going in an armoured puff-puff all the way to France. Fleischmann's brother is arranging that.'

We doubled across an infinity of tracks, several times almost having to carry the nervous girls to get them along, and at last found ourselves standing beside the gigantic armoured train, its great guns pointing threateningly at the sky. Fleischmann's brother had everything ready when we got there, and had even put a couple of men on guard. He smiled grimly as he shook hands with the girls.

'Hurry up and jump in. And no peeping out. Just stay in the bunk the whole time; we'll bring you everything you need. You'll have to share one upper bunk as best you can. But we'll get you little girls safely home again, you'll see.'

We lifted them up into the truck and climbed in ourselves to see where they were to live. They had an upper bunk in the farthest and most inaccessible end of the steel truck, that was filled with a jumble of arms and ammunition. We each received a kiss on the mouth from the three girls. Porta called them his baby doves, so they each gave him another kiss. Shortly afterwards we stood watching the great train as it rumbled off westwards and disappeared. Whether they ever saw France again, I don't know, but the train at least got there.

Fleischmann's brother was killed by a French partisan at Le Mans, six weeks later. Shot from behind and his pistol taken. If that French patriot had known about the three girls it would never have happened. But that is war. Senseless!

15

Our transport train rolled on ever eastwards towards the great steppes and wild, black forests of Russia. The stove in the truck was kept red hot, but we froze. Day and night we sat huddled in our greatcoats, with our caps pulled down over our ears. But however hard we stoked, however much we put on, and however close we huddled, we were still miserably cold.

In Church

It was late in the afternoon and in the midst of a snow-storm when we rolled into the station at Pinsk. We were given brown beans in the Red Cross canteen, and for once there was so much that we could eat our fill.

The Old Un got talking with one of the Red Cross Sisters, and she recommended us to go and see a magnificent old church there was just behind the station. She pointed it out herself, and as we did not know what else to do with ourselves, we trotted across to see it.

The church came fully up to her description, being both very old and fragrant with the incense of the centuries, and very lovely. It was full of massive things, elaborate carvings, magnificent gilding and Catholic snugness, little lamps and live flames, little corners with intimate saints painted in simple, bright colours, sky-red and sky-blue, many of them yellowed and primitive as the drawings of adult children, and in the corners small altars with white cloths, and in the centre a large, a huge space, high enough to let souls soar aloft and rise up to the heavenly Father of God's good children, under the zealously watchful gaze of the priests, whether mild or strict, ever-patient or eternally embittered, ascetically restrained or over-fed and fornicating.

Porta thought it pretty silly to go and gape at a church when it was so icy cold; but then he discovered the organ.

'Now you'll see me play!' he said, grinning delightedly and all at once looking like an expectant child.

We found the stairs leading up to the organ loft. Porta asked a couple of us to go behind and work the thingumajig that provides the air for organ-playing. Pluto had the strength of three at least, so he went to work the bellows alone. Porta gave us another happy grin, as he sat down at the big organ.

'Now you'll see how Joseph Porta plays!'

The Old Un had perched himself on a rail, where he sat puffing at a pipe of his own manufacture, which he now removed from his mouth:

'Let's have that bit of Bach you played for me in Jugoslavia,' he said.

Porta did not know what piece The Old Un meant, so Titch had to whistle a few bars. It was J.S. Bach's *Toccata and Fugue*. As soon as Porta realised what it was The Old Un wanted his face lit up. Then he called to Pluto:

'Treadle away, old galley-slave, and Joseph Porta, by God's grace Obergefreiter, will show you how you play this thing.'

He seemed to take a deep breath and expression drained from his face. It was like emptying a glass of a residue of stale beer, for it to be refilled with noble wine.

Porta began to play. It looked as though he were just amusing himself. The notes fluttered out into the church like flocks of birds, some small and chirruping, some with a great swishing whirr of wings. When he ended, we laughed with enthusiasm. He lit a cigarette and settled himself more comfortably. The Old Un gave me a nudge, and, never taking his eyes off Porta, whispered:

'Now you will hear things. Now he's got going.'

The Old Un was like a delighted, proud father, his heart filled with pure and unaffected devotion for something of real merit.

Porta did not disappoint him. His playing was superb. First he played lightly and carelessly with the keys; then all at once he became hypnotised by his own playing: Beethoven's *Die Himmel rühmen des Ewigen Ehre*; the anonymous *Schlafe mein Prinzchen schlaf ein*, which he played so ineffably gently that

107

tears came into the eyes of both The Old Un and me, and we felt a great melting joy at there being so much that was good in life after all, and sorrow at our being fettered to darkness.

Then Porta went wild. He pulled out all the stops and shook the church with a hurricane of sound. It was dancing and shouting for joy, it was all things live and dead united in a song of praise. A mighty, blaring fanfare, blown by a thousand heralds. The dance of the myriads of snowflakes on a still Christmas night in time of peace. The birds of the forest and field pointing their beaks at the zenith and letting their throats emit a celestial chorale.

We were as though turned to stone as we listened. An ugly, dirty soldier, and then this colossal, this all-conquering, pure hymn of joy.

I happened to look down into the church and, to my amazement, I saw that it was half filled with motionless, silent people. Beside the altar stood a tall, grey-haired priest, and a little farther on a cluster of rapt civilians staring up at the gallery. In the middle of the church sat and stood soldiers in dirty greatcoats and caps pulled down over faces sallow with undernourishment. Among them I could also see one or two Red Cross Sisters; but though such beings are usually objects of our wistful interest, I forgot them for Porta's lovely music. Eventually he stopped, and in the deathly silence we could hear Pluto gasping for breath at his post behind the organ. Porta looked across at The Old Un and me.

'Bloody fine playing in a church,' said he. 'Bloody fine.'

He, too, was happy – gravely happy.

The Old Un's voice shook with emotion:

'Porta, you ugly old idiot! You red-haired numskull.'

Shortly afterwards the priest came. He embraced the grinning Porta and kissed him on both cheeks.

Then Asmus came running up and called out that we were leaving. The stately priest held a cross over us:

'God bless you, my children.'

Then we were out in the swirling snow fighting our way back to our cattle-truck and to the little dirty straw on its floor. We covered ourselves up as well as we could, and continued on our shivering way towards our unknown goal. We were unloaded at Smolensk.

16

'Back, BACK, damn you! He's got his foot under the rollers!'

Porta's reaction was almost instantaneous. The tank jerked back and Porta leaped out of it, and together he and I caught hold of Hans who was standing, as white as a sheet, holding on to the tank. We got him inside the cottage and The Old Un lit a cigarette and stuck it between his blue lips. He shook his head as he cut the boot off Hans' crushed foot.

'Children, children, are you crazy!'

Before the Attack

We were quartered on the outskirts of Smolensk in civilian billets. As soon as we had drawn our rations we sauntered off to the big market square which was swarming with men of every possible army: SS troops with grinning death's heads in their caps; parachute troops; cavalry in buckskin breeches and long boots with spurs; infantry in queer leather jackets painted with splodges of brown, green and blue; Roumanians and Hungarians in clumsy khaki uniforms – every kind of soldier from the various armies of Central Europe was to be seen there in the market-place of Smolensk, from monocled, elegant Air Force officers to filthy, lousy infantrymen.

The place, too, was thronged with Russian civilians in wadded clothes, many of them incredibly ragged. They had shapeless felt boots on their feet. Six or seven women came trudging along, each with a sack on her back, all jabbering away nineteen to the dozen. All at once one of them stopped, straddled her legs, and the next moment there was a loud splashing and a large puddle spread across the ground between her legs. As soon as she had finished she walked calmly on.

'Well, I'm damned. Just like an old cow.' Porta looked from the puddle to the old woman. 'Well, I'm damned,' he said again.

The Russians gave the impression of being quite unaffected by the appalling cold, which had such a bad effect on us.

We stayed only a couple of days in Smolensk, then lorries took us to Bielev, where the 27th Regiment was quartered. Our company went to 2nd Battalion under Oberstleutnant von der Lindenau, with Major Hinka as No. 2. If only we had not had such a swine as Meier for company commander all would have been well.

Porta maintained that the Lord had appeared to him in a vision and said that the season for swine-hunting would soon start, and also that the company would soon have a new commander. That was what the Lord had said to Obergefreiter Porta, amen.

There was much talk of swine-hunting in the company. Meier allowed himself the most incredible liberties with us; he cheated us and did the dirty on us at every opportunity. His crowning act was to give us drill and route-marching, a blunder where troops in the field are concerned. All the officers shook their heads and thought him crazy, and from that moment we all knew that no one would be interested in the cause of Meier's death. After that, Meier was ours. He did not know it himself, but we did. We stopped talking about swine-hunting and many of us made dum-dums. There was nothing more to discuss.

One of those who took Meier's swinishness most to heart was Hans Breuer. He asked me once or twice whether we should not desert together, but I did not dare.

'Devil take it, Sven, can't you see that we must get away from all this, no matter how?' he added thoughtfully.

I looked at him. 'Hans,' I said earnestly, 'don't do anything stupid now.'

One evening orders came to prepare the tanks for action. We filled them with petrol and oil and loaded them with ammunition: twenty thousand rounds of machine-gun ammunition, that was ten thousand for each of our two machine-guns; one hundred high-explosive shells, one hundred armoured shells, fifty armour-piercing S-shells; hand grenades, flares, ammunition for our small arms, and oil for the flame-throwers.

Porta was on his belly, so deep in the motor compartment that you could just see his legs protruding, while he cursed at the bloody Army that turned people into swine. Now and again he gave a suppressed laugh and called down from his cylinders and valves:

'Hey, Old Un, I'm getting a nice bull's-eye this time. God's just told me.'

'If someone does not get in ahead of you,' said The Old Un. 'There are seven hundred in the company.'

Porta's answer was to whistle a hunting-call between his teeth. The Old Un and Titch went into the cottage to prepare our evening meal, while Pluto went to the quartermaster for our rations. Porta and I were to drive the tank close up to the house and camouflage it with branches and snow to prevent it being seen by the Russian planes which every night came flying over and threw down parachute flares.

Before we had got the tank manoeuvred into place Hans came across and told us that he had just had a letter telling him that his wife had gone to hospital with a serious abdominal complaint. He was very depressed. I still blame myself for not keeping an eye on him. I *knew* that I ought to; I just did not think, and the next moment it was too late.

I was standing in front of the tank signalling with my hands to Porta, so that he could drive the tank properly into place without knocking our cottage down. Then I heard Hans give a little cry, and I knew that he had done it. When I got to him, he was standing with one foot caught between the track and the heavy roller.

When the ambulance had driven away we discussed the report The Old Un would have to write. We agreed on saying that Hans had tried to climb up on to the tank from the side, and at that moment Porta had backed, thinking that that was the signal I had given him. As a result, Hans had slipped off the roller and his foot had caught. That sounded plausible, but it was not immaculate, since it was strictly forbidden to climb on to a tank from the side. You always had to mount from the front, where the driver could see you.

Also, it seemed rather strange that he should get his foot crushed just before we went into action.

'It's all the same, what it seems,' said The Old Un. 'There's not one of us doubts that he did it on purpose. But as long as they can't prove anything, all will be well. And they can't do that as long as we stick to that explanation.'

'We must just hope they don't soften Hans up,' sighed Porta. 'The devils.'

We then went to bed to get some sleep, as we were to move up to the front during the night. We were roused at one o'clock.

Titch managed to light a Hindenburg candle, and by its flickering gleam we got ourselves ready, though we were scarcely properly awake. Porta was sitting upright in the straw, clawing at his dirty, thin pigeon-chest, his red mane standing out in all directions. The Old Un and Pluto were catching lice, which they threw into the flame of the candle, where they exploded with a little pop and gave off a nauseating, oily smell. Within a quarter of an hour we had got our equipment on, and, trembling with cold, we climbed into the tank. We had wound our greasy scarves round our necks, and pulled our caps with snow-glasses down over our ears.

What a difference there is between the rubicund, spruce, straight-backed young hero gazing steadily into the distance, the woman-compelling male-warrior, whom you see on the recruiting posters of the whole world, and the snuffling, scared devil with a cold, bad breath and pasty face who is the reality of war. If the artists who drew those poster heroes knew how tragic was the task they were undertaking with their ridiculous art they would seek other work. But, probably, they could get none, for when you look more closely you soon discover that it is only sixth- or seventh-rate artists who take on that kind of commissioned 'art'. The military recruiting poster is the field of very minor talents.

The battalion's many engines were humming and singing all over the village. Now and again there was a brief flash from

113

a torch, otherwise everything was done in pitch darkness out of respect for the 'coffee-grinders', as we called the Russian planes because of their comical chugging noise, which were very much on the alert as they flew, invisible, above our heads, sometimes so low that we could hear the noise of their engines through the din of our own.

17

We left the village by companies. It was pitch dark and you had to be careful not to crash into the tank in front. To make it easier for Porta, who sat down beside the tank's instruments and steering-rods, Pluto and I perched ourselves up on the turret and gave him directions by telephone. We rattled and roared along at 33 m.p.h. All at once we heard a crunching sound. Half a minute later it came again, and at the same time large pieces of wood came flying round our ears. When this had happened five times, we realised that we were knocking the telephone poles down, and at once directed Porta back on to the road. A little farther on we almost went into the tank in front, which had halted because we had come to a bridge that the tanks could only cross one at a time. Two of us had to stand, one on either side of the bridge, holding glowing cigarettes to guide our heavy monster across. An inch or so more to one side or the other and the River Upa would have had the prey it was waiting for.

About four o'clock we halted on the fringe of a thicket. The motors were switched off, and a strange silence descended upon us. The only sound was the stuttering and chugging of the 'coffee-mills' up above. Every other moment a parachute-flare came floating down, lighting up the countryside as brilliantly as by day.

While our officers were with the regimental commander getting their battle-orders, we tried to get a little sleep, half lying on the steel floor of the tank. We had just dropped off when the order to fall in came. Our section commanders told us our tasks.

The Spectacle

'The 27th Tank Regiment together with the 4th, 18th and 21st Divisions, is to attack the Russian positions at Serpuchow, north of Thula. The positions are to be broken through with a view to a drive on Moscow. The tank regiment of the 12th Panzer Division will form the head of the attacking wedge, with the SS guards as reserve on the right flank. Our company will be on the extreme left flank and has the task of penetrating behind the Russian positions and preparing the way for the companies following on. 3 Company is the leading company.'

'Honour the memory of 3 Company,' said Porta, with a laugh.

'We are to move up to a battered village just behind the main fighting line. There, panzer-grenadiers from the 104th Rifle Regiment are to get up behind our tanks.

06.40 hours. Stukas attack.

06.48 hours. 3 Company attacks.

06.51 hours. Our company follows.

A barrage will be laid three kilometres behind the enemy lines at 06.50 hours.'

It was a magnificent sight. Tracer projectiles of all the colours of the rainbow passed screeching across the heavens. Woods and villages were in flames all along the horizon, so that the sky was tinged with reddish-violet. Individual shells exploded with sharp reports and white flashes, but otherwise there was that utter stillness that precedes the storm. Now and again a machine-gun crackled, sounding like furious watch-dogs, and stray bullets spattered into the ruins around us.

It was a magnificent drama. A battle is the big show, a real attraction. War with its prolonged apprehension, dirt, hunger and unheroic misery culminates in a gripping display of splendour and savagery. The scared soul frees itself and rises on strong wings and flies to meet its mighty destiny. It is the suffering civilian's great hour. His soul has never had an opportunity to unfold in riches and luxury; it has become dusty in an untidy office, where it has been fashioned to the shape laid down by the personnel officer. Nor has it found any opportunities in the world of the spirit; it was not of that calibre and money had been too scarce for a literary education and outlook. And when the soul has paid a visit to Love, perhaps it was no more than briefly in a doorway, then a baby, marriage lines, a dreary flat in a viewless street, bills, sweat, lust with clipped wings and a woman who quickly becomes the bane of life, a deadly boring woman.

In battle the little civilian mobilises all his accumulated dread, and there is much of it, and goes off to battle and liberates his soul in that great life-and-death drama.

No! The soul is not liberated. That is a caricature. Far from becoming a free human being, it is a crazy, hysterical cur it becomes, blindly obeying the prompting of his own fear of doing anything on his own. What it does is exactly what it never wanted to do, or at least never dared do, but which it had been tempted to do all its life: it kills for food.

And because it exposes itself to a crazy risk of death by doing so, it believes that its possessor is a brave man, and that he will neither have lived nor died in vain.

Such is the prosaic truth.

At any rate I do not believe in the lyric poets of war. Nobody will persuade me that war is a dashing, exciting adventure for he-men, a safari for hunters even richer and more powerful than millionaires.

The Old Un had often told me of tank attacks in which scores of tanks had been set on fire by the enemy's anti-tank guns and their crews burned to death inside them. I had also been told innumerable times that to lead an attack was an enterprise from which few emerged with their lives. And we, the penal regiment, would always be the spear-head.

'Well, Sven, have you remembered to write a few words of farewell to your mother and sweetheart?'

The Old Un's grave voice intruding upon my thoughts made me start. I got a piece of field letter paper and scribbled a few words by the faint light of the instrument panel. When I had finished Porta handed me up a bottle and said with his mocking grin:

'Take a swig of Dutch courage, then you'll forget that they're not using blanks over there. It'll be just like an exercise.'

Porta's Dutch courage proved to be pure 96 per cent spirit, honourably filched from the infirmary. I have drunk lots of it since, but never undiluted. Porta laughed when he saw my face.

'Excuse me! I forgot to tell you to push your uvula to one side and put the stuff down quickly.'

To my amazement Titch put the bottle to his lips and gulped it down without turning a hair. Porta had to wrest the bottle from him.

'That's enough. We're not at a Jesus feast with Christmas-tree and crackers, you ass.'

'Thanks for the present, dear Porta,' said Titch, and belched loudly. 'If I should happen to go up on this little trip, I'll order an assortment of angels and have them waiting for you when you come.'

'Lord preserve us,' said The Old Un. 'Listen to them. They think they're going to Heaven. No, my little ones, the feathers we get will be of the singed variety.'

From outside came the sound of muffled orders, and short-ly afterwards some grenadiers mounted the tank. They peered in at us, grinning. We lit a last cigarette.

'Ready to attack! 5 Company – forward march!'

With engines roaring, we rolled through the battered village. The hatches of our turrets were still open, and up behind us sat the grenadiers, ready to jump off when the fun and games began. Porta kept his eyes glued to the narrow vision slits, and his hands were clenched on the steering-rods. The Old Un stood in the turret staring rigidly through the round observation ring, while Pluto was ready to fire the heavy gun the moment the order to open fire was given. Titch had all the ammunition lockers open and stood ready to slam shells into the gun as the empty cases came out, red hot. Where I sat, down by the wireless set, I looked for the twentieth time to see that my machine-gun was in order, and arranged the long cartridge belt that twined about me like a broad, flat snake. A laughing voice sounded:

'No. 5 Company, 5 Company. The Staff Company calling. All tanks open fire!'

Thereupon hell broke loose. Our heads were filled with the roaring, crashing, banging, rumbling of unleashed energy.

Long, yellowish-red flames protruded like knives of fire from the muzzles of the guns. The inside of the tank was like

118

a witches' cauldron. Smoke from the shells stung and burned our eyes and throats. Each time the gun fired a pointed flame stabbed out from its breech-block. The empty cases accumulated and rolled with an appalling clatter into the well of the tank.

I sat with gaping mouth staring out at the landscape across which we were rumbling. All at once I caught sight of some Russian infantry straight ahead. Automatically, I squinted down the barrel and over the fore-sight; my index finger curled round the trigger in the regulation way – now! With cold gaze and narrowed eyes I watched where the tracer bullets struck, corrected my aim and murdered away. Suddenly, I was flung forward with a violent jerk, and if I had not been wearing a leather-padded crash helmet I would have torn my face to ribbons on the lock of the machine-gun. The Old Un swore at Porta, who had driven us into a shell-hole several feet deep.

'Just wait till I start driving your puffer, as, in my humble opinion, a puffer ought to be driven,' shouted Porta.

The Russians' anti-tank artillery began to answer back, and the first smashed tanks were already standing burning with fiery red flames licking up round their steel hulls, and cascades of thick, velvety, coal-black smoke pouring up towards the sky.

We worked our way slowly forwards, our grenadiers crouching under cover behind, ready to deal with the Russian infantry once we had thrust through the positions. About midday Ivan withdrew. As soon as we had got more petrol and ammunition we set off at full speed after the retreating enemy. Now and again we stopped at a village where Ivan had dug his heels in and from which he had to be smoked and burned out; within a quarter of an hour there would be no village left, just fire, in which we rattled round, mowing down everything: soldiers, men, women, children and animals. If there was a burning house in our way we roared straight through it, sending a cloud of sparks swirling round us, while burning beams fell over the tank and were dragged with it for some distance, making it look as though it, too, were on fire.

The Russian soldiers understood how to die. More than once we saw a handful of them occupy a strategically important point and delay our advance until their last cartridge was used, or till they themselves were crushed beneath our tank tracks. It is odd seeing a person lying or sitting or running or hobbling away right in front, and for you not to turn aside, but drive straight on, over him. Odd. You do not feel anything. You are only aware that you cannot feel. Perhaps some other day, in a week, a month, a year, fifty years. But not just at that moment. There is no time for feeling; the whole business is just something that is happening, going on, pictures and noises, most acutely perceived and immediately shoved automatically to one side to be analysed later.

We made acquaintance with the Russians' heavy tanks, enormous brutes of ninety or one hundred tons with a huge 22-cm. gun sticking out from their mighty turrets. In such fighting, however, they were no serious danger to us. They were too slow, those mastodons. We smashed them one after the other without difficulty.

After eight weeks' uninterrupted advance, our fighting power dried up and we came to a stop at Podolsk, south-west of Moscow. We came to a stop in the middle of the Russian winter, whose savagery knows no bounds. Thousands of German soldiers perished from appalling frost-bite. An endless transport had to be organised to send home those whom gangrene had robbed of a leg or an arm.

Our supplies broke down. There was no petrol or ammunition for the tanks. We were in the middle of Russia in temperatures of minus 58° C, and almost no one had furs or other winter equipment to keep the howling snow-storms at arm's length. Many a time the mad pain in our hands and feet made us scream and whimper like babies. No one could stand on guard for longer than ten minutes at a stretch; to do so meant certain death. If a man was hit he was usually found frozen stiff in the same position in which the bullet had struck him. It was a daily occurrence to find such a frozen corpse leaning up against a tree-trunk or the wall of a trench.

Now it was the Russians' turn to take the initiative, and we acquired a real respect for their Siberian troops, trained for winter warfare. They hammered away at us unceasingly and without mercy. Our many thousands of tanks were out of action through lack of petrol; but even if we had had all the petrol in the world, it would not have helped, for every single engine was frozen and useless. Steering and gear levers shivered when you touched them, as though they were made of glass.

On December 22nd, 1941, after three weeks, during which we were attacked incessantly by day and night, we retreated in a howling snow-storm. We had blown up all our tanks to prevent them falling into the hands of the enemy. Exhausted and half-blinded by the snow, we staggered westwards.

I walked between Porta and The Old Un, and I was so ill with the cold, hunger and weakness that they had almost to carry me most of the way. When I fell and remained lying, they hit me and cursed me, till they got me going again. It was thanks to their stubborn exertions that Titch and I did not share the fate of the thousands who remained lying in the snow, because it was so lovely just to be there and freeze to death. The Russians were ever at our heels. The cold did not mean anything to them. They were able to fight the whole time.

Being a penal regiment we naturally brought up the rear, as we had been in front during the attack.

A little to the south of Kalinin we were ordered to dig ourselves in in the snow and hold the position (that was the village of Goradnja) – hold it at all costs. Now followed insufferable days when the Russians literally ran themselves to death on our positions. Thousands and thousands of dead piled up just in front of us, yet stubbornly they threw fresh masses into the battle. It was one of the great mass slaughters.

We had been formed into a section of twelve men, with The Old Un as leader. One night the Russians finally broke through and penetrated over fifteen miles behind our lines.

I was lying behind a machine-gun with Asmus and Fleisch-mann, firing away at the attacking waves. We had to keep our eyes skinned to avoid mowing down our men, for both the

Russians and we wore long, white snow coats with cowls that went over our helmets. We were guided mostly by instinct.

All at once we heard a loud shout in Russian behind us. Gather up machine-gun, automatic pistols, hand-grenades and run! Away, only get away!

We ran back, all except Asmus, and he, the numskull, ran straight at the Russians.

And so did we, for we were surrounded.

18

It is with the greatest reluctance that I write this chapter on the period when I was a prisoner. I know that it will be used to support points of view for which I have absolutely no sympathy; while the opposing side will no doubt call me a liar and a swindler, a traitor to the people's cause.

Having read this chapter, the adherents of one view will get busy with red pencil heavily underlining passages and explain triumphantly: There! That's what it's like over there! See for yourself. An eye-witness! Read what an eye-witness says! Listen to the truth about Soviet Russia!

If anyone asks me whether it is 'like that' in Russia, I can only reply that I really do not know. USSR is a huge country. I have been there for only quite a short time and seen only very little of it, while the circumstances of my stay were such that it was quite impossible for me to have any proper contact or achieve any kind of overall view, let alone anything as complicated as an evaluation of how 'things are'.

I came as an enemy to a country which had ample grounds to hate me and maltreat me and otherwise be utterly indifferent to what happened to me. I, after all, was one of those who had helped to burn thousands of villages and ruin existence for millions of people.

I do not share the easy view that Nazism and the People's Democracy were one and the same thing, and that Stalin and Hitler were of the same kidney. One look at their portraits will show that that is nonsense. Hitler was a hysteric, Stalin an obstinate fellow who had sense enough not to play with revolutions, but went on his way thoroughly, scientifically and with infinite patience and infinite mistrustful watchfulness. He was no fool, and certainly not one of God's good children. But not knowing him personally, I would rather not guess. But, as well as comparing the two men's faces, you can also compare their writings, and these will also show that Hitler and Stalin were as far from being alike as two men can be.

This account of the time when I was the Russians' prisoner of war is thus not to be taken and used as an argument either for or against socialism, or against Stalin, for or against the East. As long as Hitler and his associates, both those who are dead and those who still live here and there about the world, still exert an influence, as they do, it would be a waste of effort to go all the way to Moscow to find the causes of the fears with which the whole world is hag-ridden. As long as democratic freedom remains no more than a problematical postulate we have no moral right to sweep anywhere but our own dirty front doorsteps.

Besides, you can gladly keep your freedom, as far as I am concerned, as long as I am allowed to retain my peace. My urge for freedom is not in the direction of shooting off rifles. Having tried war, I will willingly submit to even the strictest compulsion, if that be necessary, in order that we may live our lives in peace, as in fact it is. It is not enough to stand up and say: 'We want no more war' – and then think that you have done your bit. There has to be an assertion of will; somebody has to see that all get enough to eat, that all the great humanitarian plans and programmes are translated from paper into fact. And it will call for considerable toil, lasting perhaps for several generations; it will call for restraint and strict self-discipline to construct the mighty machinery that will ensure the production and distribution of food enough for all. It will call for the hardest of all compulsions: the need to subordinate oneself to the requirements of the general weal. It will require that one and all renounce comfort and ease and buckle to. It will require that people forget self, that they give up living only for themselves, and the liquidation of that form of individualism that only recognises the individual's rights – that to collect for himself – but that becomes so tired and wearied and so annoyed, when anyone takes it upon himself to remind them of the individual's duties. We all talk far too much about freedom with the implication that we wish to exterminate others. Or, what is quite infamous, that we want others to exterminate each other, while we look on and profit by it.

There are, however, two associated reasons why I shall write of my time as a prisoner despite my reluctance and fear of being misunderstood: the first is that my account of the war, as I experienced it, would be incomplete without this chapter, and the second that such a chapter is necessary in a book the purpose of which is to oppose all war, which is all but the opposite of showing what 'things are like' in the Soviet Union, a vast land which – let me repeat this – I do not know at all, but which I imagine to be just as human and irregular in peacetime as any other human society; in other words: quite ordinary and every-day.

Captivity

There is nothing that makes you more inclined to despair than being taken prisoner.

Fleischmann and I were locked up in a house in the village of Klin, and a Soviet soldier was posted outside our door. Kicks, blows and curses had rained over us all the way back from the front, until we had been handed over at the assembly point in this village of Klin. We were interrogated by an officer, who wanted to know how our regiment was made up and all the rest of it. On the way back to the house we saw them despatching ten SS riflemen by hammering empty cartridge cases into the backs of their necks. Elsewhere, they had crucified a major on a door. Others were being beaten to a pulp with rifle butts and cossack whips.

The hour of vengeance had struck.

Later in the night we were assembled in a large column of a couple of thousand men, and mounted guards drove us eastwards. We were not allowed to step out of the ranks, so we had to relieve ourselves in our trousers. Those who fell in the snow were given the whip till they got up again. If they could not get up they were run through with a sabre.

After three days we reached the village of Kimry, where we were put into a large barn and given our first meal since leaving Klin. The food was an evil-smelling, indefinable mess, which we were unable to get down despite our screaming hunger.

Fleischmann and I decided to try to escape. Prisoners were

permitted to go behind the barn to attend to nature, and on one such trip we saw our opportunity and set off full pelt across the fields. We ran across a frozen pond some three hundred yards from the barn, and on and on without feeling in any way tired. Fear was all we felt. We ran all night, taking our direction from the stars, which I knew quite well, having once been interested in astronomy. We ran through a large wood and on across a frozen lake. We had almost reached the other side, when a fur-clad soldier shouted at us from behind, but we ran on. He sent a dozen bullets after us; they whistled round our ears, but none hit us. A few minutes later we were lying in the cover of bushes.

That evening we came to some cottages and hid in a stable. There we lay and rested for twenty-four hours. We found a hen and wrung its neck and ate it raw. The next day we moved to the shelter of another stable, where we dug deep down into some old straw piled at one end.

In the afternoon, to our horror, we heard a lot of shouting in the farmyard, and when we peered out cautiously through a hole in the roof we saw five Russian soldiers with two dogs. After a lengthy palaver with the inhabitants of the farm they went away. We lay where we were for a few hours longer, and when dusk fell we thought we would sneak out.

The old man did not seem surprised to see us in his stable. He just asked in awkward German:

'Prisoners of war?'

We nodded.

He took us into his house and gave us food. In the room sat another old man and four women. They greeted us quietly and made room for us at the table. They observed us stealthily as we ate their mutton and boiled potatoes. No one spoke.

The old farmer let us sleep there in the room, so that we could get properly rested, and in the morning he gave us each a pair of quilted trousers and jacket to match. They were good, warm clothes and had the inestimable advantage of being anonymous, so that we could travel by day without the risk of being recognised by our black uniforms. We took a cordial farewell of those taciturn, kindly people.

For another four days we walked towards the west, but then early one morning misfortune overtook us. As we emerged from a small wood we found ourselves face to face with some Russian soldiers, who might have sprung from the ground. They asked for our papers. I started talking Danish, but they did not understand. Then I tried English and that went better. I told them that we were Danes, that we had been in a German concentration camp and had deserted from a penal regiment. At the Russian unit to which we had reported they told us to go to Moscow, but in making for the railway station we had lost our way.

There was a great confabulation after this, from which I gathered that they did not believe me. In the end, they took us to their commander. On the way, one of them caught sight of my wrist-watch, and after that I had no watch. Another took the gold chain Ursula had given me. The unit's commander treated us decently and interrogated us very thoroughly. He asked if we were Communists and we said that we were; but we did not dare pretend that we were members of the Party, in case that could be checked. He muttered disapproval of our not having bothered to become members, but the main thing was that we were good Communists.

The following day we were taken to the railway by two soldiers who were to accompany us to Moscow and hand us over to the GPU for further investigation. After thirty-six hours in the train we were delivered to a room in the station at Moscow. It was a big room with close-meshed wire-netting at the windows, which looked on to an enormous station hall swarming with soldiers and civilians. Several climbed up and looked in at us. We waited for several hours, then five heavily armed men from GPU arrived and led us to a large, black police car. We drove at a furious pace through the streets to a large prison.

'Now we've had it,' whispered Fleischmann. 'They'll either shoot us or send us to Siberia.'

Fleischmann's whisper cost us a scurry of blows from rifle butts that made us fall half unconscious off the bench, but a few kicks in the belly soon had us on our feet again. We drove through a maze of prison yards with grilles and stopped at a small door, through which we were literally kicked. We were driven along to an office, where a GPU officer received us with well-directed blows of his fist, exactly the same fare as the SS had given me in Lengries.

After entering our particulars in a register – we both said we were Danish citizens – we were taken up to a cell in which twenty-five others were already stuffed. Our fellows had been arrested for every conceivable kind of crime, both political and civil. A Red Army sergeant, who had cut his wife's throat with a bread knife, said with the assurance of the expert:

'You'll be sent to a labour camp in a couple of months. If you go about it in the right way you can get along beautifully there. The chief thing is to do as little as possible, and what you do must be muck. See, too, that you make friends with a GPU chap by "organising" things for him from the factory where you work; but that, of course, must be good stuff.'

There was a professor who had won a Stalin prize and was now charged with activities hostile to the State. The tariff for that was twenty-five years' hard labour. He told us that we would never get out of Russia legally, and advised us to do a bunk as soon as we could.

Only twelve of us could lie down at the same time. In one corner of the cell there was a bucket without a lid. The stench was intolerable and clung to your clothes. Then there were the lice and the hunger. But we were not cold. We sweated day and night, as though we were in a Turkish bath. If we stood on another's shoulders we could see down into a large yard, where they executed scores of prisoners, men and women, every night. The sound I associate with that prison is of volleys and the motors of big lorries. Like all transport work in Moscow, the removal of prisoners was done by night.

We were examined by a young commissar. The examination lasted five hours and we had to tell everything about ourselves and our families. Two days later we had another examination, when they asked us exactly the same questions, only in a different order. They continued with that for a couple of days, and in the end we were on the edge of a

128

nervous breakdown and so bemused that we began contradicting ourselves. Then they shouted at us that we had told them a pack of lies, and they tried to make us admit that we were SS men and spies.

For the next three days there was no examination, and then we were taken before a court of sorts and I was sentenced to ten years' hard labour and Fleischmann to fifteen, but what we were sentenced for no one told us. The whole thing took five minutes.

Shortly after this we and about two hundred other male and female prisoners were driven late one night to the railway station and loaded into a goods-train. They selected one man in each truck and made him a sort of head-prisoner, who was responsible for all those in his truck. These head-prisoners were mostly those whom the GPU men, for some reason or other, had picked on, and whom they made suffer for all real or fancied offences.

Those in our truck came from all strata of society. There was a peasant in quilted clothes and clumsy felt boots. Beside him lay an elderly man in a grey suit, dirty and crumpled, but of a good cut, and he was wearing shoes, a thing which only the highest classes do. Opposite me sat a woman in furs and smart silk stockings. Beside her was a young girl in working clothes, and there were one or two others in summer dresses despite the piercing cold.

The train was heading eastwards, but where we were going none of us knew. Thrice a day we were ordered out for roll-call. The method of counting us was to line us up in one rank, then a soldier went behind, struck the first man a swishing blow with his horsewhip and called 'One!'; and he continued thus all down the line. One morning a prisoner had vanished from our truck. This proved to be a former officer, who, during the night, had managed to get the door open and jumped out. Our head-prisoner paid for this escape with his life.

At Kuybjschev, on the Volga, several more trucks of prisoners were coupled on to our train. Every single day some of us died from cold and exhaustion. We were made to keep the corpses in the truck, and we had to haul them out for each roll-call when they, too, received their blows from the whip. One day, when we stopped at Bogolowsk, deep in the mighty Urals, the guards seemed to go crazy, for the door was suddenly flung open and a burst of shots fired right into the truck, where we lay as close as sardines in a tin. The door was then shut again with a great roar of laughter. Two of the women became quite hysterical and began to howl like dogs, their eyes rigid and staring and foam frothing at their mouths. Fleischmann and I attended to one, while a couple of former soldiers dealt with the other. We had to bring them to themselves with a ringing smack on the face, as you did at the front when someone went crazed. That is almost always effective, when it is done properly and the smack comes as a shock. Both the women stopped their mad noise, gave a convulsive start, then for a long time they sat and wept the rest of their agitation out of them.

We were let out in Tobolsk. The labour camp there had nothing to learn from the Nazis' terror camps. We were told that we would be put to work in the forest for the first few days, and then be sent to various factories and works. In our weakened state, the hard work in the forest was incredible toil, and it was a good thing it only lasted a few days, for otherwise we should not have survived. Fleischmann and I were then sent to work in an underground factory making wireless valves, and, judging by what others told us, we were lucky. Those who were sent to the ammunition factories apparently died like flies.

We were allowed five hours' sleep a day. We slept in a hut, where three men had to share a bunk that had no mattress and only one blanket. We were given miserable fish soup three times a day, but no bread. Bread was a luxury, presumably because the rich wheat country by the Black Sea had been lost in the fighting.

After some time we were transferred to a camp for free prisoners. That was a place from which you were loaned to factories and other undertakings that were not under direct GPU supervision, and where conditions were much more

130

humane and humanly muddled. You were treated decently and also given a little pay. If you were really smart, you could get the work-leader to put you down as a specialist, and that made you indispensable.

Our train sauntered along for five days till we came to Jenisseisk on the River Jenissei. On the way we passed Lake Kalunda, and there we got hold of a lot of dried fish and almost killed ourselves by overeating. It was the first occasion for a very long time that we had eaten our fill – and how sick it made us! Our debilitated stomachs could not digest such a mighty meal, though it was also questionable whether even a sound stomach could have dealt with more than thirty such fish. We were accompanied by a couple of decent elderly men of the so-called blue GPU.

The new camp in Jenisseisk was a considerable improvement, as far as we were concerned. There was not much space, it is true, but we were never more than two in a bunk. Also, we were reasonably free and not exposed to cruelty. On the contrary, there was quite a pleasant relationship between the prisoners and those in charge of them. We had to attend roll-call every morning and evening, and this took the form of reporting to a GPU guard, who wrote your name on a board. When the roll-call was over, the board was wiped clean with a knife. There was no paper for that sort of thing. If you neglected to report at roll-call, it might earn you a box on the ears, but there were no brutal beatings. Very often the GPU soldier on duty merely asked one of the others whether he could guarantee that the missing person was in the camp, and if the answer was 'yes', then the GPU man said admonishingly:

'Tell him that he is written up now, but he must come tomorrow or else I will be really mad with him. We must have a little order in things here.'

In this camp I had one of the craziest experiences that have ever come my way. This was the way in which they selected 'specialists'.

'Tell me what you can do.'

Knowing that it was vital to be taken for specialist work,

Fleischmann and I both coolly told them that we were 'motor specialists'.

That put us in the specialist group. When we drew the GPU man's attention to the fact that he had written 'specialist' instead of 'motor specialist', he smiled cheerfully, winked, and said:

'What would you do if a cook was wanted and you were down as a "motor specialist"?'

He was a practical man.

We began by making wooden spanners. No one had any idea what they were to be used for. The factory that made them employed twenty-five men on the job. After ten days we were moved to another department that made compasses and that sort of thing.

I had never in my wildest imaginings thought it possible to sabotage work to the extent that was done in that factory. Fifty per cent of all that was produced had to be scrapped. For an example, they were building an engine-shop, a job on which at least six hundred specialists were engaged. All sorts of precautions were taken to see that it was a nice building. The architects and leaders from the GPU measured what was done several times a day, and they wallowed in drawings and blue-prints. The work was followed with great interest by the entire town. When at long last the engine-shop was finished it was as squint as the tower of Pisa, and everybody, except those responsible for the masterpiece, laughed loudly and unrestrainedly, including our GPU men.

It was the same with the machines in the factories. They were continually breaking down, and then the workers shouted delightedly: 'Machine bust! Machine bust!'

No matter how tiny the fault, it was certain to take the rest of the day to remedy it, while a handful of sand in a dynamo would always give us a longer interval. If a part was needed for one machine, you stole it from another, and that replaced it from a third, and so on till the last was taken from a halted machine waiting for something or other from Moscow before it could run again. We had a big engine, and one day this broke down, making a whole department stop work. After a lengthy palaver we specialists decided that there must be something wrong with the sparking-plugs. Not having that kind of sparking-plug in the store, we had to send to Moscow for a new set. When they eventually arrived, three weeks later, there was a whole box of them, only the box, when opened, was full of screws. Another requisition was sent to Moscow. Another three weeks passed, and then another box of plugs arrived, and this time it had sparking-plugs in it. But in the meantime the engine itself had quietly vanished. There was nothing of that big engine left but the fly-wheel. The works-leader stared at the remains for a while, then he shook his head and went in to see Captain Turgojski, the GPU chief, and drank vodka.

It would be wrong to think that you can conclude from this that everywhere in USSR things were as chaotic and sabotage as rife as at Jenisseisk. The army that was put up against us functioned perfectly. If its equipment was not better than the German – as it not infrequently was – it was at least as good and also less complicated. And the human material was better. More primitive, but also more reliable. That could not have been possible in a land that was corrupt through and through. Many people would like to think that everything in the Soviet Union is rotten, as it was at Jenisseisk, but you should be careful about drawing conclusions. That things were as they were in Jenisseisk is not to be wondered at when you realise that there were thirty thousand of us forced labourers, six thousand of whom were foreigners. There were thirty thousand people who only thought of sabotaging the work they did, or, at the very least, were utterly indifferent whether or not things were produced or a decent job done. We were there and we were relatively well-off, so our only concern was to stay there. In other words, we had to see that things stayed as they were for as long as possible.

The big canals and power stations that have been built, the irrigation works completed, the development of heavy industry and expansion of general education, are all things which show that there cannot be nothing but saboteurs in that huge land. It is merely that dimensions there are so large that the mistakes and blunders, of which no community is

133

altogether free, since people are not machines, necessarily loom up huge in the eyes of the Western European and attract instant attention. Added to which is the factor that the country was at war, and for that reason alone conditions must have been abnormal.

I met a German Communist, Bernhard Kruse, from Berlin Lichterfelde. He had taken part in the fighting at the barricades after the First World War. In 1924 he crossed over into Soviet Russia and was received with open arms. He was a machine-fitter and got a good job in a factory in Leningrad, where he became works foreman and instructor of several hundred men. He was well-off, had a good salary and enjoyed all the privileges of the upper-class Soviet citizen, including that of being able to shop in the big party stores where everything was to be had. He married a young woman from Moscow. Then, in 1936, he was arrested and put in Lubjanka and kept for two years without any idea of why he was there. When an officer came to his cell during an inspection of the prison he asked the officer if he could tell him why he had been arrested. The officer sent for the register, turned to Kruse's name and read out:

'Your name is Bernhard Kruse; you were born in Berlin in 1902 and are married to Katja Wolin. You are a machine specialist and have been engineer in several factories in the Leningrad district. You have been given a diploma of honour for services in training Russian workers and you are a member of the Party.'

The officer read on. Finally, he shook his head.

'This seems peculiar,' he said.

Then, finally, he exclaimed:

'Aha! Here we have it. In 1924 you crossed the Polish frontier and entered the Soviet. That sort of thing is illegal.'

'Yes, but I had been given a Russian passport, and everyone knew how and when I entered the Soviet, and I have been here for twelve years.'

The officer shrugged his shoulders.

'You must have kept something or other from the GPU which they have now found out,' he said.

A year later Kruse was sentenced to fifteen years' hard labour for having entered the Soviet illegally and by stealth, probably in order to spy. He was informed of the sentence in his cell, and thus never so much as saw the shadow of a judge.

Many such stories were confided in me. Whether the tellers were all as innocent and unaware of the reason for their sentences as they made out is a question I cannot answer. One old Russian said:

'If anyone has really done something, they shoot him at once.'

I became really good friends with the Commissar for Distribution of Prisoners' Labour. He came to me several times at the factory and wanted something made for him privately. One day I asked him if he could get me a better job, which he promised to do. The very next day he came with a mad proposition:

'You can speak English and German. What do you say to becoming a teacher of languages? You can certainly teach the children something. When there's an inspection, you just invite the commissar to have a drink, and then he forgets to inspect. That's what we all do.'

I laughed. 'It would never work,' I said. 'I can speak Russian fairly reasonably, but I can't write it at all. You must think of something better.'

He shook his head in amazement. 'The children must teach you to write Russian in return for your teaching them English and German. I'm sure it would work.'

However, I did not become a schoolmaster, but a 'specialist miller'. If anyone questioned me, I was to say that I had been commissar for all the mills in Scandinavia.

A young Russian showed me round No. 73 Flour Mill. We went to some sieves with the whitest flour I have ever seen, such flour as was not to be bought legally. He then filled a fourteen-pound sack, tied it, tramped it flat and told me to put it under my jacket and shape it a bit, so that it should not be too obvious.

'And you can do that every morning. We all do.'

With the help of all this precious flour that I 'organised' I

135

became good friends with many of the GPU men to whom I sold it, and I also managed to get Fleischmann transferred to decent work outside the camp. Nor was it long before I had got us both permission to go about the town freely, as long as we reported for morning roll-call. For a couple of months we had a wonderful time and lived as well as any free Soviet citizen. Once a week we went to the cinema and saw Russian films, many of which were excellent, though the weekly 'news' films from the front were not. To me, these seemed bogus and stilted, sometimes even grotesque. One of them was of a Soviet soldier in the fighting at the Crimea. He was badly wounded, having had both legs shot off above the knee, while a shell splinter had knocked the eyes out of his head, yet no sooner had he been bandaged up than he jumped out of bed, seized an armful of land-mines and ran out on his stumps to continue the fight. German tanks were rolling along the street. Like a tiger, this legless, eyeless Russian crawled up on to a tank and blew it up. He continued doing this till he had smashed a dozen of them; then, when all the German tanks were blazing furiously, that brave Russian let himself be borne back to the field hospital where the doctors operated and finished him off. As the film ended, an officer on a rostrum called to the audience:

'Comrades! Thus does the Red Army fight against the henchmen of the bourgeoisie and capitalism!'

All good things come to an end sometime or other, and when I heard from a GPU man that there was talk of us being moved shortly, perhaps back to the hell of Tobolsk, Fleischmann and I planned to escape. We thought that we would try to get to Moscow and seek refuge in the Swedish Embassy. One morning I promised the duty GPU man a bag of flour if he would not notice if we did not report for roll-call the following morning. He laughed and said something about girls. So we let him believe it was that. At the mill I asked for a couple of days off as I had something to do for the commissar. I fetched a flour bag and stuffed into it all the money I had saved from my black-market dealings in flour. Then I walked calmly out of the town to our rendezvous.

I had been walking for twenty-four hours without a break, and when I eventually let myself tumble into a ditch I was so exhausted that I fell asleep at once. There is no landscape so tedious as the Russian. The country roads are long and twisty, made of just earth and gravel. On all sides is steppe and more steppe, as far as the eye can see. Now and again you may see a bird. The villages lie fifty or sixty miles apart. After two and a half days' marching I reached a railway line, which, judging by the map, must have been that between Gorki and Saratov. Feeling tired and done, I lay down on the slope of the embankment and waited. There was no shade, so I was almost roasted by the blazing sun. I began to be troubled by thirst. Specks danced before my eyes. I could not sleep, and yet I felt dead and empty inside. Time stood still and no longer concerned me. I just lay writhing in my gloom. Feeling both apathetic and savage, I hungered for a woman. Ursula, you have gone, I shall never see you again. I don't know if I wept with the hurt of it; I may have kicked the ground and cursed God and generally behaved like a spoilt child, but those were dreadful, interminable and bitter-sweet hours that I spent lying waiting for a train somewhere between Gorki and Saratov.

When one came, it was a goods-train travelling fairly fast, and as soon as the engine was past I began running alongside the trucks, terrified in case I should stumble on the loose stones of the embankment and fall beneath the wheels. I caught hold of a handrail on an open truck. Three, four times I tried to swing myself up, but did not manage it, and I was on the point of losing my head and either letting go or else stopping running and just letting my feet trail; but then I clenched my teeth and jumped again. A moment later I heaved myself in over the back of the truck and dropped on to a cart which had been hidden by the tarpaulin covering the truck.

Then I nearly had a stroke, for suddenly a ghastly face appeared over the edge of the cart on which I lay panting. Paralysed with fright, we stared at each other. Then I pulled the pistol out of my pocket. The other groaned and shut his eyes.

'*Jetzt ist alles aus!*'

'What the hell – are you German?' I lowered my pistol in amazement, and the next moment another man emerged.

They had escaped from a POW camp a hundred miles north of Alatyr. There had been four of them at the start; but one of them had fallen off the train and been run over, and another had jumped down right into the arms of three Russians. Luckily they had not searched the truck.

We studied my map and realised that when we got to Saratov we would have to be careful not to be carried on down to the Caspian Sea. We agreed that our best course would be to try and make our way to the area of the Volga, north-west of Stalingrad, where they both said our troops now were. They had both been taken prisoner a good four months before at Maikop, and since then the Germans had advanced farther towards the Volga.

When we reached Saratov we crawled out to see if there was another train we could get on to, if ours were going to continue in the wrong direction. We found a pile of boxes of raw fish, opened one and ate our fill. Raw fish is really palatable, provided you are hungry enough. A couple of interested cats had our leavings and the last three fish in the box, which we were unable to eat. Then we went back to where our train had been. It was there no longer, but we found another train, and, as this was loaded with lorries and ammunition, we felt sure that it must be going our way – to the front.

Now, for the first time, realisation came that I was on my way back to the front. Till then I had not stopped to consider what I was doing, but now the sight of the ammunition-boxes brought the fact home to me. Back to all that! Before, I had only been thinking of getting out of Russia, the Soviet Union being a dangerous place for me. But if it was my life I wanted to save ought I to be going back to the front? Back to head all attacks and be the rearguard in all withdrawals? The paradox was depressing. Why was life so pointless? Would not the simplest thing be to put a bullet into my head straight away? It was strange and inexplicable, but I felt much more depressed at this moment than I had when I travelled back from my leave with Ursula. Perhaps our marriage and my leave comprised a period of my life that was complete and satisfactory in itself; it gave me the comforting feeling that if I had had nothing else out of life I had had that. Here in the Soviet Union, however, I had not experienced anything that was a complete experience in itself. I had travelled far in it, a lone fugitive, though often helped, and that huge land had shown me in the midst of all my personal suffering how great is the world, how colourful and rich and full of adventurous possibilities. I had seen something that was on a far larger scale than was little, surrounded Germany now in the process of strangulation. I had met a woman who might have come straight from the golden-threaded, colourful carpet of the *Thousand and One Nights*. Without hesitation, she had given me what she had, and I knew that I could *always* have come again and again and always been given more, that she would never have had enough. But I would never go again; we would never find each other again. A huge country was in the process of closing its great doors behind me after a brief visit. I felt a wild urge to turn back, to return to what was life on a volcano, and to find my princess again and complete the adventure.

It was stupid of me not to do it. It would have been crazy to have done so; but it was also stupid to prefer to turn my nose towards home and the strange 'safety' of a tank in the front line. It is true that the conditions under which someone like me must live in the Soviet Union were inhuman, but so they were in a tank, and pointless into the bargain, with no distant, tempting peaks, to the feet of which you could struggle, enduring hunger and thirst, and thereafter climb. I was returning to a place where my hands would find nothing but shells, and you could not play with those. Nothing happens when you put your finger on the tip of a shell.

We took a box of fish and got up on to one of the trucks with it, and while the train rattled along with us we fell asleep beneath a couple of lorries. It poured without stopping all the next day, but we were dry under the tarpaulin, and there we sat, eating our fish, sleeping, talking dully. They were so boring, my two companions. They were Nazis and believed that we were winning. They believed that we could defeat such a huge country. One was called Jürgens, the other Bartram.

At Uvarov, east of the Don, the train stopped and was to go no farther. A little way outside the town, we studied our map and decided that we must be two hundred miles or so east of Voronesh. We would have to get at least sixty or seventy miles south of Voronesh before we could hope to find the Germans on our side of the Don, for we knew that north of Voronesh the Russians were west of the river and had control of all the bridges and fords.

The highway swarmed with soldiers, guns and lorries, but we did not dare ask for a lift, as only I could speak Russian. The Russian military police were everywhere, and because of that we hid during the day.

Near Sakmanka we were hailed by a Russian sergeant. The big lorry, in which he was travelling alone, had sunk into the soft road. After we had helped him extricate it I shot him and put on his uniform. I did it without properly considering what I was doing. It was just a thing that had to be done. We laid him under some bushes, and then I drove the lorry with the other two in the back. In the driver's cab I found a sub-machine-gun and some grenades. I kept my foot hard down on the accelerator, and we made one hundred and twenty miles before we ran out of petrol. We then left the lorry and continued on foot. I took the sub-machine-gun with me. We were approaching the storm centre.

The next day we could hear the guns. It was strange hearing them again. When night fell the horizon was blood-red. In battered Jelansk we hid in a ruin, but we did not sleep well there, only three miles from the front, for the din of the artillery was deafening, and it was so long since we had heard it that we had lost the ability to sleep in spite of it. Thus, our nerves were on edge when, after darkness had fallen, we set off to make our way to the trenches.

Shells went whining past our heads every other moment, landing with hollow smacks and exploding with great roars and sending earth and stones and steel swirling round our ears. It took us several hours to reach the Russian trenches, where we found a hole to shelter in. There we lay, keeping an eye on a lone couple with a heavy machine-gun. At a suitable moment we pounced on them and bashed their heads in; then we stormed across the parapet of their trench and ran helter-skelter for the other side. We had to fling ourselves into a shell-hole in the middle of no-man's-land, our sudden appearance having started a hysterical outburst of firing from both sides with arms of all calibres and all sorts of flares and lights. It was a long time before things quietened down sufficiently for us to venture out of the shell-hole and make the last dash across to the German positions. Just as we were almost there a German machine-gun gave a chatter and Jürgens fell forward with a cry. He was dead, which was a relief, if only because it meant that we did not have to carry him. Bartram and I ran on, shouting, '*Nicht schiessen! Wir sind deutsche Soldaten!*'

Shaking and breathless, we tumbled into the trench and were at once taken to the company commander. After a few questions he sent us back to the Regimental HQ, where we were given a meal and somewhere to sleep.

. . . and then he was so stupid as to confide in a nurse who could not hold her tongue. You can imagine the rest. One morning at roll-call the old man read out this little item for us:

'Gefreiter Hans Breuer, of No. 5 Company, 27th Tank Regiment, was, on April 12th, condemned to death for an offence against morale in that he purposely let his foot be crushed by the track of a tank. Degradation and loss of honour for all time. The execution took place on April 24th in Breslau.'

That was roughly how it was worded. The Old Un puffed at his pipe, and Porta gave a cheerless laugh: 'No, it doesn't pay to do it yourself.'

I sat down to write to Ursula and Mother and tell them that I was to get long leave in a week's time. That evening I was summoned to the company commander. Meier sat leaning back in a camp chair and glared at me in silence. At length he opened his mouth:

'How dare you have the impertinence to apply for leave over your company commander!'

'I have not applied for leave,' I replied. 'It was the colonel himself who said I should have it when I got back.'

'Your leave is cancelled. In this company it is I who decides who is to have leave. You may go.'

I was back in it.

The Swine Meier

'Noses to the Russian earth, you gaolbirds!'

All at once cries rang out and swiftly died away in a death rattle.

Tank 534 had sunk into the soft earth and crushed five men whom Hauptmann Meier had ordered to lie flat on their faces beneath it.

For a moment there was a deathly silence; then a loud growl came from the company. When the five mangled bodies were pulled out Meier looked down at them for a moment, as though the whole thing was no concern of his.

We had each been given a short infantry spade for digging up mines, and we were ready to go out into no-man's-land. It was 21.00 hours. Anything that could rattle and give us away – glasses, gasmasks, helmets and torches – we had left in the dug-out. Our only weapons were pistol, knife and some small egg-grenades. Porta had his Russian sniper's rifle, which he always lugged about with him. Just before we were to climb out of the trench Hauptmann Meier came along to see us, and Oberleutnant von Barring was with him. Meier was as insolent as usual: 'Now do your job properly, you swine,' he said.

Paying no attention to the Hauptmann, von Barring shook hands with each of us and wished us good luck.

The Old Un gave the signal, we leaped over the parapet and dashed on through our barbed-wire barricade. After that there was a long, dangerous, open stretch that we had to cover at full pelt. When we were roughly halfway across a Very light went up and transformed the darkness into dazzling white light. We flung ourselves down and lay completely still. The slightest movement is seen instantly when those light-screens are laid down, and all movement in no-man's-land is regarded as hostile. The light was an incredibly long time in sinking to the ground.

We jumped up and dashed on again, but we had only taken a few steps when there was another flare blazing above us. The Old Un cursed savagely.

'If this goes on much longer we shan't get back alive. What the devil's got into Ivan this evening, sending up all that rubbish?'

Another couple of flares came hissing down, and then there was a pause in which we reached the Russian wire. Lying on our backs, we clipped away with our wire clippers and the wires flew apart with small whines and curled up. Then followed the most dangerous part of the job: lying on our stomachs with a tangle of barbed wire above us, we had to find the mines by probing the earth with long, thin iron rods. The mines were made of wood and so we could not use a mine detector.

This was not work for tank troops at all, and that we had been given it was entirely due to the swine Meier and his urge to wear the Iron Cross. He had asked the regimental commander to give his company the job. Not only were we to map the minefields, but we were to dig some of the mines up and relay them in the lanes the Russians had left free for themselves to use in attacking. By doing this we would make new lanes, of which only we would know and which we could use when we attacked.

As I had no experience of digging the devils up, I was given the one spear we had, which I was told to stick slantingly into the ground. Within a moment or two the spear had come up against something hard.

'Old Un,' I called softly.

He crawled over to me.

'Have you got one?' he whispered.

'I think so.'

He took the spear and tested the ground cautiously.

'That's good enough. You've got a bite. Now be careful that it does not get a bite too.'

He marked the mine on the map. After that we found them in quick succession. When the whole field was mapped we dug a number of them up and re-laid them elsewhere. It was villainously nerve-racking work, for the least noise would have given us away. We had almost finished when a star-shell burst right overhead. I was walking along clasping a mine, and had to fling myself flat, and for almost sixty seconds I lay with the highly explosive thing clasped to me.

We all got back, unharmed, at daybreak. For four nights running we had to go out. We were incredibly lucky, for nothing happened to any of us.

When we reported that the work on the minefield was complete, Hauptmann Meier gave a mocking laugh.

'Finished, you say? You have lain snoring in some shell-hole or other out there, you swine. I have sent up flares several times, but there has not once been a sign of you to be seen. But you won't get the laugh of me, you loathsome animals. You will report here with your maps at 23.00 and I'll go out with you and just check your filthy work. Understand?'

'Yes, Herr Hauptmann,' replied The Old Un, and did an about-turn that sent the mud spurting over our crazy company commander.

The moon was up when, together with the swine Meier, we worked our way across no-man's-land towards the minefield. We came down into a long dip, where the Russians could not see us, but where the mines lay as close as herrings in a barrel. Meier went in front, looking out the free lanes on the map The Old Un had given him, and just behind him came The Old Un himself, also studying a map, though we all knew the entire field inside out.

Meier moved to the right. The rest of us halted and quietly lay down. He walked ten, fifteen yards into the minefield and nothing happened. Then he discovered that he was alone. He did not dare bellow at us, as he liked to do, for that would have attracted the Russians' attention.

'What the hell's the meaning of this, you stinking criminals?' he hissed softly. 'You follow me, as I have ordered, or I'll have you arrested and court-martialled!'

The Old Un half rose to his feet and said with a laugh: 'It's all finished with you and your court-martial, for within five minutes you'll have been made into mincemeat, do you understand that?'

Meier looked, bewildered, at the map he held in his hand.

'Yes, gape at your map, you—,' said Porta. 'Only there happens to be a tiny difference between it and the one we have. You, being an officer, of course had to have a better map than we, so we thought we would put a few of your red ticks on the right instead of on the left. So don't say that we don't do things for you.'

For the next couple of minutes we laughed aloud at him. Then Porta put up his sniper's rifle and called to him: 'Now dance for us, you officer-swine, or I'll put a bullet in your belly.'

Deathly pale, Meier set out step by step on the return journey, but he had only come a yard or two towards us when there was a sharp report from Porta's rifle and Meier had a dum-dum in his shoulder. He stood swaying and moaned with the pain of it, while the blood from his broken shoulder ran down his chest.

'Dance, blast you, swine that you are,' hissed Porta. 'Dance a waltz! We'll provide the drums with our little guns here, that you and yours have taught us to use!'

The Old Un pulled out his heavy service pistol and put a bullet between Meier's feet, so that he gave a jump that was like a sort of dance. Stege, Pluto, I and the others in the section also fired bullets into the ground in front of the shaking, shuffling officer.

When he fell, the first of the land-mines exploded and flung him high into the air. Five times the impact of his fall set off another mine.

The star-shells now began shooting up, for the explosions had alarmed the entire sector. Machine-guns barked, and there was the occasional dull roar of a mortar. From the German side red Very lights soared up into the air, signalling to the artillery to lay a barrage along the Russian lines; the Russians sent their signals whizzing up to call for a barrage to be laid on the German lines. Both sides believed that the other was about to launch an attack.

The storm came down upon us like a howling hurricane, and earth reared up like a wall. We flung ourselves headlong into a shell-hole, and there we lay for two hours before the duet quietened down. Shortly afterwards we jumped down into our own trench, and The Old Un reported back to Oberleutnant Barring:

'Herr Oberleutnant! Unteroffizier Beier reports back with 2 Section from reconnaissance ordered in the enemy's minefield. The reconnaissance went according to plan, with Hauptmann Meier in command. The Hauptmann was killed, because despite warnings from the section he insisted on going into the enemy minefield.'

Barring looked at us thoughtfully; his eyes passed from man

to man, dwelling an instant on each face. I have never seen eyes so profoundly human and grave as his.

'Hauptmann Meier killed? Well, that is what happens in war. Unteroffizier Beier, take your group back to the dug-out. No. 2 Section has done a fine job with that minefield. I shall send a report to the CO.'

He saluted, two fingers at the brim of his cap, and went back to his dug-out.

The Old Un smiled. 'As long as he lives, there will be no more swine-hunts in No. 5 Company.'

'Did you notice the somersaults the swine turned as our dear little mines prodded his backside?' said Porta gleefully. 'It would have gladdened the heart of his old gym master to have seen it.'

Such was the funeral oration over Hauptmann Meier, a German bourgeois who was too small to go to war and become someone.

20

'What? Weren't there two of them?'

Uttering a roar, Pluto rushed after Porta and the girls. Soon they were out of sight, but we could still hear the delighted squeals of the two buxom girls.

'We won't see them for a couple of hours,' said The Old Un with a laugh.

The rest of us lay down again in the tall grass. We lay there dreaming and watching the smoke from our pipes. Quietly we talked of our comrades who were with us no more.

Sleep Your Fill, Boys

Early in the morning, when you came from the fresh air into the crowded peasant's cottage, the stench of it was almost enough to knock you down, but you became accustomed even to that, and within a few minutes you had fallen asleep to the accompaniment of the snoring and hawking of the Russians. We knew that the wife was riddled with TB, but what of that? You accepted germs along with the rest: lice, rats and filth.

It seemed that no sooner had we lain down than we were wakened by the Russians getting up. Porta swore at them, but the old Russian answered calmly and firmly:

'Shut up, Herr Soldier, and sleep!'

An hour later a hen came in clucking, with her chicks in tow, and when it trod on Porta's face he lost patience altogether. He shot up out of the straw like a rocket, seized the hen by the neck, gave it a slap on the face with his index finger and shouted:

'Now take yourself and your illegitimate offspring out of here, you ill-mannered fowl!'

Then he threw the hen out of the window and began chasing the panic-stricken chicks out of the door. That brought the daughter-in-law running up, and she began screeching. 'I must have peace!' bawled Porta and swore at her till she lost her temper and banged him on the head with a big pot-ladle. The rest of us let out a great guffaw that made Porta quite demented. He rushed after the woman in just his shirt, the tails fluttering round his skinny legs. Out into the field he went, the Russians roaring with laughter, and shortly afterwards he came back out of breath, shut the door with a bang that shook the whole cottage, shoved his head out of the window and bawled:

'I wish to sleep, and the next person who disturbs me will be shot, bang-bang, finished, dead!'

It was nearly noon before we got up, and I fetched our food from the cook's lorry. For once we had something decent, bean soup. Our mess-kids were almost full, and we gulped it down like animals. When we had licked our platters clean we started on a parcel that Stege had been sent from home. There were crisps, small cakes and a large piece of smoked ham. We carried the things out to a table we had made down by the latrine. Porta had a bottle of vodka.

We had made our latrine in such a way that we could sit opposite each other with the table between us. Having settled ourselves, we fished out our greasy pack of cards and began to play. We helped ourselves to the cakes, and now and again cut ourselves a hunk of ham. The bottle went the rounds. Glasses, cups or mugs were luxuries that we had long come to regard as unnecessary and effeminate. So there the five of us sat with our trousers down by our knees, eating and drinking and playing cards, smoking and chatting, doing what we had come for and enjoying life. Our naked bottoms grinned cheerily at the people in the village street, for the latrine was sited on an eminence, from which we had a good view on all sides, as everyone had a good view of us. A bird was singing in among the trees, and beside us lay a dog, slothfully out-stretched in the heat of the autumn sun. Some women at work in a field were singing a Russian song.

Not till towards evening, when the Russians started coming home from the fields, did we rise from our idyll and saunter lazily back to the cottage.

One forenoon The Old Un and the other tank-commanders were summoned to the company commander. When The Old Un returned an hour later he told us delightedly:

'Boys, we're off on a lovely little expedition. We are to go to the plain fifteen miles south of Nowji and dig the old box in till only the turret is above ground. We shall be pleasantly on our own and thirty miles behind the front, so there won't be any shooting. There we are to stay, blossoming and waiting, till Ivan breaks through our positions at the front, and then we are to smash his tanks, as they come rolling along. We are to hold the position at all costs, and the ignition key is to be thrown away as soon as we have got the old box dug in.'

Porta gave a laugh: 'You said the ignition key?'

The Old Un smiled: 'Yes, that's all that was mentioned.'

'Splendid.'

We had four spare keys.

We reached our new position shortly before daybreak. It was right out in the middle of the plain, where the grass was so high that we had to stand erect to see over it. It was cold, and we wore fur-caps, greatcoats, thick mitts and leather breeches on top of our black uniform trousers. As we had only two spades and a shovel in the tank only three could work at a time, and there was great competition to do so because of the cold.

The Old Un flung out his hand, and in a lyrical tone of voice said:

'Children, children, little children. Isn't it wonderful to be digging here in the open. See, now the sun is rising, and we no longer need to be afraid of the bogeyman. It is going to be hot, and the birds will sing lots of little songs for us, and if we are very, very good the Old Man of the Steppes will perhaps come and tell us a long, dirty story. Do you not feel the kiss of the fresh wind of the steppe on your downy cheeks, and how it plays with your curliest locks?'

As the sun rose higher we lost some of our ardour. We began to sweat and removed one garment after the other, until in the end we were working in just shorts and boots.

Even so the sweat still poured off us, and our hands blistered from the unaccustomed labour of digging in the hard ground of the steppe.

'Tell me,' exclaimed Porta, 'are we soldiers or are we navvies? I only want to know because of the union rate.'

We kept measuring the tank to see if the hole would not soon be deep enough, but at noon, when we had been digging for seven hours, we were still only halfway. The Old Un began cursing the army, and Porta asked him innocently if he could not feel the soft kiss of the wind of the steppe, and if his heart was not gladdened by the warming rays of the sun and the educational effect of spade-work? The Old Un hurled the spade furiously at Porta and went and flung himself down in the shade of the tank.

'I'm not digging another teaspoonful. There are going to be no more holes in this war. Good night.'

Porta, Stege and I dug for half an hour, when The Old Un and Pluto were supposed to relieve us. After a lot of bickering we got them manoeuvred, grumbling, into the hole. The next couple of hours went all right, then the half-hour shift we were supposed to dig was reduced to fifteen minutes, and in the end all five of us lay on our backs, staring up into the air, unable to do any more.

But the hole had to be dug, there was no getting away from that, so after lying there for an hour The Old Un and Pluto got to their feet and the rest of us soon followed. At five o'clock next morning the hole was finished, and we were able to drive the tank into it. We got our tent pitched in a trice, so that we could turn in; but being in an area where partisans were reputed to be rife, we naturally had to mount a guard. We could not agree who was to take the first turn. In the midst of our noisy squabbling The Old Un suddenly said:

'I am an Unteroffizier and have no need to stand guard. You must see to that yourselves.' Thereupon he rolled himself up in the blankets and was asleep.

'And I am Stabsgefreiter,' said Pluto. 'Good night, dear children.'

'And it would make a mockery of the Army if an

Obergefreiter demeaned himself by doing anything so filthy as sentry duty,' said Porta.

That left Stege and I looking at each other.

'Don't let's do it,' said I. 'There aren't any partisans here.'

'None at all,' said Stege, outraged.

So all five of us slept.

The first to have to emerge from the tent in the morning was Stege. We wanted our coffee in bed and had drawn lots who should make it, and the job had fallen to him. Five minutes after he had got up he called out from up on the tank:

'Hurry out, the CO's coming!'

We tumbled out, not wishing to be caught asleep in our tent at eleven o'clock in the morning; but it was just Stege's idea of a joke, so we crawled back again and lay and shouted for coffee. In the end we got it, too, but no sooner had we finished our meal and Stege carried our mugs and jugs out again than he called out:

'Now, you'll have to come out. Hurry up! The old man and the skipper are coming. Hurry, you stupid swine, it's real this time.'

But we just laughed, and Porta called back that if the CO wanted him Stege was to say that Porta was not at home today, which observation Porta punctuated with a thunderous fart. The Old Un followed his example.

'Come out, all of you. This is a fine business,' said a voice outside, and it was the CO's voice.

We tumbled out all right. As we stood at attention facing the two all-purpose vehicles that stood beside our hole, our dress was hardly what could be called regulation. The CO glared at us furiously. Oberleutnant von Barring's expression was unfathomable. We looked like a joke in a comic paper: The Old Un was wearing khaki shorts, socks and a shirt with dirty tails. Porta wore his drill trousers with the ends stuffed into his socks and a fiery red silk handkerchief tied round his neck. Pluto's shirt was hanging outside his trousers and he had a green scarf wound round his head like a turban.

'Are you in charge of this tank?' roared the CO at The Old Un, his monocle glinting ominously.

'Yes, Herr Oberst!'

'Well, what the hell are you thinking of? Am I not to have a report?'

The Old Un ran across to the CO's car, smacked his plimsolls together and in regulation fashion bellowed out into the silent steppe:

'Herr Oberst! Unteroffizier Beier reports that 1 Tank of No. 2 Section has nothing special to mention.'

The CO went purple in the face.

'So you have nothing special to mention,' said he. 'But I have . . .' and then we got a dressing down.

Later, von Barring came back alone. 'You're the most bloody awful lot in the whole Army,' he said, shaking his head over us. 'Surely to God you could have mounted guard the first day. You must have known the CO would come and inspect. Now you're each getting three days in jug, to be served when you are relieved. The hole you've dug is not satisfactory; and you are to dig another thirty feet farther back; and I can guarantee that the CO and I will be out in the course of the evening, so you would be wise to get started at once.'

We sat for a long while silent after he had gone. Dig another hole? Never. But what then?

It was Stege who had the idea. 'Dear little children,' said he suddenly. 'You should render thanks unto God that you have an intelligent man in your midst, who can help you when thought is required. What we have to do is to take the old tinbox and drive back to Oskol, say good day nicely and invite the Russians for a ride; as their contribution to the festivities we will ask them to bring their spades.'

We rattled into the village, which lay plunged in Sunday quiet, and had no difficulty in finding more volunteers than we could use, thus it was with a load of nearly forty men and women that we rattled back. The Russians thought it the greatest fun having a ride on a tank, and to the accompaniment of much singing and joking the new hole was dug in two hours, even though they kept throwing down their spades and starting to play and sing or dance, kicking up a cloud of dust. We were so occupied with this new type of Sunday entertainment that no one noticed Oberleutnant von Barring arrive. He stood and watched the gay gathering in some amazement. Then he shook his head:

'You don't get bored, I must say,' said he; then, with another shake of his head, he drove off again. Later, in the evening, we drove those gay Russians back to their village. Porta had found a couple of girls and had them almost hanging round his neck, so it was not at all easy to drag him away.

Was it unpatriotic of those Russians to help us against their fellow-countrymen? I suppose it was. But I am not certain that what they did was not more effective than the efforts of either the partisans or the regular troops. Such acts of fraternisation did more than anything else to make the German private fed up with the war. I know of many who were well and truly cured of their belief in the idiotic myth of the Master People through discovering that the 'enemy' was no enemy of theirs and, still less, an inferior being. The ordinary German private extended his knowledge of men and people. Such encounters planted in him the seed of sympathetic solidarity with the ordinary people. Slowly but surely he was divorced from his sham, inflated ideals, his hysterical Führer, his arrogant generals. He learned actively to hate the SS, whom before he had merely feared with an oafish, grovelling fear. You have no wish to shoot at people with whom you have been dancing the day before, whether there is a war or not; so you are more than likely just to shoot up in the air, unless an officer is actually standing behind, watching you.

21

Smiling, he handed us our leave papers and said: 'If you hurry up and get ready, you can drive with me to the train. You have fourteen days' leave plus five days for travelling.'

We sang and exulted; we were wild with joy. We danced to our cottage and fought for the old razor-blade that we had used at least sixty times already. Porta kissed the old Russian mother fair and square on her wrinkled mouth and danced round with her, so that her slippers went flying. The old girl cackled like a hen and almost fell down, she laughed so.

'You're worse than the Cossacks!' said she.

988th Reserve Battalion

We reached Gomel twenty-four hours late. The leave train for that day had already gone, so we had to wait till the following day. An NCO told us that hell had broken loose up at the front. Apparently the Russians were attacking along a line that stretched from Kalinin to the Don basin, and they had managed to break through in several places.

'We've been bloody lucky, and just got away in time,' said Porta.

The Old Un shook his head. There was a worried expression on his face. 'Don't forget that in a fortnight we'll have to go back into it, and it's scarcely likely to be any better by then.'

'Oh, shut up, you old wet blanket,' said Stege. 'You're a crazy old chap. A whole fortnight at home with Mother. The war can be over before we get back.'

We spent most of the night elaborating on what we were going to do when we got home. I thought of Ursula's firm, rounded body, remembered the hug of her arms and the way her hands travelled down my back. I became silent and expectant.

Our train was supposed to go at 18.40, but we were already on the platform by five o'clock. We felt like kings as we held out our leave papers for the Military Police to see. We found a good place in the train. Porta and Pluto climbed on to the luggage racks to sleep there, and we three removed our boots and made ourselves comfortable. Gradually the whole train filled with noisy soldiers going on leave. They lay down on the floors of the compartments and of the corridors. Schnapps bottles went the round, and the sound of music and singing came from more than one compartment. Porta produced his flute and played the tune of a forbidden song, and that set us off and we bawled out our whole repertoire of forbidden and dirty songs. Nobody appeared to take objection. We old sweats sang what we liked. If anyone had tried to say anything he would have been flung out of the window without further comment. We cheered as the train moved off.

Some time in the night the train stopped in the station at Mogilev. Quiet had descended upon us by then, and most were asleep and dreaming of their leave. For many it was the first for several years.

There was a jerk and the train began to move; but it only went a short distance and then stopped again. Shortly afterwards we heard shouts coming from one of the carriages, and almost simultaneously the doors of ours were flung open and a couple of helmeted military policemen stumped in, calling:

'Everybody out and take your equipment. All leave is cancelled. The Russians have broken through, and you are to be formed into a temporary reserve battalion and sent in.'

There was a dreadful commotion. We called and shouted, all at the same time, and told the policemen to buzz off with their bad jokes.

But, unfortunately, it was not a joke. Sleepy and furious, we had to form up in the open space in front of the station: gunners and tank crews on the left, the others on the right: infantry, airmen, marines, no matter what, all on the right. Our leave papers were taken from us, and then came the order:

'Column – by the right – right turn – quick – MARCH!'

All night we struggled along. The going was heavy with

snow, and an icy wind blew in our faces. We still could not believe that this incredibly filthy trick could be true. You do not play such tricks on a soldier, do not turn him out of the train that is taking him back to a fortnight's hard-earned leave, and send him marching along a confounded country road, hounding him back to the front to fight with tanks, flame-throwers and shells. That destroyed the little morale or will to fight that any of us may still have possessed.

For six days we made our way forward through snow and snow and snow. Then we became engaged with enemy forces, a little to the north of the village of Lischwin. The shells made such a strange plop in the snow. Slowly we yielded to the attack of the Russian infantry, who came on quite indifferent to losses. Slowly and surely our new-made formations came nearer and nearer to dissolution and obliteration. We, who had no business in the Soviet, could not stand up to these people who were determined to clear their country of us. They had the moral right, in that they really were defending themselves against an attack. To tell them they were defending themselves against an aggressor was not a device of propaganda, like those Hitler tried on us and those people thought they could use after the war.

Our unit was called the 988th Reserve Territorial Battalion, and the joke of it was that it had everything in it from airmen and marines to Home Guard, but only one territorial. All sorts of shoulder tabs and flashes were represented, but one thing we had in common: we all execrated the 988th Reserve Battalion and longed to get back to our own units.

East of Volkov we got involved in bitter fighting, in which the Russians sent in tanks and fighter planes. In a ruined house there, in Volkov, we found a red cat, sitting in a cart wailing most pitiably with cold and hunger. We forced some schnapps down its throat and gave it something to eat, and when we had to leave the house we took it with us. Being red, we called it Stalin.

Stalin went through the Volkov campaign sitting in Porta's haversack. Pluto and Stege made a complete uniform, trousers, tunic and cap, which latter was tied on with a piece of thin string so that it could not fall off. Being a penal regiment's cat Stalin naturally could not wear the Nazi fowl on his chest. At first he loathed being in uniform, but gradually he got used both to it and to schnapps, and became as drunken as we. You may call that cruelty to animals, yet Stalin never left us, his fur quickly became glossy, and he himself cheeky and impudent, as a cat does when all is well with its world.

By the approach of Christmas the battalion had shrunk to a single company, and then it was disbanded. We five got marching orders for Godnjo on the River Worskla, where the 27th Tank Regiment then was. Three days later we reported to our rear HQ, and the next day we were sent up to the front line, where the tanks were. First, however, we were given our post.

I had a whole bundle of letters from Ursula and my mother. We devoured our letters, read them again and again, and finally read them out to each other, while we dreamed and longed and let each word seep down into our devout, thirsty souls. In one of her letters Ursula wrote:

Munich, December 9th, 1942.

My own darling!

I suffer with you over the beastly unfairness that has been done to you and your companions; but do not let yourself be daunted because they have stolen your leave. Hold your head high despite the bloodhounds' filthy tricks. Before we know it, this nightmare will be over, and the feathers plucked from the Nazi fowl, which soon all and sundry will be wearing on their chests.

I pray to God that He may hold His hand over you and protect you from all the horrors out there at the front. Although you call yourself a pagan and say you do not believe in God, I know that He loves you as well as He does the best of His priests, and when the war is over I shall be able to convince you of that and melt the hard shell of cynicism with which you poor wretches in the fowl-less units have to encompass yourselves. Remember, darling, that sooner or later there must be peace, and then all our lovely dreams will become reality.

I have thought that by that time I ought to be able to have a nice practice here in Munich or in Cologne, and my great hope is that you will train as a dentist or something like that. One thing only you must promise me, that you will not stay in the Army if there should be an opportunity of making a career there.

In six months I shall have completed my special training as a surgeon, and then I shall begin to save for our home. I hope that I shall be able to have it all ready, the day you come back.

But – no. I hope it won't be as long as that, before you come to me for ever. I wanted you to come today. Now.

Father and Mother have now grown accustomed to the idea of having a son-in-law. At first, of course, they were dumbfounded, and you should have seen Father's face when I told him that you had been in prison and a concentration camp and were now in a fowl-less regiment. At first he thought I had gone mad, but when I explained a little more and told him that your 'crime' was political, he accepted it without reservation and said that, as long as we loved each other, nothing else mattered.

I cannot write about political developments, which I am sure you will know of, for I expect you are pretty well informed out there. I comfort myself with the thought that, since it is not going to be so long before we two can be together for the rest of our lives, one leave does not mean all that much.

Besides, leave now would also be torture, for I would be thinking the whole time that you were having to go back to it all again, and you would be thinking of that too.

I am sending you with this a little gold cross. I have worn it round my neck next to my skin ever since I was a little girl, and you are to have it. Wear it, as I have done; it will protect you from all evil out there. Kiss it each evening, as I kiss your ring. Darling, darling Sven, I love you so that it makes my heart ache, and I weep with joy at the thought

159

that we shall soon meet again, and then I shall never let you go. You are mine, only mine, mine alone. I am well aware that now and again you fall a tiny bit in love with a Russian girl, or with one of the German women you meet on troop-trains, but I also know that you cannot fall in love with them in the same way as you are with me; and therefore I forgive you in advance if you kiss other women out there and find comfort for a brief while. I am not going to ask that you live like a monk – only you must promise me not to embark upon anything that you cannot tell me about.

You have no idea how I cried when that wonderful friend of yours, The Old Un, wrote and told me that you had been killed. It was the loveliest, though also the saddest letter I have ever read. But, shock though it was, it was nothing to that I got eleven months later when your letter came telling of how you had been a prisoner. I fainted for the first time in my life; my temperature went up and I had to spend a week in bed. It was quite a collapse. But, heavens, how happy I was!

You say that you don't believe in God, but I believe that it was He kept his hand over you, because you are a very proper person, as are your friends. You have your faults and weaknesses, but you are human and purer of heart and more honest in your thoughts than many of those who are never without a rosary in their hands. Do not think that I don't share your loathing of hypocrites and those priests who are mere sanctimonious servants of masters, who do not know, or are recognised by, the true God and genuine Christianity. But He who preaches mercy cannot help these hypocrites being there, and you must not think that by listening to what He has to say to us all you are making common cause with vicious priests. That is what I so badly want you to understand, and one day you will, I am sure of that.

But now I must stop, my dear, beloved husband, and lastly let me beg you to look after yourself out there. I know that it is difficult, but don't let yourself be affected too much by that cynical indifference that is so characteristic of you front-line soldiers. Keep on believing that there is goodness to be found in the world as well. Be careful, when you can; that will always help a bit towards my getting you home alive. And now may this New Year be one that brings luck and happiness to us both, and to all others.

Your devoted wife,
URSULA.

We had counted on being relieved before Christmas Eve, but our hopes were belied. Not only that, but we had to act as infantry and go through some hard fighting in the front line.

At seven o'clock on Christmas Eve I was detailed for sentry-duty in the advance posts, some way out in no-man's-land. We were one man in each foxhole, with about fifty yards behind each. The idea of these advance posts was that we should be able to give the alarm in time if the enemy should send a night patrol across. But, however good a look-out we kept, these patrols got across and back again time after time; and it was only when it grew light that we would discover that they had been across by finding our outposts with their throats cut. Or we would find a hole empty, the Russians having taken its occupant back as a prisoner.

We had drawn lots who was to go. Von Barring had insisted that sentry-duty on Christmas Eve should be allocated in that way. On that one night he wanted not to have to order anyone out. The lots were put in his helmet – and not only the privates, but the whole company, including himself, had to draw a lot. One of our lieutenants had to go on duty from 22.00 till 01.00.

Thus I spent Christmas Eve 1942 in a fox-hole in no-man's-land. In front of me, on the rim, I laid my grenades and sub-machine-gun ready for use.

You become fearfully sleepy when you are on guard like that. Not only is the continual straining to catch and inter-pret all the faint little sounds and imagined sights of the lurking darkness tiring, but the isolation also acts as a soporific. You are quite alone. First and foremost, however, you are paralysed by a sort of longing for death. The idea of going to sleep and being rid of it all, of falling asleep and never waking up, is very attractive – so easy and painless. All the things you feel it should be worth living for have dissolved into a sort of unreality, have become a ghostly sigh, a remote, wearied plaint, something it is far too much trouble to conquer back.

All at once the sound of steel on steel made me go rigid. It was a very slight noise, but from that instant my senses were strained and on the alert. I clutched a grenade in one hand and listened; but all was still. Then my blood curdled and turned to ice in my veins; something had gone gliding past just beside my hole. I began to tremble. I imagined that I could already feel the knife at my throat. I bit my lips till they bled, and stared out into the darkness till my eyes smarted and watered. Then I thought I heard the slither of skis over snow. Shouldn't I fire a Very light? I asked myself; but I did not dare risk making a fool of myself. So strong is convention that in certain situations you will act in accordance with it, even if to do so may cost you your life. To have sent up a light, of course, would have revealed my whereabouts to any Russians who might have been lying out there with their long knives ready. Away in the distance, a couple of wolves were howling heart-rendingly, but otherwise there was nothing but the frozen silence of the winter's night. Then a piercing scream rang out, followed by a ghastly rattle; and at the same moment another voice cried: 'Help! Help! Ivan has got me!' The shout broke off abruptly, as though a hand had been clapped over the shouter's mouth. The hair rose up on my head, and, as I thought I could make out some figures, I furiously flung some grenades at them, and fired a burst from my gun. Frantically I fired off Very lights, and in a short while the whole sector was blazing away.

Nine of us had been out there. Six did not come back. Five had had their throats cut; the sixth was just not there.

The Christmas post we had been expecting had not arrived, and at midnight came the explanation from the loudspeakers over on the Russian side:

'Hallo! Hallo, 27th Tank Regiment! We wish you a merry Christmas. If you want your Christmas parcels and letters, just come across to us. We have them here along with your runner. There are parcels for . . .'

Then the voice called out all the names of those for whom there were letters or parcels. As soon as that was finished, the voice went on:

'Comrades of the 27th. We shall now read a little of the letters, so that you can see they are good letters. Here is one, for example, to Kurt Hessner. "Dear Kurt," it says, "there was a raid this evening . . . a bomb fell . . . father is . . . dreadful grief!" If Kurt Hessner wishes to hear the rest of the letter let him just come over here.'

They read out bits from letter after letter, so that we should think our people at home were either killed or maimed, or that some other horror had befallen them. Many nearly drove themselves demented wondering and worrying, and the end of it all was that five did go over.

When day broke we saw three dead Russians lying in front of the hole where I had been, and only six feet from it were ski tracks.

One day Porta disappeared without trace. We received permission for fifteen of the oldest and most experienced men in the company to make a raid. Leutnant Holler himself insisted on coming. He took off all his badges and pips before we set out. We lay for a while in front of the Russian trench listening so as to discover where their sentries were. Then we dropped down over them, flung a couple of mines into their dug-out, and let our sub-machine-guns and flame-throwers play along the narrow trench. The whole thing took a couple of minutes at the most, after which we were on our way back with two prisoners. As soon as we had got back to our lines we began interrogating our prisoners, one of whom was a cornet. As soon as we described Porta they burst out laughing.

'He's absolutely crazy,' laughed the cornet. 'At this moment he is sitting drinking our commissar under the table. He wants to buy a bearskin coat and a case of vodka and has five thousand cigarettes with him to pay for it.'

To our amazed questions how he had got there the cornet said that he had been captured by a patrol.

Two days later, when we were relieved, we had still seen no sign of Porta, and sincerely we mourned his loss.

A week later he came sauntering into our village wearing a heavy Russian officer's fur coat and carrying a Russian brief-case, that appeared to be very heavy.

'Bloody fine weather today.'

That was all he said. We stood round him in a ring, gaping.

'I hope I'm not late for dinner. That would be a shame, as I've brought some schnapps.'

There were six bottles of vodka in his case, and he had also brought the five thousand cigarettes back.

'Russian commissars are hopeless at vingt-et-un,' said Porta, and that was all we could ever get out of him about his peculiar trip across to Ivan, so there is no rational explanation of what happened that I can give.

Six bottles of vodka, a case to carry them in and a brand-new officer's fur coat.

What a strange thing war is.

22

Because of the heavy losses the 27th Tank Regiment had suffered a lot of promotion came the way of us veterans. The CO had been killed, so Oberstleutnant von Lindenau became Oberst. Major Hinka became Oberstleutnant and our battalion commander, von Barring became Hauptmann of 5 Company. The Old Un was made Feldwebel and platoon commander. The five of us now had a new tank of the type called 'panther' which was to be platoon tank of 3 Platoon.

Porta was to have been made an Unteroffizier, but he refused point-blank to let himself be promoted. There was a tremendous fuss, but it ended satisfactorily. Oberstleutnant Hinka said:

'All right, you red-haired monkey, you shan't be Unteroffizier, but Stabsgefreiter. Will that satisfy you?'

It did, for Stabsgefreiter was a superior private, not an NCO.

Our cat, Stalin, who now had a miniature soldier's book, was made Obergefreiter and had the regulation two stripes sewn on the sleeve of his new tunic. He, too, became fantastically tight to celebrate this occasion.

Death Rolls Up

'Here, Sven, have a schnapps. Take a decent pull. The swine! The bloody swine. God help them when we are finished here and get back!'

Porta asked what had happened.

'Now I'll read the letter to you,' said The Old Un. 'And here with the schnapps, so that Sven can drink and forget. But he mustn't drink alone.'

The Old Un unfolded the letter from Ursula's father.

Munich, April 1943.

My dear son!

I have grievous news for you. You must take it with as much composure as you can, and promise me not to break down or do anything rash when you have read this.

165

Our beloved, brave Ursula is dead. The Nazis murdered her. When you come to Munich I shall tell you all the details; till then this brief account must suffice.

A famous Gauleiter was to address the students at the university, but his speech was interrupted by an overt demonstration. A number of the young students were arrested and with them our beloved girl. A few days later they were brought before the People's Court and condemned to death. When the sentence was pronounced, Ursula replied: 'The day is not far distant when you, our judges and accuser, will yourselves stand accused, while our comrades will be your judges. Be assured that on that day your heads will also come under the axe.'

This is what she said to her Nazi judges, and she will assuredly be proved right, if there is any justice left in the world.

I was with her the day before she was murdered, and she asked me to tell you that she would go to her death with your name on her lips, and she asked you to believe in God and that you two would meet in Heaven.

Even the prison warders were impressed by her proud courage, and they brought her many forbidden things on the last few days, though she shrank from receiving anything from people who wore the hated uniform.

A friend of mine witnessed the execution of these young people, and he told me that they sang a couple of forbidden songs, so that they resounded throughout the prison, and the other prisoners sang with them from all the windows. Neither threats nor blows were able to silence them, and when the last had been executed, there was a thunderous roar from those in the cell windows: 'Vengeance! Vengeance!' and then they sang *Red Wedding*.*

Burn this letter, as soon as you have read it. I am sending it by a good friend, who is going to the front near where your regiment is. I enclose a locket with her picture and a lock of her hair.

* A revolutionary song. Wedding is a district of Berlin.

Dear son-in-law, Ursula's broken-hearted mother and I have, of course, never seen you, but we ask you to come and visit us as soon as you can. We will regard you as our son and ask you to regard our home, and all that is ours, as your own. We send you our most cordial greetings and hope most profoundly that all may go well with you. May we see you here with us soon!

Yours very sincerely,

When The Old Un finished reading, we all sat silent, smoking, while the dusk grew thicker in the room of the dirty little cottage. I kept shuddering, for the whole time I could see Ursula's head rolling into the basket with the sawdust, the blood spurting from the neck in a thick stream, her lovely black hair stiff and sticky with blood, the glazed eyes, wide open and expressionless, staring up at the Heaven in which she had believed. I knew exactly how her warm body had twitched and finally been flung indifferently into a grave.

Oh, I knew so exactly how it had all happened. I knew all the details, for I had seen it so often.

Before my companions could prevent it I had undone the safety-catch of my revolver and shot the wooden crucifix and the picture of the Madonna on the wall to pieces. Then I put the bottle to my mouth and emptied it at one draught. The Old Un tried to quiet me, but I was in a frenzy. He had to fell me with a blow on the chin.

When I came to, we sat down to drink; and I drank as I have never drunk before. For days I was doped with schnapps. I put the bottle to my mouth the moment I wakened and drank till I fell over again. In the end it became too much for The Old Un. He and Porta hauled me out into the yard and put me in a trough till I had become normal again, and for the next few days they never let me sit idle for a second. I was dead tired and black and blue when I went to bed, and as soon as I woke in the morning they took me out to the trough and roused me with icy water. That helped. Slowly I began to become clear in the head again – clear and cold and dead.

I became a man-hunter, angry and slightly crazy, for all the clarity of my thoughts. I took to standing in the trench with a sniper's rifle with telescopic sights knocking the Russians down in their trench. I was delighted each time I saw one of them leap in the air, as a bullet went home. One day Hauptmann von Barring came and stood just behind me, watching me in silence. I do not know how long he was there. I laughed and told him that I had bagged seven in half an hour. Without a word he took the rifle from me and went. I wept a little, and for a long while stared vacantly in front of me. He was right, of course.

I remember the following day most distinctly. I was having my mess-kid filled with broth, elderly cow broth, when there was a bang and something scaldingly hot struck my leg. There went your leg, I thought, but it was half the hind quarter of the old cow the explosion had flung at me. The whole cook's lorry was smashed and round about it lay five or six bodies swimming in their blood and the soup. A yard from me lay a leg with a boot and all the rest of it.

I swung the hind quarter on to my shoulder and walked back to our billet, and there we had a feast.

'One man's loss, another man's gain,' said Porta philosophically.

It would never have occurred to anyone to do other than what I did: carry off the meat and feast on it. It was not cynicism that made me not stop to help the wounded, but war. War is like that. There were others there to do the helping. Apart from your immediate companions, you do not know one another in war.

Fighting flared up again when spring came, and the roads and fields became dry and firm enough for such activities.

The bottle of vodka goes the round for the last time. The Old Un sticks a lighted cigarette between my lips, and greedily I suck the smoke deep into my lungs, while with forehead pressed against the rubber sheathing of the periscope I stare out at the riven earth.

'All tanks – open fire!'

The roaring hell begins. The heat in the tank becomes appalling. We pour across the Russian trenches like an avalanche. On the open steppe countless tanks stand blazing, with pitch-black smoke welling up from them towards the smiling blue heavens. Tanks cannot take prisoners, only kill and crush. We were no longer human beings, but automatons performing movements we had learned by rote.

The T34s came rolling up in a counter-attack, and so we no longer had time to murder the fleeing infantry, but had to fight for our own lives. The turret with its long gun barrel turned, and shell after shell was hurled at the roaring T34s.

I was on the point of suffocating. There was a tightness round my forehead and chest, as though I were in the clasp of iron rings that were slowly crushing me. I realised that in a short while I would be able to control myself no longer, and must fling the turret hatches open and jump out of that hot steel monster. Then there was a thunderous roar and the tank stopped with a jerk. At the same moment a blue-red flame shot up from one side of the tank. As through a haze I saw Pluto and Porta leap out of the forward hatches, while Stege shot from the off turret hatch. The whole thing lasted perhaps a second, then I came to myself and acted, as I should: up with hatch and out in a mighty leap.

Colossal flames were pouring from the tank. All at once it bulged out like a balloon and exploded with a bang that made us gasp, and red-hot metal was flung high into the air.

When we got back to our unit on another of our tanks Porta had the cat Stalin under his arm. Stalin had had his fur singed, but not so badly that he seemed to mind. He lapped up his vodka with evident delight.

We were sent to Dnepropertrovsk to fetch new tanks, and a couple of days later we were back in the battle that was raging with undiminished fury, although in its tenth day. Everything was flung into the fighting and consumed. Endless columns of reserves came hastening along the roads in the rear and vanished when they reached the front. It was like stoking a fire.

*

From Senkow, once a village but now a conflagration, comes a T34 at full speed. Like lightning I aim and adjust the gun. It is either them or us, whoever gets the first shot home. I take aim right at the collar beneath its turret, which is the T34's weak spot. The numerals in the periscope dance before my eyes. Then the opposite points of the sighting mechanism meet, and with a roar a shell speeds on its way, followed by another almost before the first has left the muzzle. The T34's turret is flung into the air, and even before the crew have time to get out the whole thing explodes. So that is that.

There is savage, furious fighting among the burning houses. From one house a Russian machine-gun is firing at our infantry. Porta swings the tank round, a cloud of bricks and plaster flies in all directions as we thunder through the wall. The terrified Russians squeeze up against one wall and are mown down by our machine-gun, and so we roll on through the house and out through a haze of lime-dust. And that is that.

Farther on a dozen infantrymen try to get under cover. They squeeze themselves flat to the greasy earth, then they discover us trundling at them, leap up and rush towards a house. One of them gets a foot caught in a fence, and before he can free it he is a gory pulp beneath our tracks. So that's that.

We tumble trees, burst through walls, over people in brown uniforms. You have to be inside a tank and hear the bang when a shell hits your turret before you know what a bang is. The gun that is shooting at us is behind the cover of a stone fence.

'Give them a kiss with the flame-thrower,' said The Old Un. 'Then give them a high-explosive shell for dessert.'

Hastily I adjust the flame-thrower, and at the same time as it shoots its jet of flame at the gunners a 10.5 HE shell from our gun explodes right among them. Three minutes later, when we trundle across that place, there is nothing but a twisted, unrecognisable mass, about which flames are dancing and all is scorched and black.

On. On. Forward. Where the tank's broad tracks pressed into the ground no life remained. When you saw the slaughter of men that took place in the spring of 1943 you realised how well the grinning death's-head suited the uniform of the tank regiments. At intervals we halted to replenish our supplies of petrol and ammunition, and to see to our motors. Woe betide the tank whose motor broke down during a battle. It would be holed like a sieve in three minutes.

We were engaged with a big force of T34s. Those dreaded Russian tanks were wonderfully powerful and speedy, and it was only with our new types, such as Tigers and Panthers, that we dared accept their challenge. Both the Russian and our infantry kept under cover during this roaring battle of the land battleships, the greatest tank battle of the war. Darkness fell, but despite appalling losses of men and material the fight continued across the Ukrainian steppe. We had a few hours' badly needed sleep while the supply crews replenished the tank, then we were shaken awake, tottered, still half asleep, to our tank, where the supply men hung our equipment on us and helped us aboard. Dimly I saw a Feldwebel lift Stalin the cat up to Porta; then the motor started with a roar.

When, after four days, there at last came a pause in the battle, the 27th Tank Regiment was almost annihilated. The burnt-out wrecks of our tanks littered the steppe. Of forty tanks we had two left. Out of the whole regiment's four hundred, there remained eighteen. Most of the crews lay charred and dead in their tanks. Everywhere for a depth of two or three miles were T34s still burning.

Those who escaped a hero's death by burning and reached hospital only half roasted shrieked with the pain, not for days, but for months, some for years.

They were bringing up fresh tanks and crews during the night. Our still serviceable tanks were to be kept ready, together with those from other regiments. We tried to sleep while there was still time, sitting in the tank, our heads leaning against periscopes and guns; and the next day the tank battle continued, and it went on, day after day.

A continual stream of fresh cannon-fodder came from the reserve battalions in Germany and the depots in the occupied countries, boys of seventeen and eighteen with six weeks' training behind them. They were very good at drilling and saluting smartly, and they died doing it. Others were elderly men of fifty, come from the concentration camps. Hitler was scraping the bottom of his barrel. The hospitals also had to provide their miserable quota – pale, thin, often feverish wounded suddenly told that they were well and fit to be discharged; and, I suppose, bandages are no obstacle to being slaughtered.

In Kubjansk on the River Oskol a T34 and us fired simultaneously. Both shells went home; but the Russian tank took fire, with its turret stripped off, while we escaped with five links torn from the near track and two rollers damaged. This was a stroke of bad luck, for the company was on the point of withdrawing, and thus we had to be left to our own resources behind the enemy lines. We hid in some bushes till it grew dark, and then we set about replacing the damaged section of the track and the two rollers. It was a fantastic labour and most nerve-racking, for the whole time we had to keep an eye on the endless stream of Russian tanks thundering past along the road only a hundred yards away.

It was far into the night before we had the tank ready to move. Then we had to await our chance. Porta and I sat in the turret wearing Russian caps, ready to reply in Russian if we were accosted. We had smeared our markings with mud. At the right moment we moved in behind three T34s, and thus we drove for mile after mile, till we were just behind the battle-line; there our three companions swung leftwards towards a village, and we continued straight on. There was a shell in the breech ready to be fired at the first who interfered with us, and Stege stood ready with several more to send after it. The machine-guns and flame-thrower were likewise ready for instant action. We reached our regiment.

At daybreak the alarm was sounded again, and our platoon was sent to hunt down some T34s and KW2s which had broken through our lines and were then making havoc in the rear. They had roused a whole battalion from its slumbers in its rest billets in Isjum, and by all accounts were behaving like a herd of obstreperous wild boar.

Like hounds that had picked up the trail, our two tanks stormed through a little wood in which were the marks of broad tracks that could only have been those of T34s or KW2s. From the top of a rise we saw them on the fringe of a village a good two miles away. According to the map that must have been the village of Svatov. We could see only the three T34s and presumed that the others had gone elsewhere to do more damage. As soon as the three had disappeared in among the houses we went full pelt down the hill to come up behind them. We drove round behind a pond and into some thick bushes, in which we hoped we would be able to get up close, before they discovered us. Our second tank took up position behind a long building, a school or something of the kind, to lie in wait, and we then drove forward till we were only fifty yards from two T34s.

The Old Un crawled down beside me to make sure that I had set the gun right, for a bad shot would have meant our death. Then the shot roared out. The breech flew back and Stege flung the next shell into the barrel. Swiftly the turret swung round till I had the second T34 in the periscope. Again the gun roared and at that short distance the shell literally stripped the turret off the T34. The two T34s were in flames as we plunged out of the bushes at full speed to go to the help of our companion who, judging by the violent firing, was obviously getting it in the neck. We had only gone a couple of hundred yards up the road, however, when we caught sight of one of the KW2s, which are mighty brutes of ninety tons with an armament of five machine-guns, a flame-thrower and a 15-cm. gun protruding from a huge turret. It had halted athwart the road and was letting its machine-guns play through the village. It was also firing its great gun, so that our ears sang, and the great shell was like a hurricane rushing through the air.

Stege flung an S-shell into the gun, the only type of shell capable of penetrating a KW2's thick hull. A conflagration of flame spurted from the muzzle as we fired. To my horror I saw that I had aimed too low. The shell had exploded on the monster's track. Porta and The Old Un cried out at my clumsiness, and the great monster's turret began to turn towards us. Luckily a KW2's turret is slow to turn.

'Shoot, blast you!' shouted The Old Un. 'What are you sitting there snoring for?'

Again our gun roared and an S-shell landed on the brute's side. For an instant the turret halted, then it went on turning.

'Porta, move on, blast you!'

The Old Un pulled me away from the sighting apparatus and seated himself behind it. In a flash he swung the turret round and sighted; then our gun roared another five times. There was a thunderous explosion inside the monster, which strangely enough did not catch fire, although its turret was torn from its seating and hung out over one side. Three men leaped out, but were mown down by our machine-guns. The Old Un gave the KW2 two more S-shells, after which smoke and flames were pouring from it.

Thus the whole day passed, and by the end of it we had no tank left, but had to sit up behind von Barring's as he drove back to our lines. Three days later, after eight days' uninterrupted fighting, our regiment was taken out of the battle and we went into rest billets in the village of Achtyrka.

Perhaps to some people this account of the fighting will seem romantic and exciting. Any duelling with death, in whatever manner, is dramatic; it takes you away from, or beyond, the everyday. But you can try a throw with death in other ways than by going to war, and you will experience the same liberating drama, only with this difference: that the purpose of it is sensible and the intention to save life.

Only a few find war exciting and romantic. To most it is dirt, suffering, interminable monotony; and its highlights consist in pressing a button that releases what you long to experience, many miles away. War is a bad way of experiencing the heights of life; it leaves you disappointed, and when you come back from it you discover that you have not had any sensible purpose and have lost contact with that to which you have returned; you have become restless, as it is called, and your nerve has gone. That is true both for the victors and the vanquished. Perhaps the tragedy is greater for the victor.

He has been victorious, but whom has he vanquished and for what has he conquered? He cannot make head or tail of it. It was so different when he set out, for then he believed in a simple truth; but that proved to be hopelessly involved, once it was stripped of the proud words in which it had been presented to him.

After the Russians had been driven back to Bielgorod on the River Donetz, the German spring offensive came to a halt, swamped in blood, and the entire front from the Arctic Ocean to the Black Sea became static. Even the aeroplanes of either side remained inactive.

It was a lovely summer.

23

'First I would have a bathroom made,' said Porta. 'There would be a shower, so designed that the water fell in gentle summer rain; and when I had had rain enough a pack of stark and dainty maidens would come and carry me up to one of my thirty-seven rooms. They would all be hot on me and would take it nicely in turn to sit beside me and play with father's southern fruits. Then the next team would come, fine specimens too, and would have a hundred pipes filled with different kinds of the finest tobacco obtainable. The maidens would light the pipes for me, and hold them to my mouth, so that I only needed to lie and suck the smoke in and puff it out again. Now and again one or two of them would hunt my tongue down my throat. One and all would smell of violets. When I wished to eat, the girls would cut my food into nice little pieces and blow on them, and if there was anything that needed chewing they would do it for me, so that I didn't have that fag.'

'I suppose you would have another team wipe your behind when you had been to the bog?' said The Old Un.

'Have you read that last letter from Asmus?' Pluto put in. 'If only half of it is true, I wouldn't have a thing against having both legs and an arm cut off. He says as well that it doesn't hurt any longer. Just imagine having the bog brought to you in bed, and a darling nurse to give you beauty treatment when you've messed yourself. And Asmus seems to get mashed potatoes and masses of diced ham every single day, and on Sundays two eggs! They're bloody well off, the wounded are!

'What luck that Asmus has had!'

Separate Peace

The Russians bombarded us with leaflets and propaganda pamphlets. In one of them we read that Hitler had died a week before and that Stalin was seriously ill. Hitler had been shot by a general, but his death was being kept secret by the

Nazis, as Stalin's illness was by the Politburo. The pamphlet concluded with this appeal:

> Men of the army and of the fleet of the Russian and German forces!
>
> Get together for a free Germany and Russia! Turn your weapons on your true enemies, the SS and Gestapo, the murderers who guard the prisons in Germany, those who are prolonging the war, the loathsome ones who like war. German soldiers! Cast the yoke of slavery from you! Wait no longer, but do it now. And you, soldiers of the old holy Russia, shoot the GPU and the commissars! How much longer will you be led by these brutes, who rape your wives, sisters and sweethearts at home, while you shed your blood at the front? Soldiers of the Russian and German armies! Stop shooting at your brothers; instead turn your arms on the murderers in the SS and GPU!
>
> FREEDOM ARMY

This leaflet was read and discussed with excited seriousness. We were all more than eager to believe any statement, however unreliable, asserting that Hitler was dead and that we could soon go home and settle accounts with his crowd. We took the revolution as given, and assumed that it would be quickly won. Porta said thoughtfully:

'First we'll have to clear up some of all this mess we've made and hand the place over to Ivan nice and neat. Stack all the bricks nicely, so that he can just throw his gun away and start building his houses up again. Also we had better restore one or two bridges and some of the other damage we have had to do, so that the place doesn't look too bad when we hand it over.'

'And what about all our towns in Germany?' exclaimed The Old Un. 'You can take your oath that Tommy isn't going to help us by stacking bricks for us.'

'Don't you be so sure,' replied Porta in a tone of conviction. 'Otherwise it may well be that Ivan and we go and teach Tommy manners. But, naturally, our airmen will have to go across and clear up the mess they have made over there. That's only reasonable.'

Pluto mentioned France and all the other countries, where we had made a mess and would have to clean up, and Porta became thoughtful.

'It looks as though we're going to have the hell of a lot to do in the immediate future,' said he. 'But, whatever happens, all generals and officers will have to strip off their shoulder tabs and come and dig too. It would be a good idea to put Goebbels and Goring and Adolf and Himmler and that chap Rosenberg and the other gentry to tidying the Warsaw ghetto. They should be made to weep tears of blood.'

We knew better a couple of days later. The war was to continue, and not just for a short time. Our battalion was going to be used as infantry and was to relieve the 14th Jäger Battalion, which occupied a sector along the Donetz. The front was quiet, and we did not hear a shot as we moved into the lines by night. Stalin sat on Porta's pack, dressed in a thin uniform of white linen, thoroughly enjoying the trip. He was the only Obergefreiter in the German Army who had put on white tropical uniform, but the Kommandofeldwebel had entered written permission to do so in his soldier's book, which he carried in regulation fashion in his right-hand breast pocket, so the 'bloodhounds' could come and look as much as they liked. Everything was in apple-pie order as far as Obergefreiter Stalin of the 27th's No. 5 Company was concerned.

As we took over, the men of the Jäger Battalion's 7th Company said:

'Don't you go shooting at Ivan, now. They're a stout lot over there. We don't have any such crazy nonsense as shooting, here.'

We thought they were mad.

Shortly after sunrise we heard a tremendous commotion over on the Russian side, shouting and calling and hallooing. They were obviously enjoying themselves, we could hear that; then some of them appeared on the parapet of their trench and shouted good morning across to us, and we gaped in amazement. At the same time, they asked politely if we were the new lot and if we had slept well. They hoped their dog had not disturbed us with its barking. Then things became really lively on the Russian side: the whole lot of them came pouring out, stark naked, and dived head first into the river, while we hung half out of the trench staring at them with our eyes popping out of our heads. The Russians in the river called and shouted and splashed each other and bawled up at us:

'Hurry up and come in. The water's lovely and warm.'

Headed by Porta, stark naked but for a forage-cap, we rushed down. Porta jumped in with Stalin in his arms, and the Russians nearly drowned themselves laughing, when they heard that our cat was called Josef Vissarionovitch Stalin.

'This is the proper sort of war to have, don't you think?' shouted a Russian NCO, and we agreed with him. They gave three cheers for Germany, and we three cheers for Russia.

The Old Un was as delighted as a child. 'This is bloody fine,' he cried, his eyes sparkling. 'At home they would think it was a lie.'

The day brought more incredible surprises. It transpired, for example, that there was a regular agreement that the Russians fired off a few shells every day between four o'clock and five-thirty, while we fired ours from three o'clock to four-thirty, each shell dropping nicely in no-man's-land where it did nobody any harm. That satisfied the generals. When there was any shooting with machine-guns or small-arms they were naturally fired up into the air. If the Russians sent up a four-starred red Very light it meant that there was a staff officer inspecting them and that for the sake of appearances they would have to do a little shooting with their automatics. When the inspecting officers had gone they sent up a green Very light. We had all sorts of signals that helped to make life pleasant for everybody, and of course we visited, inviting each other to dinner and vodka. We swapped and bartered to our hearts' content; schnapps, tobacco, tinned foods, rugs, arms, watches, newspapers and magazines. Illustrated maga-zines were much sought after, and if we came across any pictures we found especially interesting we would make a trip across to have the text translated, and, of course, the Russians did the same.

Otherwise those summer months passed quietly and smoothly in monotonous work. When in our quarters at Achtyrka we had to help train the recruits who kept pouring in from Germany in a never-ending stream. Training recruits is a boring job, especially when you cannot see the point of what you are doing.

We had one magnificent coup, when we relieved a lorry of eighteen bottles and a fifty-litre keg of good French brandy. On this sound foundation we arranged a feast. We exchanged five of the bottles for thirty eggs, three chickens, ten pounds of potatoes, some tinned plums and tomatoes; then we stuffed the chickens with the plums and tomatoes and various other things, and poured a whole bottle of cognac over them, and invited the Russian owners of our billets for a drink. Porta borrowed a Cossack's horse (he was one of the Cossack volunteers fighting with the Germans), but as Porta had never been on a horse before, the episode ended by the horse breaking its neck. The Cossack became troublesome, and in the end we had to tie him up and put him together with his dead horse on a timber-raft and set him adrift on a river that ran through the village. One of the Russians asked us if we would shoot his cat for him, as it was stealing hens, and this too Porta arranged in a way that earned general approbation. It is true that the cat did not die of his efforts, but when the hunt was called off for lack of ammunition Porta had bagged one dog and three hens, wounded a cow and a goat, and sent a bullet through the hat of the old Russian who owned the cat. The Russian comforted Porta by telling him that the cat was a most unusually difficult one to hit.

One night we stole a 400-lb. sow from the 89th Artillery Regiment in the neighbouring village of Starja. After that we sat on our latrine eating boiled sow, drinking vodka and playing cards for seven hours at a stretch.

The Old Un also pulled one of Porta's teeth. He had had

appalling toothache for a long time, but did not dare go to the dentist. We tried the old trick of tying a thread to the tooth and a door and slamming the door, but the thread broke. Then our old Russian produced an aged pair of dental forceps, so we tied Porta up and The Old Un wrenched the tooth out of his head. But it was the wrong tooth, so the performance had to be repeated. That left Porta with just the one tooth, the black front one, so The Old Un had that as well, before we untied his bellowing patient. We had to keep the two apart for many days, but in the end Porta had his revenge. He managed to tie The Old Un up, whereupon he removed his boots and socks, lashed each of his feet to a pole, rubbed the soles with salt and invited two goats to have a lick. While The Old Un shrieked, Porta drank beer and kept the rest of us at bay with a long Cossack whip. The goats licked and licked, The Old Un sobbed and bellowed and laughed convulsively.

That was a summer for you!

24

Far away in East Prussia there was a great gathering of all the German corps commanders. There were Generalobersts and General-feldmarshalls with blood-red stripes down the sides of their well-pressed trousers. The gold braid on their red collars competed in brilliance with the jewels of the Ritterkreuzs that dangle round the necks of such gentry.

With monocles screwed well in, they bent over large maps of the huge front. They spent hour after hour moving little coloured flags on pins. Each pin indicated a division of eighteen thousand to twenty thousand men. To be the object of the screeching little Führer's satisfaction meant power and honour.

'. . . and I would ask you to convey my greetings to the many thousands who will be granted the proud fate of dying in battle, fighting for the Fatherland and the honour of our army.'

Thus our army commander to his divisional commanders, among whom was the commander of the division to which the 27th Tank Regiment belonged. The be-medalled, fat mass-murderer with the monocle then saluted and drove back to his HQ far, far behind the front, while the divisional commanders returned to their divisions to prepare for an offensive, so that the be-medalled ones might be able to go on playing with their little flags and nice big maps.

'Regiment! For prayer – KNEEL!'

The chaplain was in officer's uniform with purple tabs. He had the rank of major and was thus on a level with the staff officers. On the left side of his tunic an Iron Cross hung and glinted.

'Holy Father! Bless these proud arms, that stand here in Thy honour! Let them crush and torment the red barbarians, we beg Thee, Our Father in Heaven, give us strength to be the instrument of Thy punishment of these red marsh-dwellers.'

Later, I shall relate what happened when Porta and I got hold of this chaplain during a big battle.

The Proud Fate

'Out, out,' shouted The Old Un. 'And quickly. This is the end of the 27th Tank Regiment.'

Twenty minutes later our six hundred tanks were mere twisted burning wrecks. Another twenty minutes later Oberst von Lindenau drove up in his all-purpose vehicle and, having had a look at the smashed tanks, said in a tired voice:

'All those who are fit make their way back to our old quarters. The 27th Regiment no longer counts, now that the air force has made that mess of it.'

The air force was our own. By some deplorable mistake we had been bombed by our own Stukas.

A few days later we were in action again with new crews and new tanks brought up in a hurry from Charkov.

It was then that I discovered to my horror how war poisons your mind.

I have always hated war, and I hate it today; and yet I did what I ought not to have done, just what I hated and condemned, and which I regret doing and still cannot understand how I did it.

In my periscope I saw a Russian infantryman jump out of a shell-hole and make a dart for the next hole. Quickly I got my sights on him and gave him a short burst from the machine-gun. The bullets kicked the earth up round him, but he was not hit. As our tank approached, he darted out of this second shell-hole and ran like a hare to the next. Again the bullets spattered round him. Pluto also began shooting at him, but neither of us hit him. Porta howled with laughter and held Stalin up, so that he could see out of the observation slit:

'Have a look at the work of our crack shots,' he said to Stalin.

The Russian must have been crazed with fear, for he now ran round in a circle. Again our machine-guns chattered at him, yet to our amazement we still could not hit him. The Old Un and Stege laughed almost as much as Porta, and Stege said scornfully:

'Good God, can't you even lay the pale—— horizontal?'

I swore to myself, and as the fellow jumped into yet another shell-hole I turned the flame-thrower on to it and sent a jet of flame roaring across the ground. Then I turned to The Old Un and said:

'He won't get up after that.'

'Won't he?' said The Old Un. 'Take a look in your periscope!'

I could scarcely believe my eyes: there was the fellow, blackened with soot from the flame-thrower, running and just disappearing into a house. A mighty roar of laughter came from the other four.

It now became a point of honour for me to kill that man, so I fired at the house till I had it blazing.

A point of honour. How could I? How could I kill a man just for the sake of my pride?

But that is what I did, and I regret it. War with its everlasting murdering and noise and flames and destruction had stealthily poisoned me.

Even the most fanatical Nazi now had to admit that the Germans had lost the great offensive, for we were preparing for a withdrawal on a grand scale. One last superhuman effort was made to wrest victory for German arms. Our company reached as far as Birjutsk, where we surprised a whole cavalry unit in rest billets. At short range, and in a short time, we transformed men and horses into a shrieking, bloody mass of terrified men and kicking animals. Then we had to withdraw, because a large force of T34s was sent against us.

Everywhere there was heavy fighting and heavy losses.

We massacred one regiment that had been surrounded, but, like our 104th Grenadiers, had not been able to bring themselves to surrender. We drove our tanks into position and shelled them for three hours. Their screams were ghastly. When they were destroyed it was a grim sight we saw: everywhere were smashed lorries, weapons and fantastically mutilated soldiers, every one of whom was a woman. Many of them were young and pretty, with white teeth and red varnished nails. That was a mile or so east of the village of Livny.

The Old Un was white in the face: 'Let us promise each other that those of us, or the one of us, who escapes alive from this will write a book about this stinking mess in which we are taking part. It must be a book that will be one in the eye for the whole filthy military gang, no matter whether German, Russian, American or what, so that people can understand how imbecile and rotten this sabre-rattling idiocy is.'

Our orders were that, while retreating, everything was to be destroyed. The result is almost impossible to describe. Bridges, villages, roads and railways were blown up. Foodstuffs of every kind that we could not take with us were soused with petrol or tar, or the contents of a latrine. The vast, magnificent sunflower fields were burned or rolled flat with tractors. Pigs and all the animals were shot and dragged into the sun, so that within a few hours they were stinking and rotten. Booby-traps were left everywhere, so that, for example, a cottage was blown up if anyone opened the door. You saw desolation everywhere, an ugly landscape of death.

As usual, the 27th Tank Regiment dwindled to vanishing point in a few weeks, for, of course, we were the rearguard and fighting a running battle with the Russians' superior tank forces. Now, however, we were not sent replacements. The regiment's survival was a question of weeks, perhaps of days.

As we came rolling up a road behind the hastily retreating German troops it was sometimes impossible to make headway because of the dense columns of fleeing cavalry, infantry, artillery and tanks. Endless strings of lorries, tanks, guns, horses and men toiled desperately along the sandy roads, where dust and the heat made life a feverish dream. In the fields on either side of the road was an equally dense and equally long column of people and animals, but those were civilians. They made use of the strangest vehicles, to which might be harnessed an old horse or a cow, or both, or a dog or a donkey or a person, or else they trudged along with their possessions on their backs. All were possessed by but the one idea: to get away.

Strangely enough we never saw even the shadow of a

Russian plane, otherwise the war would have ended a year earlier than it did. When one of our vehicles broke down, whether it was a small car or a tank, there was no time to repair it. A tank toppled it into the ditch, where it would not interfere with the traffic. Innumerable exhausted soldiers had flung themselves down in the ditch, from where they implored us to give them a lift, but lifts were not allowed. It was heart-rending to hear their entreaties without being able to deaden the voice of conscience by taking at least one of them with us. No one stopped and picked anyone up. Tank after tank thundered past them, sending huge clouds of dust swirling across the fields. The refugees also fell by the hundred and lay as though dead in the broiling heat. And no one bothered about them, either. From the driver's seat at the bottom of the tank Porta roared:

'This is something like a retreat, boys. It's worse than when we were making war in Frogland, where all the French and Tommies were haring it away from us. In those days our muckcarts didn't have such a good turn of speed, but we're putting up a much better performance now. I'll eat my left leg if Goebbels ever says a word about this magnificent little race. If we keep this up I'll be in Berlin for my birthday. Stalin, old puss, you shall have a fine set of civvies instead of the filthy uniform you are forced to wear, and you shall be given a good scratch at Adolf's behind. And you're all invited too; and we'll have mashed potatoes and diced pork and afterwards potato cakes and sugar and jam and all the stuff you can swill down. And we'll fetch that legless ass, Asmus, from hospital with his wooden leg and private bog.'

He circulated the bottle and told us to drink to a happy defeat for the Prussian Nazi armed forces.

East of Charkov we were thrown into a great rearguard action, in which our tanks were all knocked out, and so we became infantry.

Porta and I were by ourselves, a quarter of a mile from The Old Un and the others, manning a heavy machine-gun. As we lay there letting the machine-gun hammer away at the advancing Russians, a figure came dashing along and would have rushed on across to the Russians if Porta had not caught him by one leg.

It was the chaplain – the chaplain, who had prayed that prayer so full of love and charity before the retreat began. Porta sat astride him and gave him a ringing box on the ear.

'Where are you off to, you bloody crow? Not deserting, by any chance?'

'We have lost the war,' sobbed the chaplain. 'We had better surrender voluntarily, then they surely won't do anything to us.'

'I'll surrender you all right, you filthy Jesuit animal! Have you forgotten your edifying little address, when you told us to murder the red swamp-creatures? Now you're bloody well going to help work this machine-gun or I'll hammer a cartridge case into your forehead, even if we die of the stink! Now you shall have a taste of the murdering you recommended so warmly to us, you cowardly— !'

Porta gave him a black eye, then butted him with his steel helmet, so that he folded up like a wet rag.

'This is – insubordination,' the chaplain cried hysterically. 'I'll see that you are court-martialled if you don't this moment—'

I struck him in the face with my clenched fist and pressed the muzzle of my pistol to the gold-embroidered cross he wore sewn over his breast pocket and shouted:

'Either you're on the other side of that machine-gun in three seconds handing us ammunition, or you're a dead chaplain.'

Sobbing with terror and fury at his humiliation, he crawled over to where we pointed. We showed him no mercy, but gave vent to all our pent-up thirst for revenge. Each time he fumbled we struck him hard on the fingers with our pistols.

'That's for Hans Breuer!'

'That's for Asmus!'

'And that – and that – and here's another – for Ursula!'

And another because I killed a dozen men in an hour with a sniper's rifle, that time when I was beside myself with grief at Ursula's death!

And another because I killed that poor devil it was almost impossible to hit, the other day.

There was a flickering before my eyes, and I saw red. I let him have it. Porta, too, had a longish account to settle.

'Now you've got into human hands, you swine, and we're not letting you go.'

When we had finished with him we made him start off across to the Russians and shot him in both legs when he had got two-thirds of the way. Three Mongolians crawled out to get him. We stopped shooting till they had fetched him in.

'I don't know about you,' said Porta, wiping the sweat from his face, 'but I feel a new and a better man.'

When we returned to the company we put in the regulation report that Chaplain von Wilnau of the 12th Panzer Division had deserted to the enemy, and that we had shot at him and wounded him while he was doing so. Thus, even if he should happen to get away from the Russians, the Germans would shoot him as a deserter.

'Were they Russians or Asiatics who got him?' asked Pluto.

'Asiatics.'

'Then he'll have had a sound, healthy blessing.'

There was general satisfaction at the chaplain having fallen into the clutches of warriors from the more barbarous parts of the Soviet Union. It was not every day they got a genuine Nazi priest to play with.

I would like to be humane. I would like to be able to say that I had no bloodthirsty instincts: but even today I still see red when I think of, let alone meet, those who incite to war, all the idiots who directly or with treacherous insinuations, fan dissension and belligerent instincts. I have seen the result of the infamous activities of these propagandists, commentators, fanatics, cold business brains and lusting politicians. They are noxious vermin and, as such, should be destroyed. They must be got out of their holes and crannies, and so, away with them! I know that our treatment of the chaplain was barbaric, but we could not do otherwise. I have no compassion for those who want war, who want to make millions of peaceable people cast all human consideration aside. They are dangerous, and I know that they should be opposed with the utmost energy. I know that, as in his heart of hearts, does every German. Oh, if only the Germans could get that well and truly into their heads and have the courage to act on their knowledge. A German united revolt against war, a merciless settling of accounts with the spirit and creatures of militarism – that would put things in their place.

Before we left Charkov for good the engineers destroyed it utterly. Charkov was a big city; it covered an area as large as Copenhagen and at the outbreak of war had a good eight hundred and fifty thousand inhabitants. Charkov was one of the loveliest cities of the Soviet Union, and it had the same prestige as Moscow or Odessa. Of its inhabitants some three hundred thousand were killed. As General Zeitzler proudly stated in an order of the day, it was '*restlos vernichtet*'.

Should I have pity on a so-called priest?

I just can not.

25

'I know it only too well, my dear Beier.' Barring gave his head an anxious shake, as he set his hand on The Old Un's shoulder. 'The whole thing's impossible. It isn't war any longer, but pure and simple suicide. We have to wage war with the help of children and the aged, but you must realise that it isn't easy for them, poor devils, to be sent like this, untrained, into the worst of the filth. So I would ask you to be a bit nice to them. Suppose it was your own father or kid brother; you would have a little consideration for them. One or two of you have also blubbed when you were fifteen or sixteen, I've no doubt. If you would like to do something for me, be decent to them. Help them find their feet, as far as that's possible under these crazy conditions. I don't think we ought to make things worse for them; they least of all have deserved that, for if anyone is without blame it is these boys. One thing at least is certain, judging by the recruits they are now sending us, the bottom of the barrel will soon have been scraped, and so we can assume that the war will come to a halt.'

'Oh no, Hauptmann,' said Porta with a laugh. 'Then they'll send us all the girls. Couldn't we put our names down now for a good assortment of film extras? I would gladly train a section of those. I have some very stimulating exercises in the prone position—'

'Porta, I shall certainly put you in charge of the film squad if it comes to that,' interrupted von Barring, smiling. 'Meanwhile, do me a favour and remember what I have just said. That is merely a suggestion on my part, but I am sure you won't mind acting on it.'

The Armoured Train

After the fall of Charkov the 27th Regiment was withdrawn and sent to Dnepropetrovsk, where we were allotted the armoured train 'Leipzig'. As soon as we were installed, we and another armoured train went to Charol, 100 kilometres west of Poltava, where we did some firing practice to get acquainted with our new guns. We five were allotted a coach: The Old Un was coach-commander; Porta was in charge of the eight machine-guns and three automatic cannon; and Stege was in charge of No. 1 Turret and I of No. 2 Turret with its 12-cm. long-barrelled gun, one of which Stege also had. Pluto was in charge of the wireless and communications. For crew we were given twenty-five recruits, who had had four weeks' training. The youngest was sixteen, the eldest sixty-two. They made a pitiful sight.

We went up towards the front without knowing exactly where we were to go. It proved to be Lwow, where we shot a village to smithereens and engaged Russian artillery with our automatic arms. After that we went south-west. Day and night we thundered along the hundreds of miles of track, stopping only to take in water or oil, or to wait in a siding to let past a train coming from the opposite direction. We were able to stretch out and sleep in our coach and had a wonderful time. War, we thought, was not really so bad, if only you could sleep your sleep out every now and again. It was the continual lack of sleep, to which we had been subjected, that made it all so intolerable and our nerves raw.

In Krementschug we were sauntering round the station area, when suddenly a woman's voice shouted:

'Sven! Sven!'

We turned round in amazement. There stood an empty hospital train, and in one of the doors stood a nurse waving to me:

'Sven, come here and say how do you do!'

It was Asta. She hugged and kissed me. I scarcely recognised her in her uniform, and also because, in the days when I knew her in Gothenburg, she had been reserved and a bit boring, though pretty. I could see that war had roused her. There was no hesitation in her eyes or movements. She pulled me up into the train, while two of the other nurses took Porta and The Old Un in hand.

Asta had married and been divorced from a man twenty-two years older than herself. Then she and a friend had volunteered for the German Red Cross, and then, and then. Heavens, how randy I was. And, heavens, how randy she was. We gazed at each other, and did not say what we wanted. Then another nurse came and whispered something into her ear.

'Come,' said Asta and took me along to another coach and shoved me into a lower bunk and pulled the curtain and undressed with swift, practised movements. In one twist she was out of her dress, and there was nothing to talk about – we both wanted it equally badly, and it was good and lovely to be presented out of the blue with a clean, well-washed, firm-fleshed girl, who knew what it was all about and that a quarter of an hour is plenty of time, if you do not waste it talking about the weather or thinking of what you do not dare. We were so starved for it, so avid and in harmony, that we managed it twice, for the simple reason that we did not stop to consider, but acted, unhesitatingly, obeying the accumulated urge of many months. Strange that life, naked and unashamed, should also choose to waylay three dirty soldiers and give them a reminder of its existence, its very near existence, in a railway station, just any old station. That shows that you can always run across something good, and when you do a quarter of an hour is more than time enough, if you wish it to be.

I can still see, and smile at, the slightly comical picture of us three dirty soldiers not unproudly trotting back to our armoured train, our backs stubbornly turned on a hospital train that is on the point of pulling out. We did not look back, but I always imagine one window of a carriage filled with girls with tender, moved expressions. It was not three nurses, but the women of a hospital train, who had bestowed their gifts upon three men and received a good return. It happened so swiftly, and it was so complete.

With laughing eyes we boarded our train.

Was it good?

It was indeed.

Even Porta was silent, which shows that there is more than just salacity in the world.

The Old Un began humming to himself, and Porta took out his flute. Then we burst out laughing and just let the others gape.

'The poor girls,' said The Old Un. 'Such an awful lot of lice they must have got.'

And so we played that piece about the king who got a flea.

It had been a poetic miracle, as natural and surprising as when, while lying in the grass on a summer's day, you suddenly discover that a leveret is sniffing at your fingers.

The armoured train moved up to the battle area during the next twenty-four hours. At Bachworat, near to a tributary of the Donetz, we were told our task. We were to support an attack, and then penetrate as far as we could down the Lugansk-Charkov line and create as much havoc as possible in the enemy's rear. We were then to withdraw, destroying bridges and track behind us. Should the train be put out of action, we were to blow it up, and all survivors were to try and get through to our own lines.

Oberstleutnant Hinka's voice spoke across the radio-telephone to all coaches:

'Make ready. Prepare for action.'

The covers were taken off the guns, shells laid ready, and each man stood at his place. Slowly the train gathered speed, until it was rocking, the wheels humming and now and again screaming and whining on a sharp curve. Then the loud-speakers barked out the order:

'Train! Get ready to engage!'

The breeches of the big guns flew open, shells and charges were slammed in. There was the rattle and clang of steel on steel; the wheels for altering the setting of the guns turned, and the automatics were duly loaded. At the same time we pulled our asbestos helmets down over our heads. I stared through my periscope at the countryside. Ahead and to one side lay the river, broad and dirty yellow in colour, twisting like a ribbon among grey slopes. At considerable speed we rattled through an abandoned village, and so swayed and rumbled across a large iron bridge. The river far below us was like a huge yellow corrugated iron roof.

We were a good five kilometres beyond the river before we made contact with the enemy, who suddenly fired a couple of shells at us. The train at once put on speed, so the noise of the heavy wheels almost drowned the howling of the shells. Then the alarm bells shrilled in all the turrets, and the order to open fire was given.

Each coach commander was informed of the target and in turn instructed his turret commanders. The big guns turned their black mouths to face the woods and fields lying there bathed in sunshine.

Then came the order: Fire! and there was a deafening, tremendous, rolling thunder, as our thirty heavy guns struck up their song of death for that smiling, summery landscape. It was not long before we were shrouded in smoke and dust. Each time that all the guns fired together in a great broadside, the train swayed so violently that we thought it was going over on its side. The Russians began to answer, and shells struck crashing against the sides of the coaches; but they were too small to do any harm. It was not long, though, before our fire was being answered by heavy 28-cm. guns, and some of their shells took effect, striking down on us like hurricanes. We at once changed target and fired at the Russian artillery instead. Suddenly the train stopped. Soon it was being rumoured that one of the fore coaches had had a direct hit and one of its bogies been smashed. Some of our engineers had to slip out and, under cover of the train, tip the damaged coach off the line. It was imperative to get moving again as soon as possible, for a stationary armoured train is a helpless prey for the enemy's artillery. Before they had got that coach off the track, however, the Russians managed to smash another coach, killing its entire crew.

This violent artillery fire forced us to withdraw towards the big iron bridge across the river. As we went we blew up the track behind us with tremendous bangs. Then our HQ on the far side of the river sent us orders to halt one kilometre east of the bridge and to cover the infantry while they were crossing it. Once they were over, we were to get ourselves across and the engineers would then blow up the bridge. Another armoured train, the 'Breslau', was being sent up to reinforce us, and as soon as it had taken up position by the bridge Oberstleutnant Hinka wanted to make a thrust with our train down the Rostov-Voronesh line and do what he could to harass the enemy. Hinka thought that we ought to be able to get to the lesser town about twenty kilometres away, where there was a Russian divisional HQ. 'Breslau' was to remain halted by the bridge and fire at the enemy, in the hope that they might not discover that 'Leipzig' was on the move in their rear.

For the first few kilometres we tore along at full speed without being fired on, but then they turned their heaviest guns on us, and within fifteen minutes several of our coaches were badly damaged, though still able to fight. Then our locomotive itself received a couple of serious hits, and we had to retreat, crawling slowly back the way we had come.

Some big tanks moved up on us, and we had to dip the guns' barrels and engage them. It was a fantastic sight seeing them being hit. Our 12-cm. shells smashed such tanks to smithereens, sending steel plates flying through the air like feathers from a burst cushion.

Shells fell incessantly round our locomotive, which was losing steam through innumerable holes with the result that our speed was reduced to a slow, jerky progress. It was more than doubtful whether armoured train 'Leipzig' would get back.

When I think of all the fantastically costly material, both enemy and our own, that I have helped to smash, my mind boggles at the mere values involved. When you think of it, you must just laugh, loudly and shrilly, otherwise you would burst into tears and put a bullet through your brain. Do people understand nothing? Do you, who read this, not realise what fantastic wealth is lying waiting for you to exploit, that if you used the military to your own advantage your material and cultural position would be that of the well-to-do today? You would be able to afford to live well, eat well and have a car each, or whatever it is that you want to have; you would be able to travel all over the world; you could go out and enjoy yourself; you would be able to set up house without fear or anxiety. There is enough, more than enough for all.

Nobody believes that – or, rather, nobody dares believe it. What is this curse that makes us all so inert and cowed that we cannot pull ourselves together and deprive the generals of their grants? We are oafs most of us, lazy and ignorant, and we nod our heads and are satisfied when we hear a lot of profound nonsense about 'balance of power' and 'interplay of forces' and all the rest of the jargon. Balance of power? If every Tom, Dick and Harry were to exert himself and demand that the money should be spent on making him better off instead of on arms and war there would be no war and we should all be better off. But the Toms, Dicks and Harrys must first bang their fists on the table and let it be known who holds the power and how that power is to be used.

But the fact is that Tom, Dick and Harry are not educated enough, and so they have to rely on their emotions, and that is not enough. Things will be all right, they say, and we're pretty well off as we are; and, anyway, we don't understand politics, and politicians only do the dirty on you as soon as they get their fingers on the spoils. If you tell Tom, Dick or Harry that they could get a car for nothing and tax free, and that petrol need not cost more than a few pence a gallon, they just laugh, because they do not know. And if you begin to work it out for them and show them what everything costs, then they become angry, for that is tantamount to showing them that they are silly idiots paying their money away unnecessarily.

It took only a few hours to smash an armoured train equipped with guns, the barrels of which alone were worth a fortune. We were encompassed by howling shells, and though we smashed tank upon tank, they gradually closed in upon us like ghastly attacking insects.

Then the fire-control centre fell silent. Feverishly Pluto twiddled his knob, but he could not make contact even with the other coaches. From then on The Old Un himself had to fight our part of the battle. We were now only eight hundred metres from the bridge and 'Breslau'; but in the meantime 'Breslau' had been transformed into a blazing wreck and all its guns were silent.

A tremendous explosion shook our coach and made our heads sing. Some of the crew began screaming, screams that jabbed at our nerves, and smoke and flame poured from No. 1 turret. It was a direct hit. We tackled the resultant fire with our extinguishers, and then counted: four killed and seven wounded. Fortunately Stege was unhurt except for a few minor burns on his hands.

Now mine was the only gun left able to fire. We sweated as we moved about the overheated turret, into which flames stabbed at every shot we fired. One after the other the coaches were smashed, and finally the whole train came to a stop, so that the enemy was able to get the range exactly. Then there was a bang like the Day of Judgment, and a searing white flame filled the turret. I received a violent blow on the chest and everything went black before my eyes. I groaned. It felt as though my body was being crushed. I had to breathe very carefully, but even so each breath was like being stabbed with knives. I could not move. I was caught in a vice consisting of the gun, that had been forced from its seating, and the steel wall of the turret.

I was spattered with blood from head to foot. Whose blood it was I did not know, but I presumed that it was my own. Beside me lay one of the gun crew, the top of his head shorn off like the top of a boiled egg. My face and shoulders were covered with his brains. There was an insufferable stench in my nostrils: that of steaming blood and guts, mixed with the acrid smell of ammunition. Then I vomited. Then there was another tremendous bang and flames shot up on all sides. The coach began to heel over, and it looked as though it were going to overturn, but something caught it and it remained poised at an angle of forty-five degrees. This second hit had shifted the gun slightly, so that I could now move my legs and one arm, and so I was able to wipe some of the sticky brains off my face. Behind me lay Schultz, a lad of sixteen, both his legs smashed to a red pulp. Above my head hung a

197

torn-off arm, on one of whose fingers was a gold ring with a blue stone. My head began to swim, and I started to scream. I quickly came to my senses, however, and shouted for The Old Un and Porta. Shortly afterwards I heard a voice through the thick steel plates, asking me to tap to show where I was. And them came The Old Un's comforting voice:

'Help's coming now, old man!'

With a cutting apparatus they made a hole, through which Porta stuck his blessed, ugly mug:

'Hallo, hallo!' he said, grinning. 'Coming out for a stroll?'

Carefully they cut me free. Of the coach's crew nine were still alive, and while we were bandaging one of these another shell came and shut us in.

Porta and Pluto went at the armoured door with a couple of heavy sledge-hammers, and we managed to get it opened wide enough for us to be able to squeeze out. Armed with our sub-machine-guns and some grenades, we ran for the bridge, keeping under cover of the embankment. Some Russian tanks rushed ahead to cut us off, and we found ourselves engaged in a life-or-death race, which those who came through will certainly not have forgotten. We got there first. The charges of explosives were got ready in a trice and the fuses lit. Then we set off full pelt across the bridge, between the steel sleepers of which we could see the river far below, churned up by shells and bullets. The Russians sprayed the bridge with their machine-guns, and several of us were hit and went swirling down into the turbid yellow water. We were almost across, when a tremendous bang took our breath away. Slowly the bridge began to sag.

'Hold on to the rails,' shouted Porta.

Most of the bridge fell into the river. Sleepers rained down like leaves from a tree in an autumn storm. The rails broke with a whining noise, and nuts and bolts were flung in all directions like projectiles from an automatic cannon.

Eventually the din subsided. With the help of some wires Porta and I managed to get up on to a pier, and from there we balanced along a swaying rail and reached the bank and the others.

Von Barring was fearfully burned about the face and in appalling pain. Oberst Hinka had had his nose and one side of his face pared off.

As soon as we got back to our depot we fell asleep.

26

We pulled down our goggles and tied silk handkerchiefs round our necks. Von Barring lifted Stalin, the cat, up to Porta. Then The Old Un's voice gave the order through the radio to the other cars:

'Start engines. Prepare for action!'

The automatic weapons were loaded, the long cartridge-belts fed in. The car commanders reported themselves ready; then The Old Un's voice sounded again:

'First Armoured Reconnaissance Platoon – forward – march!'

The engines sang, the gravel crunched beneath the heavy tyres.

Hals-und-Beinbruch

'Is it bad, Old Un?' I managed to whisper.

'A couple of little splinters in your tummy and legs. It doesn't look bad. Just you cheer up. You'll see, you'll be all right again in no time. We are taking you and Stege to the casualty clearing station. Stege copped it in just the one leg.'

I winced as the car bumped.

'It's hellish sore, Old Un. Give me a mouthful of water.'

'You mustn't drink anything till the doctor has had a look at you,' replied The Old Un and stroked my hair. 'You know yourself that it's strictly forbidden with stomach wounds.'

'Won't you have a look at it. It's driving me mad.'

'We've already bandaged you. There's no more to be done till the doctor's seen you.'

The car stopped. The Old Un jumped out and Porta came up to me.

'Now, old boy, take a good bite on the old ivories, for Pluto and I are going to heave you out of the old box and hand you down to The Old Un and Titch. That done, the worst will be over. Just think, old fellow, of all the little nurses who will wash your vital parts with clean linen cloths four times a day, as they do with our legless friend Asmus.'

My lips were bleeding when at length I was lying on the

200

ground with a gasmask-case under my head. All at once it had become important to be devilish brave and all that, and not cry out. When they put Stege down, he groaned aloud, because his leg bumped on a wheel of the armoured car. Our companions bent over us to say goodbye. The Old Un pressed his bristly chin to mine and whispered:

'Keep yourself in garrisons till the war's over.'

Porta squeezed our hands and held Stalin out, so that he too could bid us farewell; then just before he disappeared into the car again he called out:

'You lucky devils! Kiss them all from me and tell them that I shall attend to my complexion every day, so that I'll be just as handsome when they see me again.'

Then the powerful engine gave a roar. The Old Un, Titch and Pluto waved to us from the open turret, and then they and the armoured car had disappeared in a cloud of dust.

Apart from the pain, I felt apprehensive and alone. It was good having Stege to feel alone with.

A couple of medical orderlies carried us into a large hall, its floor strewn with straw and covered with wounded soldiers in tattered, dirty uniforms. Stege took hold of my hand as soon as we had been laid down in the straw.

'Is it bad, old man? You'll see, it will be better soon, when the doctor has had a look at you and given you a shot in the arm. We must wangle it so that we can stay together the whole time.'

'Yes, we're bloody well not going to be parted, whatever happens. God, this hurts. It's like having one's guts stripped. But how's your leg? Did it cop it badly?'

'Oh, it hurts a bit,' said Stege, attempting a wan smile. 'It's worst in the foot. But to hell with a leg, they can cut that off. It's worse with your stomach.'

A doctor came along with a couple of medical orderlies, who wrote out cards for each patient to the doctor's dictation. He just cast an indifferent glance at Stege's bandages and said:

'Shell splinter in left leg, transport 6, fresh bandages at once and 3 cc. tetanus.'

He put a fresh dressing on my belly: 'Shell splinters in left leg, right foot and stomach, transport 1, 3 cc. tetanus, 2 cc. morphia now and the same just before transport.'

I braced myself and asked if Stege and I could not stay together.

'Whether you snuff out here or in the hospital train doesn't much matter, as far as that goes,' he replied callously. 'But stomach wounds go with transport 1, and he there with transport 6. There's nothing I can do about it.'

Then he swept on, white coat fluttering. I do not think he was arrogant or brutal, just overburdened. In exchange for a good English pipe, our cigarettes and tobacco, the transport Feldwebel promised to see what he could do for us. I had my injection and dozed off on billows of sleep, out of which I only woke when I was lifted up on a stretcher and pushed into an ambulance. In it were four stretchers on racks one above the other. Stege was under me, so the Feldwebel had kept his promise.

When the ambulance bumped or swayed we knocked up against the stretcher above, or, where the topmost was concerned, the roof. There was only an inch or two between the stretchers, so that you felt stifled. On the top rack was a gunner with a broken pelvis; he screamed and screamed and asked us to ring, for he was afraid he was bleeding to death. Stege repeatedly pressed the button of the bell that rang in the driver's cab, but neither he nor his assistant paid any attention. When the time came to load us into the hospital train the gunner was dead. The orderlies callously hauled him out, tipped him on to the ground and pulled a tarpaulin over him; then they set about unloading us.

The hospital train was one of the notorious 'auxiliaries' – no more than an endless string of goods-wagons with straw on the floor and forty men in each, only roughly classified. The train kept stopping and starting again with a series of jerks, as though they were trying to shake the wagons to pieces. Eleven of those in our wagon died. I almost went off my head with pain and thirst, but Stege kept the water-bottle well out of my reach. It would have been death to have drunk.

That journey took three endless, horrible days and nights; after which we were laid in lines on a platform of Kiev Station with a tarpaulin under us, a greatcoat over us and the eternal gasmask container under our heads. All afternoon we lay on the soaking platform, while more died. I was only hazily aware of what went on around me. Stege lay beside me, and we held hands as if we were a couple of little boys and not hardened, tough old sweats, well accustomed to seeing people die, screaming like animals. Late in the evening, we were fetched by some medical orderlies and Russian prisoners of war and driven in ambulances to 13th Field Hospital, which had been set up in the suburb of Pavilo. There we were carried straight down to a cellar and de-loused. This was done by Russian prisoners of war, and I have never had more gentle and dexterous nurses. If they ever got a wrong hold and made us moan they were so touchingly horrified that for their sake alone we gritted our teeth and did our best not to show our pain. We wounded were generally agreed that, if only we could be looked after by those big, good-humoured creatures, we would be well off indeed, and gratefully we gave them what cigarettes we had. They had been in the trenches like we; and though they were of another race and nationality and we had once shot at each other, because those in authority had decreed that we were enemies, there was a sympathy between us stronger than any decrees which had long since proved quite without connection with any reality that the private soldier could be interested in.

I and four others were lying in the operating theatre awaiting our turn and watching a companion in misfortune on the table beneath a glaring light. Four surgeons were working on him like lighting. They were amputating a foot. As soon as it was sawn off, it was thrown into a white bucket, in which there already stood a leg, sawn off just below the knee, and an arm, the gory stump of which protruded above the edge of the bucket. It nauseated me and I was sick, or rather I tried to be sick, but only a little blood and gall came up.

The next patient was a young fellow with a broken back. He appeared to be unconscious. An elderly surgeon with a monocle kept cursing the other surgeons and orderlies, but he seemed wonderfully expert, for he worked like lightning, with never an unnecessary movement. When they had been working on the young chap for some ten minutes the old surgeon exclaimed angrily:

'But, hell, the bugger's dead. Away with him and bring the next body. And get a move on.' He gave one of the orderlies a push.

Before I knew what was happening I lay tied to the operating table. I was given an injection in my arm and another in my belly. One of the surgeons clapped me on the shoulder.

'Now grit your teeth, old chap. It won't take very long, but it will probably hurt, for we can only give you a local anaesthetic. So be brave and we'll soon patch you nicely together.'

Shortly afterwards I was aware of a cut across my belly and heard a faint clatter of instruments. The next moment, it felt as though all my guts were being pulled out. It burned and seared and tore like red-hot pincers. I had never thought there could be such pain. I screamed like a madman and thought my eyes would start out of my head.

'Shut up,' roared the old surgeon. 'We haven't properly begun yet. Keep your howls for when there's something to howl about.'

When I got 'something to howl about' I don't know; I only know that when they were finished I had been in a world of torment to which few go. I was broken, crushed. They wheeled me into a ward, put me on a bed, gave me an injection and I fell asleep.

For the first fortnight I was aware of little that went on round me or happened to me; but very slowly my strength began to return. In the next bed lay an airman with bad burns. He was called Zepp. Then there were six badly wounded, of whom two died in the course of a few days. I had no idea what had happened to Stege, and no one could tell me.

Three weeks after the operation I was pronounced fit to move. I was put in a proper hospital train with real bunks and large windows out of which you could see, or rather those in the middle bunk could. As I had to have my dressings changed frequently, I was given one of these sought-after middle bunks. Above me lay my new friend Zepp, whose good spirits were a great help to me.

We were taken to Lwow, where Zepp and I were sent to No. 7 Reserve Hospital. The doctor said that my wound looked really well, and he smiled. The tempo there was no longer frantic, and the doctors had time to smile and talk to you properly. He pulled a couple of splinters out of my leg, making my nerves quiver, but then to my relief the nurse put the dressings back again. I was given nothing but gruel, and I came to so loathe it that I almost went mad; yet when I asked the doctor if I could have a little variety in my diet he patted my cheek and said, 'Later, my friend. Later.'

Zepp and I were in a ward for badly wounded. Day and night there was moaning and groaning, and it often stank appallingly of pus and putrescence. One day a young chap, who knew he was going to die and had already taken three tortuous weeks about it, got up, dragged himself out into the corridor and flung himself down the steps. It was horrible, because we could not get up and stop him. Zepp did try, but he fell a few steps from his own bed; we others rang the bell till it almost cracked.

That was a wretched time.

My stomach caused me appalling pain, and it was no joke, either, when the doctor dug about in the flesh of my leg to find little pieces of shell splinter. My temperature rose instead of going down, but even so the doctor said that I was making progress. 'All very well for you,' I thought sourly.

I woke in the middle of one night. My bandages felt wet and sticky. I asked Zepp to ring. The next moment a nurse came rushing in.

'What's wrong with you?' she whispered irately. 'Are you crazy ringing like that at this hour of the night.'

'My wound's burst open,' I replied. 'It has bled through the dressing.' I was almost beside myself with fear and in my mind's eye I could see my mother receiving the laconic card from the Army:

'He died like a hero for Führer and Fatherland.'

She pulled the covers to one side. Out of consideration for the others she did not put on the light, but just used her torch. Quickly and deftly she undid the bandages. It was quite quiet in the ward. A young chap at the far end muttered something in his sleep. Zepp sat up in bed, but the nurse shoved him back and told him to go to sleep. 'Sven and I can manage this much better alone,' she said and went for a basin of water. I gave Zepp a frightened look, and he looked back at me, equally scared. She came back and, without saying a word, washed me. She was smiling slightly to herself and gave just one look at my frightened face. 'This is nothing to be frightened about,' said she.

'That's all very well for you to say,' said I. 'You haven't got the haemorrhage.'

She did not reply, but just smiled rather mysteriously.

'Perhaps it isn't so bad?' I queried.

'It isn't bad at all,' she replied.

When she had finished she covered me up again. Then she stood there a moment looking at me.

'It wasn't blood,' said she.

'Wasn't blood?' said I. 'But I could feel . . .'

It will be long before I forget her little smile. I went red in the face and felt horribly embarrassed.

'You were dreaming, my friend. You are certainly getting better.' She gave me a pat on the chin and walked off with her basin.

'It must have been you he was dreaming of, Nurse!' chuckled Zepp.

'Now go to sleep, both of you!'

Then she was gone.

27

In the end I had to ask him to keep the rest till the morning, so that we could get some sleep before the entire night had gone. But it was not many minutes, before:

'Sven, are you asleep?'

I pulled my head right under the blankets.

'Sven!'

'Yes. What is it this time?'

'Margaret says there will be special one-year students' courses for the demobilised once the war is over. Do you know anything about that? Sven, come on and smoke a last cigarette with me. . . . Don't you think that Margaret is . . .'

'Oh, for God's sake!'

That night I almost got nicotine poisoning. He kept getting out of bed every other moment to come and sit on the edge of mine and explain everything that he and she were going to do once the filthy war was over.

Wishing You A Long Illness

It was one Thursday morning early in December 1943 that I was declared fit and told that on Saturday I was to leave and rejoin my unit.

'I am sorry to have to do it, my boy. By rights, you ought to have been here for at least another six weeks. Now you will have to manage as best you can. I don't know if you get much to eat up there; but you must eat what you can whenever you get a chance. You will only be able to stand up to it if you eat well and, preferably, a bit more than that.'

Thus the head doctor at the hospital in Truskawice. He was a good doctor and ran his hospital on the system that his patients were to stay there till they were fit, and when they were he tried to find excuses to keep them a bit longer. Now, however, he had had orders from the very highest quarters that at least fifty per cent of all patients were to be pronounced fit and sent back to their units. Yet, according to the regulations, if a man were pronounced fit when he was not, the doctor could be court-martialled – so that just shows how they can perform miracles up at the top. You take a certificate of fitness, a rubber stamp and a court-martial and – lo and behold! – the sick are fit and well. That these 'fit' men could be a catastrophic burden on their units by forcing their fellows to do nursing as well as everything else in the middle of a battle, was not a thing that occurred to any of those at the top.

The head doctor shook his head sorrowfully when he said goodbye to me.

Barbara wept when I came and told her the sad news. I was so bitter and depressed that I felt no urge to comfort her. It would have been false to have tried anything so silly as comforting a woman in love whom you love. That at least is what I thought at that moment. I confined myself to drowning it all in fierce sensualism. The door was not locked, but I believe that neither of us would have worried if the entire German people had walked in. We were in the right. The people had required – or at least they had let it be done in its name – so much of us that we had a right to demand a little in return: and we asked only that, but that they must let us keep, and it was not a thing we took from anyone. I remained lying on her bed when she hurried off to her ward on duty, and there I smoked a cigarette and calmly thought over my position.

Actually there was nothing to think over, unless I intended to desert. I was not afraid of doing that; but neither was I really afraid of going back. I was no longer afraid of anything, only possessed by a cold, fierce hatred of all that we all hated under the common denomination: 'the filthy war'. No longer being afraid of anything, I might just as well go and study the phenomena from the angle of calm, disinterested bitterness, from which you can observe accurately.

As I was in the middle of my cigarette Margaret came rushing in and flung herself sobbing on to her bed, without noticing me. She had a letter in her hand.

So Hugo Stege had been killed.

I said that to myself and felt no surprise. I had no need to read the letter. Hugo was dead.

Without speaking, I shoved cigarettes and matches across to her. She started up in a fright.

'Oh, are you there? Sorry, I didn't see you.'

'Skip that,' said I. 'Lock the door while I get dressed. I shan't be two minutes.'

So I dressed, while she lay there sobbing. Then I unlocked the door and read the letter:

Eastern Front, November 1943.

Feldpostnummer 23645
Feldwebel Willie Beier.

My dear Miss Margaret Schneider,

I am writing to you, as Hugo Stege's friend and comrade, to tell you the grievous news that he has fallen. He has told me so many nice things about you, so that I understand only too well what great and awful grief this letter must bring to you.

Perhaps it may be some comfort to you to know how it happened.

Early one morning, when we were out on patrol with our armoured car, we were suddenly fired on. A bullet struck your fiancé right on the temple, and he was killed instantly. In death he was still smiling that fine smile of his, so you will see that he did not suffer. Now, you must not despair; you are young and you must promise me to forget as soon as you can. Life undoubtedly holds many bright, happy days for you yet, and the wisest and only right thing for you to do – though at the moment you may not like my advice – is to find a young man whom you will come to love as much as you now love Hugo. For the sake of your fallen beloved and my friend, don't cry, for that will only make him sad, if he can see it. No, smile, and just think how much he has been spared. It is an ill wind – What happens to our dead ones we do not know, but we *do* know that they are well off.

209

With my whole heart I sympathise with you.

Yours very sincerely,
WILLIE BEIER

How like The Old Un that letter, with its paternal kindness, was. The same post had also brought a letter for me.

Dear old boy,

Thanks for your letters. We got five in a batch. Unfortunately there is only time for a short card, for we are in the midst of some pretty good filth. If Ivan isn't attacking, we are. There's no peace. It's pure hell. Do what you can to stay in the rear as long as possible.

Stege is dead and Titch missing without trace, having vanished during an attack. As far as that goes, I have written to Margaret telling her that he fell with a bullet in his head – but you know how a tank soldier leaves this vale of sorrow. Poor Stege had both legs burned off. It wasn't pleasant listening to him, during the ten or twelve hours it took him to die. It's incredible where they get the strength to scream so long.

Before this rotten war's over we will probably all have kicked the bucket, and so the Party bigwigs, the generals and the rest who have kept out of it will get all the laurels – and everything else.

We are due to march now, so, dear Sven, keep in the rear ranks in your hospital, so that at least one of the right sort is somewhere, where he has a chance of surviving. And don't forget that we have promised each other to write a book about this whole filthy business.

Kindest regards from
Porta and Pluto and your Old Un.

That last evening we had avocat and cakes and there was nice, soft music on the wireless. Barbara had been let off duty. But we could not get the party going. There was a storm howling outside, and rain lashed the windows in angry scurries. Zepp gazed sadly into his glass and said:

'On such an evening I am almost glad of my paralysis. Think of being in a trench in this weather.'

Margaret went up to Elizabeth's to sleep so that Barbara and I could be on our own that last night. As Margaret was about to go out of the door with her night things she put her arm round my neck, and, looking at me with tears glistening in her eyes, said gravely:

'Sven, you must be careful out there. The Old Un mustn't have to write to Barbara, too, in a few weeks' time.'

Then she gave me a kiss and vanished swiftly through the door.

The next morning I dragged on the hated uniform and long grey overcoat. My haversack was heavy with good things the girls had stuffed into it: two big cakes Barbara had made herself, two jars of jam from Elizabeth, smoked ham from Margaret, a tin of pears from Zepp. Tears caught in my throat, and, with the best will in the world, I could not see how I was ever going to want to eat any of it. Then I strapped my heavy army pistol round my waist, hung the gasmask container over my shoulder, and, last of all, set my little black forage cap on my head.

All three girls came with me to the station. I kissed tears from Barbara's eyes.

'Don't cry, Babs; you should laugh. Remember,' I went on urgently, 'this isn't farewell. It's au revoir.'

'Sven, promise me to take care of yourself.'

When the whistle blew, all three kissed me, a last pledge of friendship, of love.

Farewell, Truskawice! Farewell, my oasis. Farewell, you peaceful rooms with clean, cool beds. Farewell, you women with fragrant, glossy hair.

I pressed my forehead to the cold, damp window-pane in the compartment, and the tears rolled down my cheeks.

28

An icy hand clutched at my heart when I saw how changed he was. His hair was quite grey, his skin yellow, and there were black rims round his tired eyes. He was thin and bent, and his uniform hung on him, now far too big. Poor, poor Old Un!

Pluto looked just like The Old Un.

Von Barring looked just as they did.

They all looked like that.

All?

There were not many left.

We had been six thousand strong when we first came out.

Now there were seven of us – seven men.

The War Continues According To Plan

They sat for a moment looking at the cake, as if it were something sublime and sacred. Eventually Porta plucked up courage, but The Old Un hit his fingers with a spoon.

'A cake that has been baked by real girls must be eaten with morality, decorum, and feeling, not with mucky fingers.'

And so we laid a proper table, with a couple of towels for a cloth and the lids of our mess-kids for plates. We washed and cleaned our nails and did our hair, brushed our uniforms and polished our boots, and so, twenty minutes later, we sat down to table and solemnly ate Barbara's cake and drank Margaret's avocat.

'Was it nice?'

'Yes, it was very, very nice.'

We looked at each other. I looked at their expectant, furrowed, tense faces. Now you must give the best that is in you, I told myself. I considered for quite a while before I began:

'Their clothes were cleaner than any clothes you have seen.

When they bent over your bed to make it, or pulled the sheet tight under you, you smelt a smell of freshly ironed, slightly starched linen that has just been taken out of a linen cupboard. It smelled entirely free of dirt, dry, almost as though very slightly scorched. When they were not on duty they wore their own clothes, and those were just as clean, and they smelled of something light and warm and yet at the same time cool. They had dresses. I saw a light-blue silk dress with white and light-grey birds on it. It had short sleeves, and it was gathered at the neck in a mass of puckers, so that it fell in folds over her breast and back. When you pulled a white silk cord, it fell off her shoulders, but then you had forgotten the two small strings on the short puff sleeves. That was her dress, the one I had. Margaret, who was Stege's, I remember best in a flame-red dress of some thin woollen material, that clung to her body, as though it were painted on her. She was like a flame. And there was a girl who wore a skirt that swung on her hips and was always a quarter of a revolution behind when she turned. The one in the light-blue silk dress,' I went on in what was almost a chant, while I shut my eyes and concentrated on seeing Barbara, 'that is, the one I had, when you had pulled that string and she had pulled the two small ones, and you had found the two press-studs and the hook and eye at the side and undone them, then the whole dress fell as something airy and soft, and she stood there inside a ring of light blue that had formed round her feet. The girls were just as clean as their clothes, and smelled wonderfully of mitsouka perfume . . .'

'Mitsouka?'

'Yes, Porta; let me explain, so that you and the others will understand. The girls were as clean as a gun just before parade in barracks. Their hair glistened like the Danube on a winter's night, when the moonbeams are making the ice gleam like a million diamonds. And their bodies smelled like the forest behind Beresina on a spring morning just after rain. Can you understand that?'

For several hours I had to tell them of the wonderful world where I had been. They could not hear enough.

'There is one thing I cannot rightly understand,' said Pluto.

213

'How is it that you, who have been living like an oriental prince, who have guzzled cakes and roast duck and swilled wine and have had a harem to feed you the fat of the land in suitable small bits, how is it that you are as thin as a rail?'

So then I had to tell them how, after my wounds had healed, I, Stege, Zepp and another man, had bought some water for three hundred cigarettes and drunk it. Two kinds of water, to be truthful; one with typhoid, the other with cholera. 'Didn't Stege tell you?' I asked. 'We became ill with a vengeance. Zepp is still paralysed below the waist, and the fourth man died. I was unconscious for nineteen days, and after that I refused to eat. Barbara and a Polish wardmaid forcibly fed me, one spoonful at a time, for a fortnight. The doctor gave me up five times. They gave me injections of all sorts of medicines and salt water and glucose. Now I have been discharged six weeks too early. Heil Hitler!'

'Did they have stockings with slipper heels too?'

'French heels? Yes.' The others shook their heads and looked despairingly at each other.

'You know, Sven, that all leave is stopped,' said Porta concisely, as though that explained something, though what I did not understand.

'Porta,' said I, 'there's one thing I don't understand.'

'What is it?'

'If only I knew. Something has happened to you, I don't know what. You have been through quite a lot, I can see. There's a pretty strong smell of filth on this sector. But it can't be that alone. There must be something more. It was the same with Barring when I reported back. Why haven't I heard one word of filth from you, Porta?'

They looked at me. Then they looked at each other; or, rather, they looked past each other, as you do at the mention of things of which you do not dare speak. The atmosphere in that dusky, lousy cottage became unreal and terrifying. Porta got up and stood with his back to us, facing the window.

'Old Un,' said I, appalled, 'tell me, what's wrong? You look as though you were at your grandmother's funeral. As if you were dead.'

214

At that word 'dead' something went click in my brain. I am not superstitious, and what happened in my thoughts is not in the least remarkable or inexplicable.

I suddenly realised that they were dead, dead without there being any sensational mystery about it. They had given up hope of ever getting home alive. They regarded everything, including their own lives, as hopeless. To them my tale must have been about something that did not exist. Their dreams of the glorious great collapse had been shattered. The revolution there was to have been when they got home, and which was to have been over in fourteen full and bloody days, was a chimera, a phantom ship on the black sea of death. Porta's one firm anchorage in existence, his refuge, the warmth of the female belly, even that had lost its significance. That does not mean that Porta's behaviour had become less immoral, for whenever he glimpsed a rounded backside he still smacked it, and both took and gave. But, as he himself said, a few days later – he had just been with the farmer's girl and was describing the proceedings in his usual graphic manner, when he suddenly stopped in the middle of a sentence and looked round at us:

'It used sometimes to be as though I stood there watching myself. I don't do that now. I stand and look out of the window, while Herr Porta, by God's grace, lies there rogering. If there only were something interesting to look at through the window: the fire brigade practising, or if Hitler were having half his moustache shaved off before going to make a speech – but there isn't anything to look at, and I would be quite unmoved, even if there were. You don't understand, of course, but that doesn't matter, as I don't either.'

For many days I went about trying to cast off this grim conviction that they were dead men, for I could not very well discuss it with them. Then one day I asked them point-blank if what I felt was sheer imagination or whether they really were so utterly passive as they appeared to me, even though on the face of it we were spending our time just as before.

'I don't really know what to answer,' said The Old Un.

'All leave is stopped,' said Porta.

'There are seven of us left out of a regiment, which numbered six thousand men when we set out in 1941,' and he ticked them off on his fingers: 'Oberst von Lindenau, Oberstleutnant Hinka, Hauptmann von Barring, plus the honoured members of this company. Allah is great, but the casualty lists are greater.'

'Halleluja and cross your— !'

'Amen!'

'Yes,' said I, and my voice was a shade shrill, while I took a breath, with fear in the pit of my stomach. 'But you can't let down the book we have promised each other to write.'

They looked at me. My gaze flitted in panic from one to the other. They did not know me, or rather they knew me better than I knew myself, and they had the profoundest, calmest sympathy for me, because I still cherished stupid hopes and had an anxious, pounding heart, over which the winds blew.

'When you write our book,' said Porta, screwing his flute together, 'give all the girls my kind regards. There won't be a soul that will bother to read it, for you can't offer the esteemed public books that aren't about little Miss Switchboard and the boss's stalwart son in a double-room. Or she's a nurse and he the head surgeon. But in any event, none of the characters can be lousy. As I said, you'll never get rich off our book. People just don't care. So you'll have to put your hand in your own pocket when you drink yourself tight on our account the day you finish it.'

29

Whilst in these positions Christmas 1943 came, and we tried to make it as festive as we could. We had planted a little firtree in an empty ammunition box . . .

Soviet Propaganda At The Front

The propaganda sent over from the other side was fantastic in its invention. At times it presented us with such monstrous tales as no normal person could have swallowed, but none of us was normal, so they never failed in their effect. It put us into a ferment, filled us with doubt and depression at our desperate situation, our unworthy circumstances, and its Russian authors could record a rich harvest. By that I do not mean so much the men who ran across and let themselves be taken prisoner – sometimes whole units went, headed by their NCOs. Those could be counted. As far as most of us were concerned, Prussian discipline and Goebbels' propaganda about the horrors of conditions in the Soviet Union had us in a stranglehold; and even without that, the little common sense we still retained told us that, considering the way in which the German Army had spoiled and ravaged the lands of Russia, we could scarcely expect to be received with such open arms as the blandishing of the trench loudspeakers sought to persuade us would be the case. What I meant was that the Russian propaganda had a paralysing effect on the men who preferred to remain where they were. It left our minds torn and drained.

Mostly the Russians made use of the penetrating, objective argument that stuck in your mind, however much you said to yourself and the others: propaganda! It was propaganda, but it was well founded – they had their proofs.

The Russian loudspeakers bawled out:

'German comrades! Come across to your Russian friends! Why lie there freezing? Come over to us and get a warm bed and a decent room. Pretty women will see to it that you lack for nothing. You will be given rations three times what the Nazis give you. Grefreiter Freiburg will now come to the microphone and tell you that what we say is true. He has been with us for two years. He has visited all our prisoner-of-war camps and seen that they were not in the least like prisoner camps, as you imagine them. Our camps are in big hotels or holiday camps, and the most is two men and two women in a room. But here is Grefreiter Freiburg, so you can hear him for yourselves.'

Shortly afterwards a hearty voice roared out:

'Hallo, Comrades of the 27th Tank Regiment. This is Grefreiter Jürgen Freiburg of the 309th Grenadier Regiment. I was born on May 20th, 1916, in Leipzig and lived at Adlerstrasse 7 in Dresden. I have been a prisoner of the Russians since August 1941, and it has been a lovely time. I have been in almost every camp in Russia, and we have everything the heart can desire.'

Then for over an hour he described the paradise in which he was. Among other things he read out the menus for a whole week, which included caviare, roast pork, goose and pigeon. Our mouths watered at the mere mention of such food.

One evening they rigged up a big film screen on the parapet of the trench and proceeded to show a film that made many of us quite sick and crazy. We saw German prisoners of war sitting in an elegant salon. We then followed a couple of them from the moment they were taken prisoner, saw them being waited upon like princes in splendid rooms, where were huge tables laden with mountains of glorious food, that was photographed from every conceivable angle and from quite close. Many of us sat munching without realising it, as these wonders of photography were displayed, and I almost believe that if they had kept showing those pictures of food the entire 27th Tank Regiment would have rushed the screen.

The next scene was played in a luxurious room dominated by an enormous bed. A pretty young woman slowly undressed in front of a German infantryman. She slipped off garment after garment, turning and twisting in front of the soldier. When she was quite naked she undressed the soldier; and then followed a pornographic séance that it would be difficult to match for lewdness. There was silence over the German lines. Many sighed and uttered little noises without realising it. It was dreadful to listen to.

'Bravo, bravo, Ivan!' we shouted. 'Let's have it again. Encore! Encore!'

We shouted and clapped rhythmically.

Then the loudspeaker crackled and we fell silent:

'Comrades. Don't let yourselves be murdered for a cause that is not yours. Let the SS bandits and Göring's drawing-room heroes, who are enjoying life in the occupied countries, let them fight for Hitler and his gang. You old veterans of the proper German Army are too good for this swinishness. Come over to us, come on! Those of you who would like to join the Red Army and fight for your true rights will have the same rank as you now hold. But for that you must come now!'

At other times they demonstrated, objectively and without comment how Hitler had broken all his fine promises. Or a Russian doctor told us how to simulate illnesses or contract real diseases.

'Comrades, throw away your weapons and come across to us! It's stupid of you to go on fighting. Cannot you see how you are being misused by the Nazi swine? Don't you know that one-third of the German Wehrmacht is now enjoying life for the fourth year in the occupied countries, eating themselves fat, while you must hunger and freeze? The second third is at home in Germany sleeping with your girls, while you, the last third, have to endure hellish privations here, in the great fatherland of your Russian comrades.'

'Hear! Hear!' we howled, and flung our helmets into the air to show our enthusiastic agreement with so truthful a statement.

A whole Saxon Division went across, headed by its colonel. A Thuringian Reserve Regiment in the sector next to ours went over with all its officers.

But it also happened, and quite often, that Russian deserters came across to us, and that Germans who had been taken prisoner made their way back, as I had once done. Naturally they had no tales of luxury hotels to tell, nor of splendid holiday resorts. Most of them had been through a lot, as I had: in some camps they had been treated decently, else-where appallingly; in some places the Russians had been eager to realise the object of their propaganda and win the prisoners of war over to the ideals and doctrine of socialism; in others they made no attempt to do so at all, and elsewhere again they were quite inhuman, often animated with a thoroughly understandable desire for vengeance, which I cannot find it in me to condemn. The way the Russians were slaughtered, for example, when the SS went into action beggars all description and reason, so when the day of wrath dawned for the beaten Nazis the sorely tried victors exacted vengeance for a large sum of torment and suffering. I do not mention this in order to make excuses or embellish a tragedy, or explain anything away. I mention it so as to show that it is not difficult to find proof for what are euphemistically called 'Russian conditions' – but with that kind of proof you can prove that 'Russian conditions' prevail in every country that has been at war.

Sometimes things happened that left us open-mouthed with amazement. For example, during one attack some of our sixteen- and seventeen-year-olds were taken prisoner. The very next day the Russians sent them back, having first lopped the legs of their trousers, so that they were like boys' shorts. On the back of one was pinned this note:

The Red Army does not fight against children; therefore we are sending these back and request you to send them on – home to their mothers, so that they may finish being suckled.

Greetings from the Red Army.

Or that business of the old Unteroffizier.

In No. 3 Company they had an elderly man who was an Unteroffizier. One day he received a telegram informing him that his wife and three children had been killed during an air raid on Berlin. He went at once to his company commander and applied for leave; but although his company commander did his best, the application was refused.

In his fury and despair the elderly Unteroffizier deserted, but to our amazement he was back again the next day. He told us that the Russian divisional commander for the sector facing us had himself given the Unteroffizier leave. We thought that the old man had gone off his head, but to our surprise he had both a sealed letter addressed to our colonel and a complete set of Russian leave papers, properly filled in and signed, made out for fourteen days and travelling time to and from Berlin. The Russian had even filled in the correct times of the trains he was to travel by. Von Barring later told me what was in the letter to Oberst von Lindenau. The text was as follows:

Dear Oberst,

We are profoundly surprised that things are now so bad with the German Army that you cannot even give leave to a poor Unteroffizier, who, like this one, has lost everything. The Red Army, however, will give its prisoner fourteen days' leave, and at the same time releases him altogether.
I am fully aware that you, Oberst von Lindenau, will perhaps now punish this Unteroffizier for fraternising with the enemy, but I suggest to you that for this once you wink at what has happened and see to it that he is able to go home on leave. Personally, I consider that he has been punished enough already through having lost everything during that raid on Berlin.

STEPAN KONSTANTINOWICH RADION
Lieutenant-General
Commanding 61 Infantry Division of the Red Army.

This letter and the man's Russian leave papers were sent to our divisional commander, Generalleutnant von Rechtnagel, for him to decide on so extraordinary an affair as that of this Unteroffizier who had gone across to the enemy and by him been granted leave. For the next few days the entire 27th Tank Regiment waited anxiously for the outcome. The Russians kept asking through their loudspeaker whether the man had been given his leave, and each time we had to answer no. Bets were made about it. Most of us thought that the man would be shot. They were simply bound to punish him. That could not be avoided without rewriting the entire military code.

Finally our suspense was relieved: the man was granted his leave and sentenced to three days' strict arrest for having left his post without authorisation. This was to be served when he came back from leave.

The Russians had other, more robust means of making propaganda. For example they had what they called 'radio transmissions'. These began with a skit on a German wireless programme, often pretty coarse, but none the less witty and effective. Then came the request programme. A well-trained speaker's voice said:

'You will now hear a request concert of various instruments. First a composition on lighter instruments.'

At that a score of machine-guns and light mortars started firing and tore the parapet of our trench to pieces, sending earth spurting round our ears.

'And now, honoured listeners, you will hear a phantasia on the Stalin organ.'

The next moment it was as though the world were coming to an end; the nerve-shattering rocket shells of the famous 'organ' came howling down upon us and exploded with deafening bangs.

'And for a festive finale we have chosen a potpourri of all instruments in our large and well-rehearsed symphony orchestra.'

Oh, that smiling, chatty voice!

The whole sector quivered with horror during the hurricane that was then unleashed upon us. As we crouched down, each kept an eye on his next-door man, ready to knock him out the moment he showed signs of falling victim to the frenzy of shell-shock.

There were various units of Russian volunteers in the German Army. As well as General Vlasov's notorious divisions of traitors, there were some Cossack regiments that were sheer devils when it came to mishandling Russians who fell into their clutches. The most horrifying of all, however, was a women's battalion. These harpies used to pull the clothes off their prisoners and tie them to a table or a bed, whereupon they excited the poor wretches till they were willy-nilly able to satisfy the others' bestial sexual urges. The usual end of the debauch was that either they cut off their victim's penis and stuck it in his mouth, or they crushed his testicles with a hammer. This last Porta one day witnessed, and what he saw earned seven of the women a bullet through their heads from his sniper's rifle that same night.

When the Russians got hold of any of these Cossacks or *Flintenweiber* they paid them out in their own coin. The most appalling sadism flourished and spread like fungus. There were also Ukrainians enrolled in independent battalions in the SS, and others incorporated individually in German regiments and known as Hiwis (*hilfswillige*), and one and all grew more and more desperate and unhappy the nearer the war drew towards the inevitable, and to them fearful, end. They had put their money on the wrong horse, whether out of conviction or calculation, and the realisation was making mad beasts of them.

It naturally happened that some of these Russian deserters grew tired of the German discipline and deserted back to the Russians. What happened to them then we never succeeded in discovering. Presumably they were hanged for high treason. Then the Russians put a sudden and radical end to this traffic. They returned all Russian and Ukrainian deserters to us by the simple expedient of flying them in over the German lines and there chucking them out. In the breast-pocket of each was a yellow service envelope and delivery note:

Military Police Unit 174 hereby returns
   SS Volunteer Boris Petrovich Turgoiski
   born March 18, 1919, in Tiflis.

He deserted on December 27, 1943, at Lebed from 18th SS Battalion and was taken by 192 Rifle Regiment of the Red Army.

This deserter is being returned to the German Army by Lieutenant Barowich, pilot of the Red Army Air Force.

Receipt

Receipt is hereby acknowledged of deserter

Rank . . . . . .   Name . . . . . .   Unit . . . . . .

It is requested that the receipt on completion be returned to the nearest unit of the Red Army.

Such atrocities had a stupefying effect on one. For a long time I went about in a state of queer, dull resignation and was on the point of being infected by my companions' belief that we were all doomed and that nothing mattered at all, since all men were evil and sinister without exception.

Hauptmann von Barring began to drink.

30

Only the machine-guns had been removed. We got hold of the farmer and asked him how the devil the tank had got into his barn. Delightedly he showed us a paper on which was written in German:

'We, the crew, have sold this tin-box to Farmer Peter Alexandrowich for a cow, both being in a good serviceable state.

Heil Hitler!
A Kiss on the— , dear Party Member.'

In almost every farm of the Ukraine, big or small, you could expect to find a German car or vehicle of some kind.

Retreat From Kiev

The reason they gave was that a SS-Untersturmführer had been killed just outside the village. As a warning to others the SS commander had ordered that every man and woman between the ages of fourteen and sixty be hanged. They were hauled up into a couple of lorries, which backed in under some gallows; ropes were placed round their necks and the lorries drove away.

A loud, distinct growl rose from our ranks as we marched past. The SS squinted nervously at us and took a tighter grip of their weapons, while our officers urged us on, so as to avoid a clash.

The conflict between the Army and the SS was on the point of becoming an open one. Himmler had crushed all attempts to create an organised underground movement against the régime, whose watchdog he was, but to no purpose, for he had not identified his enemy. In fact, he had crushed the wrong ones. The real enemy – though naturally he could not know that – was the weapon of terror that he thought he could use as he saw fit. This, in fact, was employed quite without plan, and in the end it became his undoing. It was this that roused German resistance until it became an underground movement, whose chronicles have not been written, and never can be, because there are no records. It was not an organised movement, but it was there, and it did its work in the same inconspicuous and seemingly fortuitous manner, as when we liquidated the swine Meier.

The Russians had occupied half Kiev when we moved in. In the city we divided up into small combat groups, which penetrated independently into the different streets. I rattled along in my tank just behind those of Porta and The Old Un. We went down Wosduchffotskoje, then crossed a railway line and along Djakowa Street, all the houses in which were occupied by the Germans; then we turned out towards Pavolo at the northern end of the city. Down narrow streets and alleys we drove, and then, just as day was breaking, we reached an old factory.

In the great yard we discovered eighteen T34s and five KW2s lined up side by side, while their crews were paraded for roll-call in front of their tanks. The sudden apparition of our three tanks not twenty yards away paralysed them.

I pulled our inexperienced Unteroffizier away from the sighting apparatus, and flame-thrower, machine-guns and gun roared out together. The nicely paraded company went down like ninepins, and within a short space of time all the Russian tanks were ablaze. After that we drove full pelt down a couple of side streets, encountered a company of infantry and disposed of them, using first our flame-throwers, then machine-guns, while the steel tracks of our tanks attended to the few survivors.

On we went, crushing everything that came in our way. Suddenly there was a loud bang and The Old Un's tank stopped with a broken track. I swung round at full speed and thundered down a side street to get in the rear of the Russian anti-tank gun. This, and its crew of eight, I simply ran down; but they had already set fire to The Old Un's tank and killed two of his crew. The Old Un came into my tank, and the other two went into Porta's.

We continued thus all day. It was exhausting, monotonous, and a constant strain that nearly drove us mad. When we got back we learned that No. 5 Company had lost all its tanks and that Oberst von Lindenau had been burned to death.

Kiev was burning.

There is no more nerve-racking or brutal form of warfare than street fighting. You never really know what you are up against, as you dart from door to door, sometimes suddenly having to get into cover behind a cement lamp-post, because howling, whistling, banging things are being hurled at you from the houses.

On several occasions we had to leave a house because it had collapsed under us, so that we fell three or four stories. We fought savage hand-to-hand battles, using knives and spades, and the whole time the city was burning; always there were flames round us, and bangs and shrieks, and people getting frost-bitten because the temperature was minus 40–50°C.

The huge iron bridge across the Dnieper had been blown up, and only twisted bits of steel protruded from the water. The city's pride, the wireless station with its steel masts, was a pile of broken iron and twisted cables. In the great abattoirs thousands of carcasses were drenched with acid. Hundreds of tons of sunflower seed and millet-oil were spoiled with petrol and set alight. The huge locomotive shops resembled an elephants' graveyard.

During the withdrawal our hatred of the SS flared up and found open expression. Things reached the stage that no SS unit dared move up during an attack if ordinary army troops were behind it. It happened repeatedly that when Russians and Germans were blazing away at each other from their respective sides of a street, and an SS unit came creeping up it, there would be a pause in the fighting to allow the Germans to mow down the SS. Once they had been dealt with the fighting would be resumed.

Early one morning, shortly before daybreak, we reached a sector near Berditschev, where things were about to happen.

As well as our regiment, there was a reserve infantry regiment there. Having lost our tanks, we were being used as infantry.

We of the 27th Regiment at once crawled out into no-man's-land, which was always our place. We dug ourselves narrow one-man fox-holes, in which we could lie with impunity while the Russian tanks rolled across. The idea was that, once the tanks had passed, we were to engage the infantry following them with our machine-guns, flame-throwers and possibly close-combat weapons, bayonet and spade.

In the trenches behind us our grenadiers were being subjected to violent shelling. Hour after hour passed and the artillery duel only increased in intensity; then at three o'clock there was a sudden, brief pause and the barrage was moved to just behind the front lines and resumed with the intensity of a hurricane.

The sight that now met our horrified eyes almost made us swoon. Through the low-lying mist great herds of T34s came thundering towards us, and behind them stormed a brown mass of infantry with fixed bayonets.

Suddenly it became dark in my hole and some earth trickled down over me. A cold sweat broke out on my forehead and my knees began to shake. Again a tank rolled over above me, and as soon as it had gone, another was there.

Then the machine-guns began, accompanied by the rumble of the guns. That meant that they were engaged by our grenadiers and anti-tank guns.

I did not dare stick my head out of the hole and have a look in case a T34 should come along and decapitate me, but when the machine-gun in the hole next to mine began to chatter I had to straighten up.

About fifty yards away I saw a Russian heavy machine-gun in position with twelve men lying round it. In an instant I had my flame-thrower aimed and pressed the trigger. There was a hollow rumble as the red flame shot at them. Two of them reared half up and dropped again, blazing furiously. Then I came under fire from another machine-gun a little to my right, and I had to duck quickly, stopping the flame-thrower.

228

Carefully I eased the muzzle of the flame-thrower over the edge of my hole, used my periscope to aim it and pressed the trigger. The machine-gun fell silent.

Then came the next wave of tanks, and this time it was worse, for they knew that we were in the holes. The method of close-combat between the infantryman and the seventy-ton tank is this: the infantryman, fearless in accordance with the regulations, jumps out of his hole, rushes at the tank from *in front* and flings himself on to its bows, clinging fast to its big towing-hook with one hand, while his other clasps a magnetic bomb.

The violent effort of heaving myself up on to the huge tank that was tearing along at full speed made me break out into a sweat. Fortunately for such as I, the crew of a T34 can see nothing within a radius of ten feet from their tank. Several times I was almost thrown off, my hands were torn and bleeding and my nails broken. But the dauntless warrior got up and stuck the bomb against the steel rail that runs round the rear-most part of the turret. Then he pulled the release-cord, jumped off and flung himself into a shell-hole, where lay a dozen of the grenadiers with a machine-gun. Five seconds later there was a hollow roar from the tank, which stopped with its nose in a shell-hole. Its entire crew were killed instantly by the blast of the powerful magnetic bomb.

When the next T34 came thundering along the fearless soldier picked up one of the mines the grenadiers had with them and swung himself neatly on to the tank, breaking several more nails. That sort of thing becomes almost routine. How effective the routine was I only realised when a piece of tank-turret, having described a curve through the air, dropped a foot from me with a mighty smack. It cannot have weighed less than half a ton.

Our anti-tank artillery drove the enemy tanks back, pursued by mines and magnetic bombs. Then the Russian guns began to speak, and the grenadiers and all the new boys in the 27th Regiment went off their heads. They took to their heels and ran in headlong flight in all directions. Even we old sweats were infected, and followed their example. The

Russian infantry at once set off in pursuit and came storming after us with wild shouts of: 'Uray Stalino! Uray Stalino!'

An elderly major tried to halt us and force us to turn and face the Russians, but his automatic pistol was wrenched from his hands, and he was trampled to death by panic-stricken soldiers. What suddenly brought us to our senses and made us halt I do not know, but halt we did; and so we fought the Russians hand-to-hand. I seized a Mongol's rifle with both hands and tried to wrest it from him. We bit and snarled at each other like two animals, for we knew that one of us must die. Possessed by a mad frenzy, I got the rifle and, like lightning, plunged the bayonet into his back. He fell forward with a bellow, tearing the rifle from my hands. I had to put my foot on him to pull the bayonet out. Having kicked him off it, I stormed on, bellowing like a bull and screeching like a mad-man, the bayonet held horizontal in front of me. I ran into a Russian with such force that the bayonet protruded from his back. He screamed, with his mouth wide open. There was nothing but these bellows and screams, all animal noises, and contorted faces.

Suddenly the blood froze in my veins. With mouth agape I stared up into the sky, where a dense shoal of howling, glowing rockets came driving at us with flaming tails of fire behind them, screeching worse than all the evil spirits of Hell, a ghastly noise that seemed to be slowly pulling every nerve out of my body. Every one of us lay pressed to the ground, and we howled with nameless terror, bit and kicked. It was the Stalin organ, the most terrifying instrument of all time.

After thirty-six hours' fighting the Russian attack flagged and ebbed, and the final result was that both we and the Russians were back in our former positions. Then began a tremendous artillery duel, a hurricane that lasted for six days and nights and cost many their reason. A small wood was razed to the ground in two hours, so completely that there was nothing to show that there ever had been a wood at that spot. We sat in our dug-outs staring into space with sickly bloodshot eyes. Talk was impossible, for you could not make your neighbour hear, even if you bellowed at the top of your voice.

It was the sight of Porta and The Old Un that saved me from going off my head. I had only to look at them sitting quite unaffected by the exploding, deafening inferno, and I became calm. The Old Un puffed at his pipe, and Porta played on his flute, with the cat Stalin curled up on his lap. No one, not even Porta, could hear a note of what he played, but he played on in grave concentration, paying no attention to the uproar. Perhaps he had achieved such a degree of detachment that he actually could hear what he was playing.

In the forenoon of the fourth day von Barring appeared in our dug-out. He looked more ill than ever. The Old Un had told us that he was suffering from pernicious dysentery and had to spend most of the day sitting with his trousers round his knees, and also something had gone wrong with his kidneys. To all appearances he had not long left.

He gave The Old Un a paper on which was written:

'We must get the men a meal. I have already sent four parties for rations, but they have not come back. Will you and your two comrades try it? We must have the food fetched. You three are my last hope.'

We looked at each other and at von Barring, who sat there exhaustedly, his head in his hands. The Old Un shrugged his shoulders and nodded. He was given a report to take, telling our HQ that our telephone had been shot to pieces.

It was an indescribable sight we saw, as, with the food-buckets strapped to our backs, we dived out into the shattered trench. It was like a ploughed-up lunar landscape. An incessant rain of fire and steel was coming out of the dark sky. The clouds hung low and threatening. The Old Un gave a worried shake of his head. Porta nodded indifferently, and then we jumped up and out of the trench.

It took us six and a half hours to cover the artillery belt that was four kilometres wide, and seven hours to make our way back with full food-buckets. It was pork and yellow peas.

We ourselves ate at the field kitchen, ate and ate and ate, till even the cooks began to have scruples. Porta stuffed a piece of

231

boiling, quivering meat into either trouser pocket, remarking that we must also think of the evening. The buckets felt darned heavy when we strapped them on again. Porta put Stalin into the pocket he had made on the outside of his great-coat, and there he sat looking out over the edge, a red cat with a forage cap tied on its head.

I have also fought deep underground. The Russians had started mining under our positions. If we put our ears to the floor of the dug-out we could hear the thud, thud, thud of their picks, as they worked down there. It became our task to dig down to them, kill their miners and undermine the Russian positions instead.

We were lying in a gallery, and we could hear the Russians working: thud, thud, thud.

All at once there was silence. We listened, all our senses strained to the utmost. Had they finished, and would we in a short while hear a muffled roar, after which the earth would cave in on us?

We listened for a quarter of an hour, and that is a long time to sit listening for a noise that does not come, when otherwise there is absolute silence.

We listened for an hour.

Then the thuds began again. It was like a new lease of life. I heard The Old Un draw a deep breath of relief behind me.

We prepared to go into action.

Softly The Old Un whispered to those who were young and inexperienced:

'Remember when you stab with a knife, never stab between the ribs, the knife just sticks there. Stab in the neck or in the belly, preferably obliquely down into the groin, cutting up as you pull out.'

Cautiously we made our way down the long tunnels that in places were so narrow that we had to crawl on our bellies. Turning one corner, we almost ran into four Russians, who were lying ten feet away busily working with their picks. Without a sound we crept up behind them and stabbed them. All round us in the communicating galleries our people lay waiting for the Russian sappers, who now came crawling up, having smelled a rat. The Old Un, Porta, I and six others crawled forward to the end of a tunnel, from which we could see a gang of eight at work. While the others hid against the side of the tunnel, Porta called in Russian:

'Comrades, hurry and come up. We're being relieved.'

The Russians peered in surprise at the dark tunnel, but did not see us. One of them called back:

'Are we all to come?'

'Yes. Hurry up! The others are all up already. They're waiting for you.'

We struck them down as they came abreast of us. Our knives glinted in the light of their sleepy torches. One of them managed to drive his short pick into the belly of one of our boys, who started to scream, so that we had to cut his throat.

They threw a lot of explosives down at us.

One day we buried Pluto. We could not find his head, but the rest was there.

It fell to the 27th Regiment to remain behind in an evacuated sector, one hundred and twenty kilometres long, to camouflage a big withdrawal. The positions on this sector were built-up above ground, and we were to see that for the next twenty-four hours the stoves were kept alight and the chimneys smoking, and every now and again we were to fire a few bursts of machine-gun fire at the Russians. Besides doing this, we were to make booby-traps. Our company was allotted twenty kilometres; there were two hundred of us. We had strict orders that under no circumstances must we leave our positions unless the Russians actually entered our trenches.

We were thirty in our platoon, facing four thousand five hundred Siberian riflemen, the most feared of all the troops in the Red Army.

We set about our preparations. Every door was connected with mines that exploded the moment the door was opened or shut. An innocent-looking piece of firewood set off a bundle of aerolite cartridges if anyone picked it up to put it in the stove. A loose board on the edge of a trench was connected with fifty tank mines a hundred yards away. It was strange going about preparing those surprises. Why did we not leave them undone? Perhaps because it was just as pointless not to make them as to make them.

The afternoon passed quietly. The Russians apparently had not noticed that facing them they had only a handful of forlorn, sad men. The ensuing night was not very pleasant. We did not dare sleep. We just sat and stared. It was fifty or a hundred yards from you to your next-door man, and you never knew when you might expect a patrol to come sneaking up – a Siberian patrol! With my head filled with such thoughts I sat in a corner with a pile of grenades ready to throw and two loaded sub-machine-guns beside me, staring and staring into the darkness.

At daybreak the Russians began to suspect that all was not normal. We sent a few bullets over at them, but they became more and more venturesome, sticking their heads over their parapets and gazing inquisitively at us. I hurried to The Old Un and said excitedly:

'Shouldn't we make off now, before it's too late? It can't make any difference whether we stay here twenty hours or twenty-four.'

The Old Un shook his head.

'Sven, an order is an order; and, above all, the others are relying on us as they trot along out there in the snow. The poor devils have a bad enough time ahead of them. Let us give them a chance to get themselves out of the trap, if they can.'

Porta now joined us and he too grumbled, but The Old Un just said that as far as he was concerned we could go if we liked, but he would remain, alone if necessary.

'Oh, shut up, you silly old Feldwebel,' shouted Porta angrily. 'Of course we shan't leave you. But don't say we didn't warn you.'

Fuming and cursing, we went back to our posts, where we stayed watching the Russians and fearing the worst. Some

Russians now got up on to the parapet of their trench and signalled across to us. We sent a couple of bursts at them, which made them jump; but shortly afterwards they were back again. Suddenly, to my horror, I saw a dirty face appear over the parapet not ten yards from where I sat. Like lightning I flung a grenade at it. The man was killed on the spot. Then things became frantic. The Russians came sauntering across in large groups, and then at last The Old Un gave orders to abandon our positions.

We tore off on our skis across the snow-covered steppe. At intervals we heard a bang behind us. That was one of our booby-traps going off. Otherwise all was still and desolate. Now and again a column of Russian tanks went rolling along the highway scarcely two kilometres away. After five days' search we found the remnants of the 27th Regiment which, at last, was being taken out of the fighting to be re-formed.

I was made Fahnenjunker, which I did not like. Hitherto I had been nicely hidden in the ranks, but now I had to stand well out in front and receive the report of the Kommando-feldwebel, who, previously, had been my superior. It was like standing out there naked. My companions grinned.

31

Some time later he said in the same whispering voice:

'When you make your revolution against the Nazis and the generals, will you give Adolf a couple of extra wallops from me?'

'We promise you that, Porta. He shall have so many on the moustache from you that you would have been very tired if you had had to apply them yourself,' replied The Old Un.

'Good!'

Then for a good while there was silence, and all we could hear was The Old Un puffing at his pipe.

'Old Un, have you got your instrument with you?'

The Old Un pulled his mouth-organ out of his pocket.

'Play that bit about the girl combing her hair. The one who was sitting on the rock combing her hair.'

The Old Un played and I sang softly, while Porta lay there gazing up at the ceiling.

> '*Ich weiss nicht, was soll es bedeuten,*
> *dass ich so traurig bin;*
> *ein Märchen aus alter Zeiten,*
> *das kommt mir nicht aus dem Sinn.*'

We wept. Then Porta whispered:

'Now Joseph Porta, Stabsgefreiter by God's grace, is going. It's a bit hard. Promise me to look after Stalin. Let me see him, before I set sail.'

The Old Un lifted the cat up and put it to Porta's face.

'Remember to smack Adolf and Himmler! Servus!'

Yellowy-black fluid trickled from the corner of his mouth, but his grip tightened slightly on our hands. Then slowly the grip relaxed. Porta was dead.

'There's A Man Lying Out
On The Wire'

Though I did not know it, my second trip to hospital was to prove a turning point. I had been left hanging on the barbed wire, but then they dragged me in, and I was sent to the rear and hospital. After my release, I was sent to the Tank School at Wünschdorff in Berlin for a short officers' course before going back to the 27th Regiment. There, in Berlin, by a strange dispensation of Providence, I became courier for the conspiracy against Hitler. But of that on another occasion.

One morning, while I was in reserve hospital in Franzen-bad, a small, stocky person of about twenty-five came into our ward and made straight for my bed, held out his hand and said in resonant Viennese: 'Old Friend, Ernst Stolpe's the name. 7th Alpine Regiment and queer in the top storey, raving mad and I've papers to prove it; here, see for yourself.'

He handed me a certificate that was as good a 'game licence' as any reasonable soldier would dare dream of wangling:

Obergefreiter Ernst Stolpe, 7th Alpine Jaeger Btn., is to be classed as gravely war-wounded by reason of three serious injuries to his head. Under no circumstances may he be put to heavy work or made to wear heavy equipment, especially not a steel helmet. In the event of an attack he should be taken immediately to the nearest military hospital.

Standortlazaret 40   Paris

Dr Waxmund, Oberstabsartz.

'Old Friend, that's pretty Heil Hitler, isn't it? You aren't crazy, I suppose? If you are, you mustn't say so, for it would never do to have two here in the one hunting-ground. I go about taking letters to various idiots in the HQs and garrisons. When I need a little holiday I dot an officer one on the snout, give him a sweet smile and show him my licence. Then I'm sent to hospital. When you're allowed up, I'll show you Franzenbad and Eger and Prague. Would you like to hear how I came to this somersault factory?'

'Yes, do tell me,' I replied. All at once it occurred to me that I had not smiled for several weeks. I had sent Barbara a telegram and she had come, and then she had got herself transferred so that she could stay at Franzenbad and look after me, but my spirits had not improved. I was so tired and exhausted. Barbara was very worried.

'Make your ear comfortable and listen, then, my dove,' said Stolpe. 'The first time I got one too much was in France. It was a tree-trunk on a railway truck, and I got it right on the nape. Fracture of the skull. Into hospital. Out again. Out for a fortnight, then I show a fellow how to ride a motorbike the way a bike ought to be ridden. Take my hands off the bars, but darn me if someone hasn't put a fence just where I wanted to go. I sail through the air like a shell and land in an iron water-trough. The trough holds. I don't. New fracture of the skull, plus a broken collar-bone. Discharged without a certificate. Six weeks and there I am again. This time it is a wagon-pole. Now, I say to myself, this time I must do it; but you've no idea how hard it is to get a certificate to say that you have a screw loose. A good German soldier doesn't have a screw loose, not a bit of it. That, I imagine, is because most of the good German soldiers I have met have *several* screws loose. Well, I got going, but I had to work at my part, till it brought me a bonus. I began by giving the house physician a broken nose. Oh, you should have seen his snout afterwards; boy, he *wept*, I can tell you. "Do you like it?" I asked politely. "My name's Stolpe." But it didn't work. Well, I thought, you must use a coarser file; so one afternoon I said to the head sister, an elderly and very shrivelled virgin of fifty or so, "Off with your knickers, Cleopatra; I want a word with you!" That didn't work either; I suppose she had still been hoping. Well, said I, but I said it to myself, a good German soldier never gives up. What I need is a hammer. So I got myself a hammer and waited till the time was ripe. So one day I discover that it is ripe; go in to a major. Greet him nice and polite and admire

238

his private room. Then I admire his watch, an elegant piece and of gold. Ask him if it is strong. The chap doesn't answer, just gapes. So I wink, out with my hammer, bring it down on the watch. No, that wasn't a strong watch at all, say I, and wipe the head of the hammer, while he rings his bell. Just cheap muck, say I disdainfully and hand him ten pfennigs. That's for a lottery ticket for a new watch, say I. Half the hospital comes rushing in, but I slip quietly down to the kitchens and wink at the girls there. Pretty hot down here, say I. Wouldn't you like me to open a window for you, girls? And so I out with my hammer: eight panes. That gives you a bit of air, eh, ladies? Then I fling my socks, three handkerchiefs and a floor-cloth into the soup and ask if they can't wash those for me while they're about it. That, at last, gave me my licence.'

I could never make out how crazy Stolpe really was; but there was certainly nothing wrong with his appreciation of the pleasant and the useful; and Barbara was overjoyed that he took me under his wing and cheered me up with his crazy ideas, which had an incredible habit of resulting in our wangling some hospital spirit.

Once I was able to get up I was given a bathchair, for I was still almost paralysed, and Stolpe delighted in wheeling me about. The bathchair proved most useful, especially when we went to the theatre or some other place where you were supposed to queue; for Stolpe just wheeled me in to one of the gangways and then came and sat beside me; there being just room for two.

We also got much amusement out of having a third person wheel us both about the smart streets of Eger or Prague, while we sat side by side, smilingly accepting the sympathetic glances of the young ladies. This led to our being invited one day to a very grand party, at which some elderly German and Slovakian garrison officers were present. They and the society ladies of Prague were moved almost to tears by the sight of us sitting sweetly in the one bathchair, Stolpe in grey-green Jaeger uniform with a large edelweiss in his cap, and I in my black Tank uniform with beret set aslant. There was no limit to what they wanted to do for us, and we had our pockets stuffed with all sorts of delicacies, which we later shared with the others at the hospital. They even photographed us so as to have a memento of when the Jaeger and the Tank soldier were united in one bathchair.

What was not so fortunate was when a couple of these kindly matrons caught Stolpe and I in an improvised bath-chair race, on which occasion Stolpe was not in the chair, but running with it down the street as hard as he could go. After that we were invited to no more parties.

When we needed money and diversion Stolpe rang up his girl friend, wife of an SS-Standartenführer, in Nürnberg.

'Hallo, my old luxury lass,' he crowed into the telephone, making everyone in the post office turn round. 'How's the beggar? Is he at home? No? Caught up in Russia, is he? A good place for him! Listen, old mare, I have learned a new position, so, if you're interested, you had better come. But it's a very strenuous position, so unless you have something very strengthening to bring, you needn't bother. And don't bring that port, you know; I've always said it was a bad lot the beggar bought. I don't want to see port until you've drunk all that stuff you have now. Well, I can't stand here gossiping with you all day. I'll expect you on the two-thirty-two.'

Thereupon he dropped the receiver without replacing it, so that it hung dangling and laughed protestingly for a few seconds before it fell silent. A couple of young girls laughed, and there was general ill-concealed merriment in that other-wise boring place. We then stood in a queue and bought a stamp, which Stolpe stuck on the forehead of a policeman farther back. He took it good-humouredly.

To my surprise the middle-aged wife of the Standarten-führer really did arrive the next day, bringing a load of black-market goods. Ernst and she spent a couple of hours in an hotel room, after which he sent her back to Nürnberg, mak-ing the excuse that he had very little time. When she had gone the whole ward drank itself tight on the wines and liqueurs she had brought.

One day Stolpe was missing. He had been sent to a special hospital. A week later I received a postcard from him:

Somersault Factory, Nürnberg. 18 April 1944

Dear Sven,

What muck I've landed in! Smoking forbidden. Going out forbidden. I do go in great secrecy to the lav, and am hellish afraid that one day I'll find that's forbidden too. Up to yesterday I ate my food under the bed, but then a nurse explained that eating wasn't forbidden. All the doors are locked, except the lav, and that's wide open. There are iron bars in front of all the windows, but whether that's to keep us who are here from making off, or to prevent anyone coming in and taking us, I just don't know.

Greetings, Ernst the Mad.

32

'Darling!'

'Darling! Oh, how good it is to see you again, Sven. I have longed so for you.'

'And I, too, Barbara. Come let me take one of those cases. I have a car waiting. Are you hungry?'

'You bet I am.'

When we had eaten we went to her hotel, where she had a bath and rested for half an hour. Strangely enough we did not fall into each other's arms. We were simply too moved, and it was so nice and secure as we were. I was calmer than I had been for the last several nerve-racking months. We had plenty to tell each other. The other thing would not run away. We went out to Potsdam and had dinner there and walked hand in hand in the park at Sans-Souci.

One of the great raids was rumbling and roaring over Berlin. Barbara nervously squeezed close to me as we stood watching the smoke and flames above Neukölln. Wave after wave of bombers came soaring in over the city to drop their loads.

Suddenly there was a high-pitched whine. Like lightning I pulled Barbara down and flung myself beside her. Another bomb came screeching down. Barbara jumped up and ran screaming down the road, quite beside herself with panic-fear.

I leaped up and ran after her, shouting: 'Barbara, fling yourself down! Barbara! Barbara!'

A screaming whine made me fling myself into the ditch. Earth rained down over me. I remained lying there for a few seconds before I got to my feet. Barbara had disappeared.

Two hundred yards farther on I found her. Her body lay on the road in a pool of blood.

I sensed nothing, saw nothing, never heard the 'all clear' go. A car stopped. A man in uniform took me to it. A rug was put in the back and in it my Barbara.

They undressed me. A doctor said something about shock. A hand took me by the wrist, a soft hand that gripped me in the same light, sensitive way as Barbara's – Barbara whom they had killed.

Company Commander

I was sent back to my regiment as Oberleutnant and commander of my old company. Von Barring had become Oberstleutnant and battalion commander. Of the old lot there were only Oberst Hinka, von Barring, The Old Un and I left. The Old Un was now Oberfeldwebel.

One cold, grey rainy day The Old Un and I were on our way back from the front line. For the last stretch to our village we walked upon some railway track. We had almost reached a temporary station, where there was a huge ammunition dump, when there was a horrible, familiar whizzing in the air. The Old Un gave me a push that sent me head first into the ditch, and he followed.

For the next half-hour it was as though the whole world were coming to an end. There was a continuous howling, banging, rumbling and thundering from a never-ending succession of explosions. Dazzling white flames shot up into the air with noises like cracking whips. Whole bundles of shells were flung, exploding, in all directions. Two railway trucks soared through the air and dropped one hundred and fifty yards out in the fields. The entire undercarriage of a heavy goods-wagon smashed through a shed and fell with a crash not far from us. Two tall factory chimneys fell. One seemed to break at several points simultaneously; the other heeled slowly over and ended in a cloud of mortar-dust on the ground. All the houses for a wide radius were razed to the ground.

The subsequent silence was ghastly. Slowly I recovered myself, stood up and looked around me. The Old Un was lying a couple of yards from me.

'Well, Old Un, I suppose we ought to get on? That was pretty grim, wasn't it?'

There was no reply.

Both legs broken; left hip a pulp, and the shoulder very much the same.

I took his head on my lap, and with my scarf wiped the sweat from his forehead.

'Old Un, old chap,' I whispered; 'do you think you can get as far as the dressing station if I carry you?'

He opened his eyes for a moment.

'The Old Un's done for, Sven. Let's rather stay here and hold hands. It won't be long. Pop me in a cigarette, if you have one.'

I lit a cigarette and stuck it between his lips. It hurt him to talk.

'When I've gone, you'll write to the wife and kids, won't you? You know the recipe: shot in the temple and no pain . . . I haven't much pain anyway, apart from a tugging in the back when I talk . . . My old pipe and patent knife are for you; the rest you'll send home together with the two letters in my pocket-book.'

For a short while he lay silent, his eyes closed, while pangs thrust through his body. I held my water-bottle to his lips.

'Old Un, here's some schnapps. Try if you can drink a little.'

He managed a couple of gulps and opened his eyes again. Hoarsely he whispered:

'What hurts most is that I'm leaving you quite alone. I hope that you will be able to get back to that little country where you feel at home and which you have told me so many nice things about.'

When it was all over I lifted him on to my shoulder and trudged heavily off through the slush, in which my boots kept slipping. I wept and ground my teeth in helpless fury each time I slipped, while the sweat ran down my neck and my hissing breath was hot.

The Russians stared in amazement as I came staggering into the room with my dead comrade and laid him on the bed. Then I went across to von Barring.

'Now he too,' groaned von Barring. 'I can't stand much more.' He seized me by the shoulder and shouted: 'Sven, I'm going mad. I feel like a butcher each time I have to give orders to attack.'

He was shaken by sobs, flung himself wildly into a chair and let his head drop on his arms which he stretched out in front of him across the table.

'Oh, God in heaven, let this soon be over! Let it soon be over!'

He poured vodka into two glasses till it splashed over, then handed me one of the glasses. We drained them at a draught. He filled them again, but as he made to pick his up I stayed his hand.

'Erick,' said I, 'let's leave the glasses till we've buried The Old Un. You must come with me and bury him now. Only we two must do it, for we knew him. After that I'll gladly drink myself to death with you.'

We tore the swastika off the flag in which we wound him.

As I tighten my chinstrap and settle my helmet I let my gaze travel along the company, whose commander I am.

In the space right in front of me once stood Hauptfeldwebel Edel. He died of typhoid in 1943.

Behind him once stood tall, good-natured Feldwebel Bielendorf, buried alive with the whole of No. 4 Platoon during the fighting at the Kuban bridgehead.

On the right of the second platoon stood The Old Un, smashed by shells the day before yesterday.

Behind him Stabsgefreiter Joseph Porta, who went to his eternal rest with his belly ripped open with a knife.

Beside him the Titch, fate unknown.

Pluto was decapitated by a bomb in the forest at Rogilev.

Hugo Stege, Unteroffizier, burned in his tank with his side ripped open by a shell splinter.

Asmus Braun, the ever cheerful; both legs and one arm torn off in February 1942.

Unteroffizier Bernhard Fleischmann, disappeared in Moscow after escaping from a prisoner-of-war camp in Siberia.

Gefreiter Hans Breuer, degraded police lieutenant, executed after letting one foot be crushed in the track of a tank.

Down by No. 5 Platoon Leutnant Huber, only nineteen years old, a real friend to his men. One morning in April 1943 both his legs were blown off and he bled to death on the barbed wire calling for his sister Hilde.

Tank-gunner Kurt Breiting, sixteen years old, died in the

torments of hell after a phosphorus shell had exploded between his hands, while we were manning the armoured train in June 1943.

Obergefreiter Willy Pallas, short and always smiling, killed on the same occasion.

Gunner Ernst Valkas, head smashed in same armoured train. It was his brains I got over me.

Oberleutnant von Sandra. Disembowelled by an HE shell in his stomach.

Leutnant Bruno Haller, thirty-five. Jumped out of a burning tank with his badly burned brother, Unteroffizier Paul Haller, in his arms, himself to die of phosphorus burns. The two brothers were buried with linked arms at Berditchev. Together they went through Hitler's concentration camps and penal regiments, and together they rest in the cold earth of the Russian steppe.

God, if you exist, then I pray that You will let this mighty army of the dead for all eternity march before the eyes of the field-marshals responsible! Let them never have peace from the booted tramp of dead soldiers! Make them stare into those hundreds of thousands of accusing eyes. Let mothers, wives and sisters stand forth and hurl their accusations against them and their staff officers, who planned mass murders in order to please an untalented little bourgeois, a hysterical journeyman painter.

With a start I come to and realise that the Hauptfeldwebel has just made his report to me. I salute and give the command:

'No. 5 Company. Company – shoulder – arms!'

The movements of the badly trained men are appallingly sluggish. So many of them have only had three week's training as recruits.

'Company – by the right – right turn – quick march!'

Squelching in the bottomless slush, two hundred pieces of cannon-fodder march out on to the road and up to their positions.

246

33

Oberstleutnant von Barring and I were sitting in my company dug-out by the flickering light of a Hindenburg candle. We were drinking.

In front of us stood a whole battery of empty and half-empty bottles of vodka and cognac.

Barring's nerves had been worn threadbare, and he could no longer bear to be sober. If he was, he fell into such a rage that we had to tie him up to prevent him doing an injury to himself or to us. To have him more or less under control Hinka and I had to take it in turn to drink with him. One of us alone could not possibly have kept pace with his consumption. Kept in a perpetual state of dead-drunkenness, he was more or less normal.

'Sven, what bloody filth the whole thing is,' said he and filled a large mug with vodka, which he drank as though it had been beer. 'When you think what Adolf and that liar Goebbels have stuffed us with, it's incredible! Are we dreaming, is it really true that so much lying and contradiction is accepted and swallowed by an entire nation? What's wrong with us Germans? We all know that we're going straight to hell, and we've known that the whole time. Are we suicides, the whole lot of us? Or are we as stupid as we appear? As blind and crazy for power, and as dull-witted? I believe we are mad . . . I know I am.'

Von Barring

'Can you remember when Adolf screeched on the wireless: "If I want to conquer Stalingrad, it is not because I like the name, but because it is necessary that this important nerve-centre in the Russian river traffic be taken from the enemy, and I shall take Stalingrad when I consider the time is ripe!" And a few weeks later, when the whole Sixth Army was captured, how the idiot stood up and shouted, to the wild applause of his imbecile Party members: "When I saw the pointlessness of taking Stalingrad, which has no significance whatever for the ultimate victory of our troops, I gave orders for a temporary withdrawal!" People cheered that speech. One hundred and eighty thousand, however, could not be withdrawn. They were annihilated in the fighting for Stalingrad, the "unimportant".'

'Tchah!' I replied. 'We can see the swindle; but what can one penal regiment do against sixty to seventy million bawling people who cannot see anything, because they do not wish to. Rather die than lose the war, that's what they are saying today, when the war is already lost. What they mean is: rather let others die than that we lose our lives. I heard a woman in Berlin say that, even if there was just one single German regiment left at the front, Germany would win, provided that regiment was the SS-Leibstandarte!'

'The women are the worst of all,' said von Barring. 'The Lord preserve me from fanatical women. But to hell with it all. Hitler has lost the war, but whether we two will see the glorious collapse is a different matter. It will be our turn soon. Fancy just living on the hope that the whole thing will go bust as soon as possible! Let's drink, Sven, that's the only thing for us to do.'

'Let's drink to a speedy meeting with a pretty woman. Fanatical or not, it's all the same to me.'

'Yes, they are all the same on their backs: an amenity. If only they weren't such a damned oppressed lot that you cannot even talk with, because they have never learned to do anything but lie on their backs and say "yes" and "amen" to everything you suggest. Have you ever met a woman who had an opinion of her own?'

The jangling ring of the field telephone interrupted us. It was to tell me that I was being sent to Lwow to fetch forty precious tanks, possibly the last the Army could rake together.

That trip to Lwow had to be postponed, however, as the Russians chose that moment to attack and gave us plenty to do for the next week.

One day von Barring came to my dug-out while making his inspection. He stood and looked about him with dull gaze.

'Now I can't be bothered any more,' said he and went.

I hurried out after him.

Outside my dug-out he began firing off Very lights of all colours, so that our guns did not know what was wanted. We overpowered him, tied him up and carried him back to the dugout. He kept shouting in a hoarse, rattling voice, and he just stared straight in front of him, his eyes wide with terror, a terror that only he felt, but that we others could imagine only too well:

'At your service, Your Majesty! Majesty Hitler, ha, ha, ha! Oberstleutnant von Barring of the Regiment of Death reporting for duty in hell. Here with the establishment's best pitchforks, Your Majesty! The murderer von Barring reports for duty, Majesty Hitler!'

I stuck my fingers in my ears so as not to hear his laughter. When I saw that he was on the point of causing a general panic among those in the dug-out, where everyone was staring as though hypnotised at the madman, I had to knock him out.

Now, of the Regiment of Death only Hinka and I were left. Barring, who once, so young and friendly and filled with genuine kindness of heart, had stood up for us, when we suffered under the swine Meier, had now broken under the strain.

Some time later, when Hinka and I were on a brief duty journey, we stopped at Giessen and went to the army mental hospital there, where von Barring was. He was strapped to his bed and grinned idiotically without recognising us. Saliva ran down his chin, and he was a loathsome sight even to us, his friends. When we were in the train again we were so shaken that neither of us dared speak for a long time. Finally Hinka gave a nervous – no, a desperate laugh and said:

'So we aren't as hardened as we thought.'

'No,' I replied. 'It was horrible.'

'In case that happens to either of us – shouldn't we agree to help each other out of it?'

He held out his hand.

THE END